7 Sanctuaries

Ben A. Sharpton

Copyright © 2012

Novel Voices Press Inc.
Radnor, Pennsylvania
Ottawa, Ontario

Novel Voices Press Inc.

Copyright © 2012 Ben A. Sharpton

This is a work of fiction. Names, characters, places, and incidents either are products of the author's imagination or are used fictitiously. Other than actual historical persons, portrayed according to the author's interpretation and understanding, any resemblance to actual events or persons, living or dead, is purely coincidental.

Sharpton, Ben A.
7 sanctuaries / Ben A. Sharpton.—1st ed.
2012948831

ISBN 978-0-9854464-4-4

www.novelvoicespress.com

Printed in the United States of America

To my brother, Pat, who went before me through high school and seminary/grad school and life, and who continues to lead the way, still.

And remembering my three junior high and high school friends, Larry, Joe, and Danny:

Larry, with the soft, clean jump shot that somehow usually found its way into the hoop—you left us much too soon.

Joe, who always asked when he could read one of my books—I think you would have enjoyed this one, but I was a little too late.

And Danny, taller than I and a much better round-ball player, and still a friend after four and a half decades.

PREFACE

The 1960s. For some, it was an almost magical time, brimming with new innovations promising luxury and convenience never known before. Just a couple of decades earlier, the United States had saved the world from an imperial menace, and now the country dominated the planet—militarily, educationally, and technologically. More children were born in the 1960s than in any previous generation. Fueled by their idealism—the idealism of youth—they crusaded for peace, prosperity, and purpose, and they challenged old norms and conventional wisdom.

For others, the 1960s were a time of rampant change threatening the views, values, and virtues that had made our country great. Authority was challenged; the sacred, questioned. Young people were abandoning their core beliefs, and our nation was being pushed toward to the edge of a deep abyss.

Religion has always been an integral part of Southern living, and this was certainly the case in the '60s. People exercised their faith in different ways. Some treated it almost superstitiously, following certain rituals and traditions to the letter. Others used their beliefs as a means for activism and personal involvement in the changing world. Faith was pervasive.

Now it's the year 2012. Over time, memories have faded and morphed, and our perception of history is perhaps not entirely in line with reality. It's easy these days to think that the impact of the '60s affected only large metropolitan areas like New York City, Chicago, and San Francisco. It's easy, looking back, to believe that college campuses only welcomed bare-footed, "Flower Power" hippies with anti-war protests and drug-induced hazes. And it's all too easy to declare that, while the American government was caught up in the fury of the time, rural America was blessedly exempt. It's easy to believe these things, but that doesn't make them true.

In reality, all of America felt the growing pains of that decade. Rock music reverberated from radios in the Big Apple, Motor City, Chi-Town, and the City of Angels— and it reverberated from radios in rural communities as well. From NYC to small-town America, young people expressed themselves through bell-bottom blue jeans, long hair, tie-dyed shirts, and peace signs. The Civil Rights Movement affected every corner of our country in every sector of life, from housing and education to employment and military service. Women's rights movements swept through cities large and small. Substance abuse was rampant in both the inner city and the wide open country.

Our country seems to encounter enormous waves of change every one hundred years or so. Settlers colonized the land in the early 1600s. In the mid-1700s, colonists revolted and gained their independence. In the mid-1800s, the American Civil War took place, nearly destroying the American dream. And about a hundred years later, in the 1960s, another wave of dramatic change engulfed the country and, ultimately, the world.

When they were faced with times of tumultuous transformation, people sought solace and comfort in safe havens—sanctuaries, if you will—to protect themselves and their loved ones from the stormy world around them. Some people naturally turned to religion and community and family. Others sought such sanctuaries in a more deliberate, conscious way, hoping to find in them a place to celebrate the new and to teach alternative thought.

We continue to seek sanctuaries when our worlds go through transformations today. We may choose from the seven discussed in this novel—family, business, nature, church, school, sports, or the world itself—or we may choose among any number of others, such as fame, patriotism, fortune, friends . . . The list goes on. Some of these sanctuaries have what it takes to stand the test of time. Others inevitably fail. We do our best to choose our safe havens with care.

Wishing you the safest sanctuaries in times of turmoil,
Ben A. Sharpton, author
June 2012

SANCTUARY ONE

Family

"A mother's love is a sanctuary
Where our soul can find sweet rest
From the struggle and the tension
Of life's fast and futile quest."

— Helen Steiner Rice

KATIE FRANKLIN
(née Marshall)

January 1938

"Even when you got nothing, you can always find a way to help somebody who's got less than nothing." That's what 10-year-old Katie Marshall's mother had always told her.

When the country was hurting real bad, and the Marshalls had to move all over the place to find work, Katie's mama always found a way to give a hand to those who had less.

In Jacksonville, she shared an old towel with a family in the Greyhound bus station. In Memphis, she gave some biscuits to a little girl standing on a street corner. When she was real sick from pneumonia and didn't have long to live, she still somehow found a way to give a friendly word or a warm smile to those around her.

Katie's daddy didn't take to charity the way her mother did. He seemed to think that everyone around him was out to take him for whatever he was worth, so he kept a watchful eye on others.

Young as she was, Katie could tell the difference between her parents' views, and she tended to side with her mama, even when things got bad. Especially when things got bad.

* * *

Chilled by the numbing cold of the harsh Michigan winter, all Katie wanted was to be warm again, back in Texas or Alabama or Arkansas, all places her family had lived as her dad moved them around in search of work.

Now, finally, Katie felt like she might find warmth: they had just received word the night before that a new job was waiting for her father in Atlanta. Clutching her father's hand and dragging her ragged suitcase behind her, Katie struggled through the ice and snow as they left her uncle's house and made their way to the train station.

As they turned the corner onto Main Street, they came face to face with Katie's best friend, Claire Washington, and her mother. Although Katie had spent hours playing with Claire while their dads worked in the factories, her father had never met them before.

"Excuse me, Mr. Marshall," Claire's mother said. "May I ask you a question?"

Claire's warm, chocolate brown eyes searched Katie's. Concern riddled her ebony forehead.

"Well, we have a train to catch . . ."

Katie stepped forward to give Claire a goodbye hug, feeling the tears well up but grateful for the chance to see her friend one last time. The girls shuffled their feet to stay warm, the cold from the snow seeping into their weathered shoes.

"It will only take a moment, suh," Mrs. Washington insisted. Then, before he could turn away, she added, "Rumor has it you could make a suggestion for someone to take the job you're leaving at the General Motors factory."

Katie could see that her father was uncomfortable with the question.

"Yeah, I could," he said slowly. "But, as I said, we need to be going."

"I sure would appreciate it if you would recommend my husband, Joe. He's a hard-workin' man, a good mechanic, and an honest—"

Claire's father cut in, "I really don't have time. We're heading for the train right now."

"But, suh, the foreman would take a written note."

Katie watched as her father took a deep breath. He

glanced at her standing next to her colored friend, snowflakes covering their hair and shoulders. Then he stepped closer to Mrs. Washington and said in a low voice, "You should go to the Ford plant. They're more likely to hire a Negro than GM, these days."

Backing away slightly but not giving up completely, she replied, "But Mr. Marshall, Joe goes to the Ford plant every other day. They ain't got nuthin'. You're our best hope."

Tears began to fall from the woman's big brown eyes as Katie's father firmly replied, "I can't help you. I'm sorry."

Katie had seen desperation often. She'd seen it on the faces of the hungry men and women who lined the food kitchens. She'd seen it on her mother's face as she neared death. But still she was struck by the intensity of the desperation in Mrs. Washington's voice.

She felt herself suddenly yanked toward the train station.

"But Dad," she protested as she tried in vain to pull back.

"Not now, Katie," he said firmly. "It's cold out. We're leaving."

Katie yelled, "You can help them, Daddy, you—" She cringed as her father veered around with raised hand, but he stopped himself abruptly. He stared at her for a moment, then turned and stalked off to the train station.

Terrified, Katie turned to look over her shoulder at Claire and whispered, "I'm sorry," before dashing down the street toward the retreating figure of her father.

* * *

Katie stared out of the frozen window as the train lumbered down the tracks. She refused to look at her father in the seat beside her. The old suitcase in her lap was light compared to the weight in her chest, the sadness she felt for Claire.

Over the years, she and her father had lived in some seedy places. He often had to leave her with relatives or friends for long hours while he worked in the factories and mills. Katie remembered how happy she was the day she met Claire, whose father also worked in the auto factories, whenever there was work to be found. When the girls weren't busy with chores, or with school when it was in session, they spent almost all their free time playing together. In a crazy world where no one stayed in one place long, and where, for most people, it was a real challenge to form meaningful, lasting friendships, Katie had found Claire—and she could not have asked for a better best friend. She would miss her terribly.

While living in Detroit, Katie and her dad had managed to share dinner together two or three times a week. It was rarely much more than bread, soup and potatoes, but it was their time together. They would set a small dining table on the dresser in the chilly bedroom that Katie's uncle let them to use.

Before eating whatever meager meal they had managed to pull together, her dad would fetch a small wooden box full of tiny paper cards, each with a different passage of scripture. He would draw a card from the top of the stack and hand it to Katie, who would read it out loud and then return it to the bottom of the stack. Those cards were the closest things to a real Bible that they owned.

A few days earlier, Katie had read a passage that said, *Then shall he answer them, saying, Verily I say unto you, Inasmuch as ye did it not to one of the least of these, ye did it not to me.* It must have been a lucky verse, because two days later her father got the job offer down in Atlanta. They packed their bags and headed south the next day.

As Katie thought back to that Bible verse, the image of Claire and her mother standing in the frozen street watching them leave flashed in her mind. *Inasmuch as ye did it not to one of the least of these, ye did it not to me.* Finally, Katie couldn't take it any more.

Looking away from the window, she asked, "Why didn't you help them, Daddy?"

"It's complicated," he replied, turning a page in the newspaper he'd found on the train.

"All she wanted was a note."

He closed the paper. "Look, Katie. This job in Atlanta might not last forever. We could be back in Detroit in six months looking for more work. I can't afford to burn any bridges."

"What does that *mean?*"

Katie could see the frustration in his eyes as he tried to explain. "Say I recommend this Negro that I don't know, and he turns out to be a bad employee. What then? If we end up having to come back here in six months, my recommendation might keep me from getting hired again. Understand?"

Katie just stared at him.

"Ah, damn. You're just like your mother."

On that day in 1938, on a southbound train to a new life, Katie made a silent but solemn vow—she would never again allow herself to ignore or mistreat *the least of these.*

* * *

February 1959

To Katie Franklin, her family's home somehow always felt warm, even in the dead of winter. When visitors came inside from the icy cold, she made sure they left feeling cozy and light. Every morning, her children dashed down the porch steps bursting with energy, and every evening, they returned drained but craving the healing and restorative warmth of home.

Katie liked it that way. She worked to make her home the best it could be for her family. She had lots of energy herself. Her husband, Ray, had once called her a 'fiery dynamo.' She always tried to outlast her energetic kids, staying one step ahead of every potential situation.

Contrary to what her Aunt Betsy had told her, Florida weather was not always sunny and bright. In fact, on the day before Valentine's Day in 1958, Tallahassee was hit by almost three inches of snow. In Springlake, where the Franklins lived, flakes of fine powder settled on sitting automobiles along their street, and the kids spent an hour scooping it into snowballs and hurling them at each other and the neighbor's cat. School was canceled on that cold Thursday, because the school buses were ill-equipped for icy roads.

Katie orchestrated suppertime at their house like a perfectly choreographed three-ring circus, everything timed just right. In the early years, nothing interfered with supper hour, and it always lasted an hour. Ray would arrive home from the hardware store at 6:30 p.m. every weekday night, and dinner would be on the table by 6:45 p.m.

Later, once television had made its way into their home, suppertime slid back to 7:00 p.m. so Ray could relax in his easy chair and watch the national news—which usually had the unfortunate effect of counteracting the benefits of sitting in the chair. But even Walter Cronkite couldn't stop the rush to her table every time she announced, "Dinner's ready!"

Ray looked tired today, as he did most nights after a hard day of work. Six-year-old Robby was arguing with his older brother Tim about something that had happened on the playground. Ray and Katie ate in comfortable silence.

Katie cleared her throat. No one looked. She cleared her throat again. No response. "I think we should go to the tent revival," she announced. Silence fell over the room like a veil.

"What?" Ray finally asked.

Katie looked around the table and repeated, "I think we should attend the tent revival. Twila Turner went last Monday night and she said that the music was beautiful, and The Evangelist Chase Andrews was the best speaker, and Elliot got saved and half the people from church were there. I thought it sounded like a good thing for us to do."

"Elliot Turner got saved?" Ray repeated. "He's the biggest drunken, whorin'—"

"Raa-aayyy," Katie admonished.

"Well Elliot Turner ain't the nicest guy on the street, Katie."

"Let's keep the conversation civil," she said.

After a long pause, Ray said, "Okay, you're right. Why not? When does it start?"

"Twila said it starts at seven-thirty, although some people get there as early as six."

"Well," Ray said. "I can't get home before six. I don't see how we can go that early."

"Then we'll plan to go tomorrow night after supper," Katie said, triumphant.

Ray sat across the table with a helpless look on his face.

Tim spoke up. "Do we have to?"

"We're going," Ray said, his mind made up.

Later that night, after turning off the lights and closing the bedroom door, Katie overheard her two sons talking.

"Tim?" came Robby's voice.

"Yeah."

"What's a tent revival?"

After a long pause, Tim whispered, "I don't know. It's kinda like a church service, except the preacher shouts a lot and people cry a lot."

"Have you ever been to one?"

"No," Tim said. "But Steve told me about it at school. He said there were holy ghosts, and women screaming and all sorts of weird stuff."

There was another long silence.

"I don't wanna go," Robby said.

Tim responded, "You ain't got no choice." Then he added, "Don't worry. I'll be there too."

Katie smiled and slipped quietly down the hall. She was proud of Tim; at only nine years old, he was already looking out for his little brother.

* * *

At 7:20 p.m. as the Franklin family pulled into a parking lot near where the tent revival was being held, they could hear someone playing on a grand piano. It was the loveliest music Katie had ever heard, even better than her Liberace album on the Hi-Fi. The tinkling music blended with the cold October air in an ethereal, almost eerie way, sending a chill through her body.

Stepping out of the pitch-black night and into the tent, they had to squint until their eyes had adjusted to the lights inside. The stage was bathed in brilliant light. In fact, the entire tent seemed to glow from the scores of different spotlights. Most of the seats were filled. They found room near the back and sat down on the hard, folding wooden chairs as the revival began.

The music began slowly, but that pace didn't last long. Almost immediately, the song leader raised the tempo and volume with vigorous arm movements, and everyone responded by standing and singing. The choir all wore bright gold robes with dark blue sashes. They swayed to the rhythm of the hymns as they sang. Soloists came forward and thrilled the crowd with beautiful melodies, and an offering was collected in giant Maryland Fried Chicken paper buckets. Then the tent lights dimmed and bright spots illuminated the stage. The piano played louder and the choir singing intensified.

Into the spotlight stepped a tall, slender gentleman dressed handsomely in a gray suit, white shirt and dark blue tie. The Evangelist Chase Andrews advanced to a podium at the front of the stage. A hush fell over the crowd.

As The Evangelist Chase Andrews spoke in the canvas cathedral, his words lilted musically, cascading from his lips and caressing the ears of his listeners. His pitch and tone rose and fell as if directed by one of the finest orchestra conductors in the world. And he was eloquent, too; Katie had never heard a more articulate and passionate speech.

He moved about the stage as he spoke, first directing his attention to one side of the audience and then the other, and in between returning to the podium upon which rested a large, gold-leaf Bible. It was as if he were wandering from his Source to impart the Truth, and when he was empty, he would go back for more. He reminded Katie of a gardener scattering seed. *How magnificent and glorious*, she thought, as she watched and listened.

The Evangelist Chase Andrews spoke for a few minutes, not more than ten or fifteen, and then he invited the crowd to come to the altar and meet the Lord. And come they did. They filled the tiny altar rail two and three people deep. Women cried. Men shouted, arms raised high in the air.

Katie turned to see how her children were reacting to this awesome spectacle. It warmed her heart to see Robby and Tim holding hands and staring ahead intently. Ray had one arm wrapped protectively around Robby's shoulders.

Katie suddenly snapped back to reality and realized that the conductor was leading the choir through another verse of *Just As I Am*. Until that moment, she hadn't noticed that the singing had resumed.

All too soon for Katie, the service ended. The lights came up and the crowd slowly crept toward the parking lot. Ray chatted with a couple of friends from their church, and nodded politely to a few of his regular customers from the hardware store.

Katie, surrounded by her family, ambled out to the parking lot, bathed in the glow and warmth of the inspirational words from The Evangelist Chase Andrews. She was silent on the way home, hoping the silence could help her hold onto the feeling and the power of the service a little bit longer.

* * *

Every mother fears that she may one day kiss her children good night for the last time. That's what Dear Abby had said in the morning paper. As Katie tucked her boys in, this fear crept into her thoughts.

"Never," she whispered desperately. "Never."

But still, she couldn't shake the nagging worry that her fears might one day come true.

* * *

April 1959

Every small town in the South had one. Katie made a point of stocking up on carrots, tomatoes, cucumbers, strawberries, and other produce every Saturday morning at the Springlake Farmers' Market. It sat on the east side of town, conveniently located between the rural farmlands and the city. Farmers would bring in fresh produce to sell at a discount to local residents once a week. Along with dozens of other customers, Katie would walk beside the long tin-roofed open-air pavilion, selecting whatever she needed for her family's upcoming meals.

One Saturday morning in April, she was looking over some cucumbers when something back in the parking lot caught her eye. A big Negro lady, wearing a full white apron over what looked like her Sunday best, was holding a wicker basket filled to the brim with bright red tomatoes. She was in a heated exchange with a white farmer. Something about the lady's demeanor—the desperate look on her face, the intensity of her gestures—made Katie curious. She broke away from the crowd and walked closer so she could hear the conversation.

"Well, it looks like you've got about twenty-five pounds of 'maters, there," the gravelly voiced farmer said.

"Feels mo' like thirty-five," the Negro answered.

Katie thought the basket did look heavy—the woman had to keep shifting and readjusting it to keep her grip.

"They won't let you sell 'em here," the farmer said. "You ain't got no membership card."

Katie could easily see how worried the lady was, her sweaty face etched with concern. "I picked these out of my garden. They's good tomaters."

"You know, ma'am, I've already got several bushels of 'maters," the farmer continued. "But I'll do you a favor. I'll buy yours from you and sell 'em myself."

"Would you?"

"Sure," he said. "I'll give you two-fifty for 'em."

"Two-fifty? They's worth close to eight or nine dollars."

"Well, that's my offer."

The colored lady clearly knew she was being taken. She took in deep breaths of fresh air, trying to figure out how to handle the confrontation. She gripped her basket's handles so tightly that some of the strands had broken.

The least of these, Katie thought to herself, remembering the pledge she'd made so many years ago. She marched over to the two people.

"I'll pay you nine dollars for your tomatoes, ma'am," she said.

"What the hell—" the farmer said, turning around in surprise. "What are you doing, miss?"

"I'm buying some tomatoes," she said simply.

"You can't buy over here."

"I think I just did," Katie said, seeing out of the corner of her eye the colored woman's face break into a gold-toothed smile.

The farmer squared off with Katie. In a hushed voice, he said, "Look, ma'am. I'm trying to do this nigger a favor. She can't sell her crops here, so I'm offering to buy them from her."

"At one-fourth their value?" Katie said. "That ain't much of a favor."

He shrugged. "It's better than nuthin'."

"It ain't fair," Katie said, staring him down. When he looked away, Katie turned to the woman, who was standing back a ways but could still hear every word. "Can you help me take them to my car?"

"Well, I never," the farmer said in disgust.

"I hope you never do," Katie retorted, reaching into her purse for the money. She handed nine one-dollar bills to the colored lady. It was more than she had planned to spend, but, she reasoned, sometimes principle beats price.

"Lawdy, Lawdy," the woman exclaimed. "I am so very grateful."

Katie held up a juicy red fruit. "I sure do like tomatoes."

The colored lady smiled her thanks as she carried the wicker basket to Katie's car. Katie found a cardboard box in the trunk, and they started transferring the tomatoes into it.

"I shore do appreciate your hep," the lady said. "I ain't never tried to sell my tomaters here before. Don't reckon I would do it agin, if I had the chance. It's just that my husband has been out wif a bad back for the last week, and we jest need a little more money to git by."

"I'm happy to help," Katie said. Surveying the back seat full of tomatoes, she added with a chuckle, "Looks like now I'm gonna have to make a big pot of stew."

"I don't mean to impose, ma'am," the colored lady said, picking up her empty basket, "but along wif my tomater garden, I sometimes help wif housekeeping chores. You know, like sweepin' and moppin' and washin' clothes. Would you knows of any work like that, that needs doin'?"

Katie paused a moment, then said, "You know, I could use some help, but only one day a week."

The colored woman's eyes grew wide with anticipation. "Fine wif me, ma'am, fine wif me." She extended a large meaty hand. "My name's Irma. Irma Brown."

Katie shook Irma's hand and introduced herself. A wonderful new friendship had begun.

* * *

There was something in the air—Katie could feel it. People were on edge, nervous.

Maybe it was the Cuba situation. Someone on the news had said that Fidel Castro was building ties with Russia. It frightened Katie to think that the Russians might be sitting just a hundred miles to the south.

Or maybe everyone was jittery because of those satellites that Russia had launched into space. People kept glancing up at the sky, Katie thought, as if they were trying to see what might be up there.

Perhaps it was the racial strife. Up in North Carolina, some colored people had staged what they called a sit-in at an all-white diner to protest segregation. Somehow, Katie could feel the tension, even down in

Springlake. White men huddled together in little groups, talking in low voices. People seemed to stare more closely at colored folks on the sidewalks and in their cars. Ray said he could feel it at work, too. He said that colored people resented having to go around to the back door to buy hardware supplies.

A few weeks earlier, Katie had shared her fears with Irma while they were folding clothes in the laundry room. The two had become close, and she'd needed to find out how her friend felt, to share and be each other's sounding board.

"Irma," she'd asked. "Do you read the newspapers?"

"You know, Miss Katie, that I don't read so well."

"It's just that there's so much going on in the world around us. Those satellites out in space, and that thing going on in Cuba, and the death of the Pope and all those storms . . ."

Irma had given Katie a blank stare. "Miss Katie, I don't know nothin' about all those things that I can't do nothin' about, and I don't intend to." The two women were quiet for a moment, then Irma added, "I just have to keep trustin' the Lord. His eye is on the sparrow, so I knows He watches me."

Irma's words had comforted to Katie, if only for a short while.

* * *

March 27, 1960

Ray and Katie enjoyed their Sundays. They let the children sleep in a little later than usual, if they wanted to. Katie usually arranged a breakfast of pancakes and bacon so her men could enjoy a nice breakfast together. Ray liked to linger a little longer with the morning paper. Then, everyone would get dressed up and head off to church and Sunday school at First Methodist Church downtown.

Ray was still in the shower when Katie brought in the paper and laid it on the table next to his place setting.

Strange words jumped off the front page: *Night of a Thousand Crosses.* A large photograph of a burning cross was beneath the headline.

Katie slipped into Ray's chair, picking up the newspaper carefully. She became so engrossed in the article that didn't hear Ray stroll into the kitchen.

"Taking over the breadwinner's chair?" he teased. His hair was wet and slicked back from the shower.

"Ray," Katie said, not turning her attention away from the paper. "Look at this."

He came up behind her and leaned over the chair. She could smell his fresh scent. In an uncertain world, small things like that were comforting.

"Ray, it says the Ku Klux Klan staged a demonstration throughout the South, burning these giant crosses as a protest against coloreds trying to visit white places, like those boys up in Greensboro who went to the diner in Woolworth's." She pointed and read: "*Hundreds of crosses were raised and set aflame throughout the South. Reports included sightings in Georgia, South Carolina, North Carolina, and Florida.*" She looked up at Ray. "Do you think there were any near us?"

Ray's face was flushed as he eased down into the nearest chair and pulled the paper to him, staring at the hideous photograph. "You know," he said softly, almost in a whisper. "Whoever did this could have bought this lumber from us."

"But nobody in Springlake would do a thing like this, would they?" Katie asked. Ray shrugged his broad shoulders. Neither of them knew what to say.

When the family was dressed and ready, they piled into the station wagon and drove to First Methodist Church. One of the ushers whispered something to Ray as they gathered in the church narthex. Other church members seemed to be burdened with heavier than normal concerns.

After church, Ray announced that they were going to take a little side trip on the way home. "Do we have to?" Robby asked. "I'm starving."

"You're always starving," Tim countered.

"It won't take but a few minutes," Ray said. He steered the car onto Main Street toward the east side of town. As they neared the city limits, they saw several cars and a Springlake fire truck parked along the side of the road. Ray slowed as they approached Wagoner's Field, old farmland that had been tied up in bankruptcy court for several years.

On a prominent hill next to the road stood the crusty remains of a burned cross. Most of the arms had burned away, giving it a stubby, disfigured look. The smell of kerosene and smoke was intense. The ground around the cross was charred and smoking.

"Wow," Robby whispered. "What happened?"

Katie turned to face him. "Some very confused and mean people burned that cross back there to put a fright into others. Some people don't care for those who are different from them, and they do things like that to scare the different people away."

On the way home, Ray and Katie were quiet. Then, a block or two from home, Katie said, "You know, Ray, I sat there in church and stared at that beautiful cross hanging above the choir loft and thought, 'How could something so awful be so beautiful at the same time?' Then, staring at that burned cross back there, I thought, 'How could something so beautiful be so ugly at the same time?'"

Ray reached over and squeezed her hand as they pulled into the driveway.

* * *

May 1960

Early one Monday morning, Katie heard a frantic rapping at her back door. The screen door made a *ba-bapping* sound as knuckles pounded on it, slamming it into the frame. Ray was at work and the boys were at school, and Katie had just sat down to a cup of coffee. She hurried to the door and was surprised to see Irma, who only worked on Thursdays.

"Miss Katie," she began. "I'm so sorry to bover you so early in the mornin', but I have to talk wif you."

"Irma! Come inside."

"I won't stay long, Miss Katie. I just need to speak wif you."

"Of course," Katie said, welcoming her friend inside and pouring her a cup of coffee. Irma squeezed into the small kitchen chair across from her. "What's on your mind, Irma?"

Irma's hands shook and she held her cup with both hands to keep from spilling. "I had a dream, Miss Katie," she began. "It was the most real dream I ever done had, and it shook me up real bad."

"It's all right, Irma," Katie said, reaching across the table to squeeze Irma's hand. "Tell me about it."

"Like I said," Irma continued. "It was real, so real, that I ain't sure now that it never happened. Are the boys all right?"

Her question took Katie by surprise. "Why, yes. They're both at school."

"Well in my dream, something terrible done happened to them, and I loves bof dem boys so much and I jes don't want nuthin' to happen to neither one of them."

Katie quickly replayed all of the events of the morning in her mind to reassure herself that her boys were okay. Nothing struck her as potentially dangerous. "What happened in your dream?"

"I don't know, Miss Katie . . . There was these bright lights flashin' on and off, like, and there was this loud siren going *wooooo-oooooo*. It was like an ambulance or an air raid siren and there was blood on the ground, and I somehow felt that one of the boys, or maybe bof of them boys, was hurt real bad."

"Did you *see* Tim or Robby?" Katie asked.

"Naw, I somehow jes knows it was them. It sounds kinda far-fetched to tell it out loud."

Katie paused, took a deep breath to calm herself, and then tried to comfort her friend. "I think you had a very bad dream, and it's upset you. But Tim and Robby are fine, Irma. It was just a dream."

"Naw, Miss Katie. It weren't just no bad dream," Irma insisted. Then, looking up from her coffee cup with pleading eyes, she whispered, "It was a vision."

In spite of herself, Katie felt a chill run through her spine.

"I think it was a vision of what's to come, Miss Katie."

Katie didn't know what to say. She didn't want to discredit her friend's beliefs, but she also couldn't accept the vision that Irma had described. She sipped her coffee.

"Miss Katie," Irma said slowly. "I loves bof dem boys so very much. You knows I'd do anything for Timmy and Robby, an' I jes don't want nuthin' to happen to them."

"Well, Irma," Katie said carefully. "Right now, the boys are doing fine. We'll both have to keep an eye on them to make sure they stay safe, okay?"

"Yessum," Irma said. "You knows I'll do whatever I can for dem boys."

"I know, Irma. We're lucky to have you on our side."

They finished their coffee and then Irma excused herself, saying she'd been so confused that she forgot to pack a lunch for Willie.

After she left, Katie thought long and hard about Irma's vision. She fought the urge to pick up the phone and dial the elementary school to check up on the boys. She asked herself if she even believed in visions at all. She tried to brush it off as the wild dreams of an overly emotional friend, but Irma's conviction and persistence made that hard.

Eventually, the groceries, house cleaning, meal preparation, and other demands of the day took over, and Katie gradually managed to dismiss Irma's concerns. At least for a while. But she couldn't get them out of her mind altogether.

* * *

There was nothing quite like the freedom of riding a bike full-out, feeling the wind in your face and the sun on your back. Katie had only experienced that feeling second-hand, since she had never learned to ride a bike herself. But her boys could ride for hours without stopping. Sitting on her porch, watching them fly by, she sensed their thrill as they passed.

But with such thrills come pain—for both sons and mothers—as bikes slide on rough asphalt and young riders tumble to the ground. On many occasions, Katie herself would wince as she dabbed Merthiolate on scrapes and wounds and blew on the bleeding spot to ease the pain.

As the boys got bigger, so did their bikes and so did their injuries. Like the time Tim got a huge gash in his forehead from trying to jump over the ditch. The boys had built a makeshift ramp out of old plywood and two-by-fours, and Tim was the first to demonstrate his cycling prowess by charging down the street and up the ramp, planning to jump over the three-foot-wide ditch on his bike. But either the ramp's incline was wrong or Tim's speed going into the jump was too slow, because his bike didn't rise high enough and smashed into the wall of the ditch, catapulting him headfirst into the gravel.

There was also the time Katie had rushed Robby to the doctor because he'd slipped while trying to ride hands-free and caught his wrist on the pavement. The seven-year-old had spent a month with his left arm in a cast after that one.

The worst bike accident, however, happened one summer day in 1960. The boys spent all summer biking around town. Katie never worried about them and they never got into any big trouble. One afternoon, however, trouble found them. Katie saw them from the kitchen window, and knew immediately that something was wrong. If it was possible for someone to limp while on a bicycle, Tim was doing it. Katie ran to the door and met them in the carport. Irma, who had been hanging sheets to dry in the backyard, hustled to the house to help.

"Boys, what happened?" Katie cried.

Neither one said anything. They both just shuffled inside. Katie followed them both into the kitchen and sat Tim down. He sported a bruise over his left eye and a bleeding lip.

"Now," she said firmly, "tell me what happened."

Robby spoke up first. "They jumped us."

"Who? Who jumped you? Where?"

"Them niggers jumped us over by the tracks."

Katie flinched at the word nigger. "No matter what happened to you, we don't say things like that." She could sense Irma's presence behind her in the doorway, and her son's language embarrassed her.

"Well they did," Robby said.

Katie turned to Tim. "Tell me what happened."

Tim hesitated at first, but then he let it all come out. "We were riding down that hill over by Broadmore. It's the only hill in town because it goes over the railroad tracks. We weren't doin' nuthin' to nobody and these five colored boys rode up on bikes. They said we were on their property and told us to get out—"

Robby broke in, "Then the biggest nigger hit Tim."

Before Katie could stop herself, her left hand shot out and she backhanded Robby across the cheek. Her hand glanced off his face, and his body bounced against the back of his chair. Katie was so stunned by her reaction that she immediately wrapped her arms around her son and apologized. She turned his reddening face to her and was appalled to see a bloody one-inch-long scratch down his cheek, where her wedding ring had dug into his skin.

"Mama, you hit him," Tim cried.

"I didn't mean to," Katie whispered. All three Franklins remained motionless.

From the doorway, Irma broke the uncomfortable silence. "Who jumped you? Was it those Jackson boys?"

"I don't know their names," Robby said. "I ain't never seen them before."

"Now you listen to me," Irma said, coming up behind Katie. "They's good white folk and they's bad white folk. They's good colored folk and they's bad colored folk. You don't let what happened today make you think bad of nobody, ya hear?"

"Yes'm," both boys mumbled.

"Did they hit you any more than that?"

"No ma'am," Tim said. "We both jumped on our

bikes and rode home."

"That's fine. You stay away from that part of town. You don't need to go messin' around there."

"Yes, ma'am."

Katie rose from where she'd been kneeling near Robby and fetched a washcloth. She soaked it in cold water and then used it to wipe her boys clean, first Tim's bruising forehead and then Rob's swelling cheek. She was scared and embarrassed and didn't know what to do next.

"Can we be excused?" Rob asked in a small voice.

Katie nodded and both boys went to their room.

"Don't be hard on yourself, Miss Katie," Irma said. "These days people are gettin' kinda crazy. They do things that they don't mean to do."

Katie looked up. "We spank the boys, when necessary, but I've never struck one of them."

"It's okay," Irma said. "These boys will bounce back pretty quick. They's like that."

By suppertime, Irma's prediction had come true. Both boys devoured their chicken and dumplings as if nothing had happened. Ray had just pulled his chair to the table when, with a start, he suddenly noticed that his two boys were battered and bruised. "What happened to you?" he demanded.

Katie quickly answered for them. "They had some trouble by the railroad tracks. Let's you and I talk about it after supper." She placed a bowl of vegetables in front of him.

Ray let it go, as Katie knew he would. While Tim and Rob cleared the table, the parents went to sit on the back porch. "The boys got in a fight with some colored boys today over by Broadmore."

Ray leaned forward in his rocker. "Who are they?" he shouted. "I'll go find them—"

Katie put a hand on his arm. "You wouldn't be able to find them now," she said. "Tim and Robby will be all right." Then, reluctantly, she added, "To make it worse, I struck Robby. He called them 'niggers' and Irma was there and . . . I just reacted. I felt terrible. I . . . handled it badly."

Ray was quiet for a moment, then he said, "They'll be all right, Katie. They rebound pretty quickly. And they love their mama."

"That's what Irma said," Katie replied.

"Well, she's a smart woman."

* * *

September 1960

For Christmas the previous year, Ray had given Katie a new Philips transistor radio, which she kept on the kitchen counter so she could tune in while she prepared the family meals. It had a cream-colored plastic front and wooden body, and too many buttons and knobs, which she never touched anyway because she always listened to the local Springlake radio station. In early September, she kept the radio on all day, anxious to hear the latest forecast on Hurricane Donna.

For Floridians, hurricanes were a feared and respected fact of life. They came, they terrified people, they destroyed whatever was in their paths. Katie was grateful, because hurricanes seemed to avoid her small town. But in 1960, Hurricane Donna bore down on Springlake. The weatherman said that she moved more slowly than most, taking her time to soak everyone and everything in her path. Her winds gusted at around one hundred miles an hour and held their speed for longer than most hurricanes in recent memory.

Like everyone in Springlake, Katie and Ray did their best to protect their family against the coming onslaught of wind and rain. They put masking tape on both sides of every window in their little concrete block house. Ray brought home fresh batteries for the flashlight and the radio. Katie bought whatever canned supplies she could find at the grocery store. Ray filled their station wagon with gas. Katie filled the bathtub with water for drinking, cooking, and washing, just in case.

And then they waited.

Katie called Irma to see if she and Willie needed

any help. Irma said they were heading to Alabama to stay with relatives.

Katie listened to the weatherman describing how Donna had churned through Cuba, causing devastation and destruction in the island country, before heading north through the Florida Keys and veering west just south of Miami. She moved parallel to the western coast of Florida for a hundred miles or so, gathering strength and moisture.

Then, after passing Fort Myers, she turned and headed northeast, as if she'd set her sights on Springlake, Florida. A hurricane alert broadcast throughout Central Florida for several days. Those who had some place to go, fled. The others dug in and waited it out. The Franklins were among those who chose to stay put.

The children stayed home from school on Friday, September 9, and played around the house. The skies were dark all day, warning of the coming destruction.

Ray had to work at the hardware store to help the other Springlake citizens who had chosen to stay behind. That left Katie to secure their own home against the storm. She did the best she could, and felt confident that the Franklins could withstand any attack.

At 5:00 p.m., Ray pulled into the driveway. He was followed by an early '50s model Ford. Ray hurried back to the Ford and helped the driver secure the car as close to the house as possible. Then he helped unload some boxes and a suitcase from the trunk. Heading to the back door, Ray motioned for his friends to follow.

Katie opened the screen door wide to invite Ray's guests inside. Once out of the wind, Ray introduced his new friends.

"Katie, this is Bill, Marilyn, and little Larry Watson. We're worried that their rental home might not be safe tonight, so I told them we could find some room for them here."

The Watsons stood timidly in the doorway, obviously frightened of the storm, of the coming damage and of being in a strange home. They reminded Katie of Claire's mother, not just because of their skin color but also because of their precarious situation.

Katie smiled as big as she could. "I'm so very glad to meet you and that you'll be sitting out the storm with us." She was relieved to have guests to focus her attention on during the storm. It somehow made her feel like she and her home had a purpose, a reason for being blessed with strength and resources.

She turned and called to the boys at the back of the house. "These are our sons, Robby and Tim," she said as they burst into the room. "Robby and Tim," she said, "this is Mr. and Mrs. Watson and their son, Larry."

The three boys headed straight to their room, where they built their own hurricane-proof house out of plastic building blocks. Meanwhile, Katie showed Bill and Marilyn to the guest room, and Ray helped bring in their belongings.

That night, dinner was a mix of different foods. Katie had planned to serve fried chicken livers, but she'd had to add a few hot dogs when their unexpected guests arrived. The boys devoured the hot dogs and the parents feasted on the chicken livers.

The conversation bounced from topic to topic. How long had either family lived in Springlake? What was it like to work in the electric company? How many relatives did each family have and what did they have in common?

When supper was over, Katie and Marilyn went into the kitchen to prepare a pot of coffee. When they brought the coffee and cups into the dining room, Ray had the boys clear the table. Then the boys went back to their plastic building block project. Eventually, they found their way to the living room where their parents were gathered, listening to the radio. Ray explained that the reception was poor on the television set because the outdoor antenna was being tossed to and fro. Besides, as far as they could tell, there wasn't that much on the television that wasn't also on the radio.

Late into the night, everyone listened to the monotonous descriptions of the impact of Hurricane Donna on small towns with strange names and obscure locations. Every now and then, one of the adults would comment on the radio broadcast. "Looks like Fort Lauderdale has been spared. Uncle Jake won't have anything to worry about." "Sarasota? That's right in her path." "I wonder what a hurricane would do to a lake the size of Okeechobee—probably scatter a few gators around the state."

Eventually, the boys fell asleep, and one by one, they were carried to bed for the night. The house was secure. Both families were safe. After a while longer, the adults agreed to turn in for the night as well, with "thanks," "your welcomes" and well wishes shared all around.

In the middle of the night, everyone awoke to the sound of smashing wood on metal. The kids stayed covered in their beds. Katie and Ray peered through blinds in a vain attempt to find the source of the crashing noise. The wind howled like a mourning ghost. Other smashing sounds echoed through the night, clues to the damage that was being done nearby. Throughout the night, never ceasing, the rain fell. It smashed against the window panes again and again. It beat down on roofs and cars. It seemed impossible for so much water to fall so steadily— an incessant, constant onslaught. But it did.

Safe in the arms of her husband, Katie finally managed to fall asleep. The rain was still falling when she awoke. She stretched over the headboard to look out the bedroom window, and saw a lake where her yard used to be.

The swing set, once perched upon a small hill, now stood in a foot of water. She noticed that an old pecan tree, once so solid, had been completely uprooted. The root system now stretched upward as if searching for soil and nutrients in the naked daylight. The tree was leaning against the rear corner of the garage, where it had apparently struck and damaged the roof. The roof could easily be repaired; the old pecan tree was lost.

And still the rain pounded.

Finally, at 10:00 a.m., the rain stopped, leaving an eerie silence in its stead. The clouds, still dark and ominous, threatened to rage once again.

Katie and Ray threw on their raincoats and waded into the backyard to survey the damage. The soft Florida soil felt squishy and slimy beneath Katie's tennis shoes. The pecan tree was indeed dead—all that was left was its tangled and disfigured carcass. Several other trees were down as well.

Water was everywhere. It looked as though it would never dry, as if the backyard would be forever submerged. Off in the distance, at the edge of the yard, they caught a glimpse of a snake, swimming through the debris, making its way to dry land. A stray dog picked at upturned garbage cans in the neighbor's yard. But most of all, there was silence.

The quiet blanketed their little world. Nothing moved. Nothing stirred. It seemed as if nothing would ever move again.

Eventually, they turned and headed back inside, stirred by the wet drops that were beginning to fall again. The rain came in tiny droplets at first, then built up to another steady downpour, strong enough to rival the first. They all hunkered down for Donna's encore.

* * *

The day after Donna, the Franklins and the Watsons ventured back to the Watsons' home. Just like everywhere else, the flat Florida land did little to hide the massive amounts of water that had fallen in the past twenty-four hours. Many houses had been reduced to crumbling wrecks, soaked through and through and entirely uninhabitable. The radio said that the eye of the storm had passed over Springlake, causing the eerie silence and calm.

Although she had never seen it before, Katie could tell that the Watson home, though not completely destroyed, was heavily damaged.

Parts of the tin roof had been stripped from the wooden beams, making the house look something like one of those skeleton costumes at Halloween. Bill and Marilyn stared at the damage for several minutes. Slowly, Bill shook his head in dismay.

Larry and Robby dashed into the house, despite Marilyn's words of caution.

"Well, it's liveable," muttered Bill. "But it's gonna take a lot of work to get back to normal."

"Do you think your landlord will help out?" Ray asked.

Bill shook his head. "He owns a lot of these old houses. I don't expect much help from him."

Katie nudged her husband.

Ray spoke up. "I'll give you a hand wherever I can. I can get supplies at the hardware store where I work for twenty percent off."

Bill smiled, looking overwhelmed but relieved. "I'd be very grateful for the help," he said softly.

With that, they all ventured inside to inspect the damage up close. The vinyl floor in the kitchen was soaked. Bill squatted down and peeled back one of the squares of material. "It looks like we'll have to replace the entire floor in here."

Puddles of water had pooled on the kitchen counter, the kitchen table and other exposed surfaces.

"Good thing you unplugged the fridge before leaving," Ray said. "Don't know what kind of damage the rain would have done to it."

Marilyn and Bill walked through their damaged home in a trance. Mattresses were saturated with water. They would take forever to dry. The sofa would probably have to be trashed. Framed photographs were streaked from moisture droplets. More than once, Marilyn broke down, crying in Bill's arms.

Seeing all this, Katie realized how very fortunate her family had been. The damaged pecan tree, the water-filled backyard, even the smashed garage roof were nothing compared to what the Watsons had lost.

The days following Hurricane Donna were filled with water-drenched chaos. The dampness just wouldn't go away. Bed sheets hanging out took ages to dry. Mud clung stubbornly to their clothes, and Katie spent countless hours mopping the kitchen floor.

Ray gave up his lunch hours and daylight time immediately after work to help Bill patch his roof. It wasn't difficult work, but it did take time. He even gave up his Saturdays to help the Watsons. Katie adjusted her schedule to allow Ray to spend more time at their place.

She wondered if the small lake in her backyard would ever recede. In time, it did, along with the small rivers that ran over asphalt roads and through drainage ditches.

Springlake would take a long time to heal. Donna had moved up the coast on her devastating trek, but the scars she left behind would remain in Central Florida for years to come.

But things did improve. Several weeks later, the Watsons invited the Franklins over for a picnic. It was a glorious day. Katie wore a pullover and pedal pushers. She basked in the warmth of the late September sunshine, watching the boys play baseball in the park while the grown-ups grilled hamburgers and hot dogs.

Eventually, some neighbors dropped by, and Marilyn introduced Katie and Ray as the guardian angels who had saved them from the wrath of Donna. She and Bill took Katie on a tour of their renovated home. New floors and countertops gave the old place a much more modern look.

"Will the owner cover the repair costs?" Katie asked Bill while admiring the wallboard patches in the living room.

"I don't think so," Bill said. "He claims that so many of his homes were damaged by the hurricane that he can't afford to pay for all the repairs."

"That ain't right. He's got insurance to cover that stuff. He's probably already turned in the claim." Katie could feel anger and indignation bubbling up inside her.

"Katie, there ain't much more I can do," Bill said. "I'm thinking about moving to those new apartments over by George Washington Carver High School. They're much nicer than this place, even with our repairs."

"Well, if you need me to write your landlord a letter, you just say the word."

"Thank you. You and Ray have already done more than enough."

But Katie disagreed.

* * *

I may never get out of here, Katie thought gloomily. The Jefferson Davis Elementary School PTA had a long list of material on its agenda. She scanned the mimeographed piece of paper in her hands again to estimate what time the meeting might end. She considered slipping out the back between the discussions on the new playground swingset and the commendation for Mr. Johnson, the music instructor with fifteen years of service. She would have left, too, were it not for the fact that she was friends with the PTA president, Sarah Palmer.

Their boys played together at least once a week, and Sarah and Katie had become good friends. Tim, Robby, Ken and John played on the same baseball teams, sat together in school and trick-or-treated together at Halloween. Sarah's husband was a foreman up the road in the Bartow phosphate pits, and he and Ray were friends.

Finally, Sarah banged the little wooden gavel to close the PTA meeting, and the ladies all began to mosey toward the back door. Katie waited even longer while Sarah gave some last-minute instructions to a couple of ladies who had volunteered to publicize the school vaccination program. At long last, they said goodbye and Sarah came to meet Katie in the back of the classroom where she'd been waiting.

Sarah could not contain her enthusiasm about the presidency—not of the PTA, but of America. "I am so excited about President Kennedy," she said, then started explaining why President Kennedy would be so great for the country.

"I can tell you're excited, but—"

Sarah went on, speaking in an animated voice, moving her hands around as she spoke.

Katie broke in again. "You might want to lower

your voice. Remember, he won by just a few votes. Some people here may have voted for Vice President Nixon."

John F. Kennedy's election had represented a dramatic change among Americans. He was the second youngest president and America's first Catholic president, which was one reason for Sarah's enthusiasm, being a devout Catholic herself. Katie liked him because he had voiced support for Civil Rights legislation during his campaign.

Sarah placed her hand to her lips. "Oh, you're probably right. It's just that he's so young and brave. Don't you think that Jackie is so attractive? It's such a great time to be alive."

"Of course it is." Katie steered her toward the exit doors and the parking lot.

When they reached their cars, Sarah said, "Well, I'm off to run errands."

They said their goodbyes, then Katie called after her, "Can we get the boys together on Tuesday?"

"I don't think we could keep them apart," Sarah said over her shoulder. "Bye!"

Katie had certainly felt the tension during the election campaign. For many, Kennedy's tenure in the White House would be seen as an exciting new era of growth and progress. For others, it was a step in the wrong direction. Katie wondered if things could possibly get more tense and unsettled.

* * *

June 1961

Nuclear peace talks, astronauts in space, a failed attempt to invade Cuba, and talk of going to the moon. Katie and Ray felt like the world was spinning out of control. Business at the hardware store was booming, keeping Ray busy six days a week. It all piled up, and the family decided they needed to get away for a while.

The perfect getaway state turned out to be Texas. The boys said they thought it would have cowboys and rodeos, and Ray said he thought it would be nothing but desert. As for Katie, she had a more realistic perspective on the Lone Star State. She had an aunt in Dallas whom she had not seen in many years, and Aunt Betsy had told the family that a new Six Flags theme park was scheduled to open in Texas that summer. As a secretary for the Arlington City Council, Aunt Betsy promised them that she could get advance tickets to visit the park in June before it officially opened.

With the lure of cowboys and a new theme park, the Franklin boys were sold, and would not stop talking about the trip. So the family had no choice but to load up the station wagon and head west. Unfortunately, one evening as Katie put the final touches on dinner, she overheard Walter Cronkite on the evening news talking about the Freedom Riders. She stopped what she was doing and went to stand behind Ray in his easy chair while Cronkite described the group.

The Freedom Riders were Negro and white civil rights activists who rode buses in the South to test federal laws that granted equal rights to colored people. In Anniston, Alabama, a busload of Freedom Riders were attacked by a mob of white people who slashed the tires and firebombed the bus. In Birmingham, Alabama, a bus was met by members of the Ku Klux Klan, who beat riders with bats, chains, and pipes. Other buses met with similar fates throughout the month of May in Montgomery, Alabama, and Jackson, Mississippi.

"Plop, plop, fizz, fizz." A commercial for Alka-Seltzer came on, and Katie and Ray turned away from the set.

"I'm afraid we're going to have to cancel the vacation," Ray said. "Every major city between here and Dallas has been affected by these Freedom Riders, and I don't feel it's safe."

"The boys will be so disappointed," Katie said. "We've always taught them to treat all people fairly. What would it mean to them if we let this cancel our vacation?"

"We have to think of safety too, Katie," Ray answered. "Maybe we can go next summer."

"Are there any other options?"

"I guess we could take back roads all the way, but I really don't know if they will be safe, either. It would make the trip much longer."

The two sat in silence.

"I know," Katie said suddenly. "We can fly!"

"Fly? We can't afford that."

"Maybe we can. I've been saving money for a rainy day, and we do have that money your mother gave us last year for special occasions. I can't think of a more special occasion than this."

"But who ever heard of a family like ours taking an airplane for a vacation? We're the Franklins, not the Rockefellers."

Katie's excitement soared as her mind filled with thoughts of planes and new adventures. "What a great experience. The boys will never forget it. After all, when will they have another chance to fly in an airplane?"

Katie's mind was made up. With Ray's eventual nod of approval, she drove to a travel agency in Orlando the very next day to book the flight. Unfortunately, most of the local flights to Dallas were already reserved, and their meager savings, even combined with the gift from Ray's mother, were not enough to cover four tickets from Tampa or Orlando.

After forty-five minutes of phone calls to various airlines, the agent reserved four spots on a flight from Tallahassee to Dallas on June 9, returning on June 16. Tallahassee was several hours north of Springlake, but it would save the family from driving through Alabama and Mississippi.

Katie called Ray at the hardware store, then eagerly wrote out a check for the tickets.

* * *

Sitting on the double bed in the air conditioned room at the luxurious Holiday Inn in Dallas, Katie wrote a note on hotel stationery to her friend Sarah Palmer:

Dear Sarah,

We are having such a wonderful time. All three of my boys are taking one last dip in the swimming pool right now. We all went horseback riding, watched a real rodeo and ate genuine Mexican food. Six Flags was so much fun—you won't believe the crazy hats Robby and Tim bought at the park. We had a great flight out here and expect another trouble free trip back to Florida tomorrow.

Love,
Katie

On Friday, June 16, they boarded the plane for their return flight to Florida. Katie wore her nicest Sunday morning dress and high-heeled shoes. Ray wore his suit and both boys wore clip-on ties. Despite her attempts to stop them, the boys also insisted on wearing their wild Six Flags hats.

The airport in Tallahassee was a much newer facility, and smaller than the airport in Tampa. When the plane landed, the boys were glued to the windows, watching the pavement race underneath the plane.

Immediately, everyone's attention was drawn to the airport terminal, which was surrounded by crowds of people. From the confines of the airplane, Katie could not tell exactly what they were doing. She could see that some were carrying signs. They were all white, and mostly men, and angry.

"What's going on, Dad?" Tim asked.

"I don't know, son."

After a few minutes, the pilot came on the airplane's public address system. "Ladies and gentlemen, we are going to wait here on the tarmac for a few more minutes to get directions from the tower. There appears to be some sort of event taking place in the terminal. Please, be patient." Katie shot a concerned look to her husband.

After about twenty minutes of anxious waiting, the pilot spoke again. "Ladies and gentlemen, we have been cleared to park near the terminal. We will unload the luggage once we have parked. I've been instructed to tell you to collect your luggage and follow the police escort through the terminal to the exit. Do not stop or slow down. This is for your own safety."

One by one, the passengers walked down the stairs from the airplane. Concerned and confused, they all lined up at the back of the plane and picked up their luggage.

Ray grabbed their two large suitcases, Katie carried her overnight bag and each of the boys had a suitcase. Along with the other passengers from their flight, they followed two Tallahassee policemen into the small terminal. Immediately, they were overwhelmed by a loud and angry mob of white people hurling insults at a small group of people in the terminal restaurant. Reporters were standing by, taking photographs and jotting down notes in small notebooks.

Robby, jostled by one of the men in the crowd, dropped his suitcase. Katie bent down to help him pick it up, only to be shoved by someone from the pulsating crowd. They gathered their belongings and pressed on.

At one point, their group had to slow to a stop. The mob had swelled in size and the passengers simply couldn't get through. Katie turned to the nearest reporter. "What is this all about?" she asked.

"You haven't heard?"

"No. We just landed."

The reporter nodded toward the restaurant. "Those people in there are some of those so-called Freedom Riders. They rode buses to Tallahassee and were planning to fly back up north. It would have been fine, except they decided to eat at this restaurant and the owner didn't want to serve colored people. He closed the place down last night, and they decided to stay until the restaurant opened again this morning."

Katie raised her eyebrows in surprise. *All night?*

"All these people are here to see to it that those liberal fascists don't tell them how they should run their business."

Katie turned to Ray. "This isn't right."

"This isn't our problem, Katie," he replied.

"I ain't so sure about that."

The noise from the crowd was almost deafening. The family was jostled around by the angry mob. Katie was pushed back against Ray's strong chest. She felt him wrap a protective arm around her waist.

She thought of her black friends back home. She thought of the example that her children were being shown. She thought of Irma, and she thought of Claire. Then, she stopped thinking.

"I want some coffee," she announced. With that, she pulled away from Ray and pushed her way to the front of the crowd.

"Katie, wait!" Ray called. He tried to pull her back, but was hampered by the suitcases and crowd.

But Katie couldn't wait. Frightened to numbness but driven by principle, she marched through the angry mob. She ducked under the arm of a large, sweaty man and wedged herself in front of him, then kept moving.

"What's with you, lady?" he yelled.

As she neared the entrance to the restaurant, the mob shifted slightly and, for a brief moment, a tiny gap appeared. Katie slipped through the opening and dashed to the counter where two black men and one white man sat, waiting to be served.

Feeling like a burglar about to be caught at any moment, Katie took a seat on one of the counter stools. She caught the attention of one of the waitresses, an attractive, older woman with worry lines across her forehead, who stood near the kitchen door. She walked over to the corner where Katie sat and said, "You don't want to be here right now, miss."

"I would like a cup of coffee," Katie said firmly.

The waitress looked perplexed and scared. She bit her lower lip and looked back toward the kitchen.

"I said, I would like a cup of coffee."

The waitress glanced toward the Freedom Riders, then eyed Katie closely, "Are you with those people?"

"I just landed. My family has been vacationing in Dallas, Texas. Look, all I'm asking for is some coffee."

The waitress hesitated, clearly trying to discern

Katie's motives. She sighed, shrugged helplessly, and then complied, placing a cup and saucer in front of Katie. She poured some coffee into Katie's cup.

"May I have cream and sugar?" Katie asked.

The waitress fetched a large container of sugar packets and a silver tin of cream and placed these beside the cup.

Katie emptied two packets of sugar into her cup and poured in a good helping of cream. She slowly stirred the mixture until it turned a soft, creamy shade, somewhere between black and white. Despite the adrenaline coursing through her and the palpable tension swirling around her, Katie couldn't help but appreciate the symbolism—blacks and whites mixing together like the creamy concoction in her cup. *If only it were as simple as coffee and cream*, she thought wryly.

The crowd had hushed.

Katie took a sip of her coffee. "That's good," she told the waitress.

The waitress smiled weakly.

"Now, I'd like a cup for these three friends of mine," Katie said.

The color drained from the waitress's face. "I—I can't. You know I can't. The owner doesn't want us to serve them."

Katie smiled reassuringly. "You won't be serving them, honey," she said. "You'll be serving me, and I'll be sharing it with them."

The waitress obviously felt trapped. She turned to the head waitress, standing near the kitchen. Then she just stood still. Katie looked at her nametag.

"It'll be all right, Dorothy," Katie said.

Moving slowly, the waitress turned and retrieved three more cups and three more saucers. She placed them on the counter next to Katie. She turned around again, got a fresh pot of coffee from the burner, and placed it next to the cups. Then she turned on her heel and went to stand with the head waitress, as far away as she could get without leaving her station.

One by one, Katie filled the cups with coffee and

passed them to the three men sitting near her at the counter. She also passed down the sugar and cream.

They smiled and simply said, "Thank you."

All four of them sat quietly and sipped their coffee. The crowd, momentarily stunned to silence, suddenly roared back to life.

"You can't do that," someone yelled.

"You nigger lovin' bitch!"

"That ain't right."

Katie just sipped her coffee, hoping that her peaceful response sent a powerful message, if not to the crowd, then at least to the reporters and, most importantly, to her children. She ignored the angry jeers as best she could, and kept her back to the crowd.

Suddenly, the Tallahassee chief of police burst into the restaurant through the kitchen and announced in a booming voice, "Your attention please." He was a heavy-set man, wearing a black fedora and exuding an extreme level of confidence, typical of law enforcement officers in the South.

The crowd outside the restaurant hushed.

The police chief continued. "You people in this restaurant are under arrest for unlawful assembly. We provided safe transportation for you yesterday from the bus station to the airport terminal, and you have insisted on causing trouble. You have left us with no recourse but arrest."

The crowd outside the restaurant cheered.

"Come with us peaceably or we will carry you out."

No one moved.

Katie couldn't stop her hands from shaking as she put the cup to her lips. Her decision to support the Freedom Riders was about to get her into more trouble than she'd ever faced in her life.

The white man sitting two stools down from her was suddenly yanked up from his seat. His coffee cup and saucer fell to the floor with a crash. "You can't do this. You are violating my rights," he yelled.

"Shut up and git movin'," the chief of police said, as two other policemen dragged the struggling man from the restaurant.

The crowd screamed their support.

A moment later, the police returned for the black man sitting next to Katie. "C'mon, boy," the chief said.

The young black man held up a hand. "Wait. I will come." He stood and followed the two police officers outside.

When they got to Katie, Dorothy and the head waitress came forward and interrupted the chief of police. "She ain't with them," Dorothy said.

Katie felt like she should protest, show more solidarity with the Freedom Riders, but she was terrified.

"She just came in for some coffee. I think her family is over there by the door," the head waitress said.

Katie turned, as did the chief of police, to look for her family. They were standing near the entrance to the restaurant. It was easy to tell which passengers were her family—Ray looked every bit the panicked husband, forced to stand by and watch because he was tied down with two giant suitcases and two bewildred and frightened boys.

"Go home, ma'am," the police chief said quietly. He turned and walked away.

Since the Freedom Riders had been escorted off the premises, the crowd quickly dispersed. Ray grabbed Katie's arm and steered her toward the exit. The boys followed, carrying their suitcases.

Katie's breathing didn't return to normal until they were about thirty miles outside of the Tallahassee city limits. Then she gulped in a deep breath of air and let out a long and loud sigh. She shook her head and blinked her eyes. "What did I just do?"

Ray, who'd been silent up to that point, actually started laughing. "Well, Mrs. Franklin, you defied the entire Leon County Law," he said.

With that, the tension broke.

"Mom, that was great," Tim said.

"I can't believe you did that," Robby said.

"That was great!" Tim repeated.

"Were you scared?" Robby asked.

Katie laughed, and then she replied seriously,

"Honey, I was terrified."

"Me too," Robby said. Tim nodded.

"We're lucky it ended the way it did, for us," Ray said a little sternly. "We could all be spending the night in jail."

Katie's hands were shaking again. She placed one on Ray's arm for support. "The next time I do something like that, stop me."

"The next time you do something like that, I'll go with you," Ray said. "You are one gutsy lady."

He moved his arm to her shoulders and squeezed her tightly as they drove south.

* * *

November 1963

Katie felt numb. No, less than numb. She felt as if the whole world around her had suddenly been given a shot of anesthesia, like she got when she had a tooth filled at the dentist's office. She couldn't feel anything. She didn't move, wouldn't *let* herself move, for fear that what she was seeing might be true, that it might not be a dream.

She stared at the black and white television screen. She had turned it on as soon as Sarah Palmer had telephoned with the terrible news. President John F. Kennedy had been shot.

Walter Cronkite was explaining on a CBS News report that it had happened while the President was riding in a motorcade in Dallas, Texas. The scene was chaotic. Cronkite sat at a desk, with a thin microphone before him, reading from one report after another on the incident. Katie couldn't turn away. She, like the rest of the country, it seemed, was glued to the television.

She prayed that, somehow, the reports were wrong. She prayed that the President was still alive. She prayed that the madness would go away. Her prayers went unanswered.

This was reality. President Kennedy had been shot,

and now, everything would change.

Tim and Robby were released from school early. They rushed through the front door shouting, "Mom, did you hear about the President?"

When they entered the living room, Katie wiped the tears from her cheeks and opened her arms wide. Her boys hugged her from either side. They all settled back on the sofa to watch the horror unfold on television.

Katie watched her distraught family closely during dinner. Just a few weeks ago, the boys had been excited about building a fallout shelter over at Wagoner's Field. Now, Tim was buttering his bread several times over, and Robby looked confused, trying to make sense of a tragedy so far beyond what a ten-year-old boy should face. Ray ate little; he just twirled his fork in his spaghetti.

Marilyn Watson called Katie after dinner, and they talked for half an hour without really saying anything. As soon as she hung up, Tim took over the phone and called several of his school friends to talk about the shooting.

Robby seemed antsy, as if he felt smothered by the silent and somber house. He moved from chair to sofa and back again, and finally sauntered toward the front door. Katie watched him step out on the front porch, letting the screen door slam behind him. A few minutes later, she went out to find him with a couple of glasses of lemonade. He sat on the porch rail, with his back against a small support pillar, staring down the street.

He took the glass and sipped his lemonade without a word. Katie sat in a rocking chair and sipped her own lemonade. She didn't know what to say. She had no idea what to do. She only knew that people should not be alone during such tragic times.

After several long minutes, Robby said, "Listen."

Katie stopped the rocking motion of her chair and cocked her head to hear . . . nothing. The street in front of their house, usually busy with passing traffic, kids riding bikes or neighbors walking by, was completely empty. If she strained her eyes, she could see the flickering glow of televisions through the Edwards' house across the street, but it was too far away to hear any sound.

Tonight, it seemed like everyone had locked themselves away, away from the awful world in which a promising leader's life had been so savagely destroyed.

Tonight, it was best to just stay home.

* * *

March 1964

Life had just about returned to normal when, on one afternoon late in November, Katie happened to be out in the laundry room on the opposite side of the carport. Tim was playing with Wayne, a neighborhood kid who, as far as Katie was concerned, needed a little more family time and a little less neighbor time.

She overheard Wayne saying something about a "nigger woman" who had yelled at him for riding his bike on the sidewalk.

"This nigger woman started shouting and yelling," Wayne said, laughing. "I laughed so hard that I cut a loud fart." Both boys burst into uncontrollable laughter.

Katie was about to scold them when a loud, familiar voice broke through the boys' laughter.

"Just who are you calling a nigger?" Irma asked.

The laughter stopped abruptly.

"Not you," Wayne managed to mumble.

"Well, you'd better not be calling *me* a nigger," she said. Katie could hear the justified anger in Irma's voice. "I am *not* a nigger," she said.

"No, you're not," Wayne mumbled some more. "You . . . ain't no nigger woman."

Katie heard him shuffling his feet, kicking at the dirt.

"And . . ." Irma said slowly. "What would you say I am, then? Well?"

Wayne sounded like he was about to wet his pants then melt away into nothingness. "You're a *nice* woman," he said.

"Oh. So niggers ain't nice?"

"Well, I mean, no," Wayne sputtered. "Niggers are

nice . . ."

"So, who are you calling a nigger, mister?"

Wayne's voice shook. "Certainly not you, Miss Irma," he said.

"Of course not," she said. "Because I am *not* a *nigger*."

After a long pause, Katie thought the kids might come bursting through the laundry room door at any moment, but Irma finished her lesson for poor little Wayne. "I am a black woman, and don't you forget it."

"No ma'am," Wayne said in a small voice.

"I don't want to *ever* hear you use that word again, Mr. Wayne," Irma said.

"Yes, ma'am," he said.

"Now, go on home."

Katie watched him sprint by her, out the door and homeward. He ran home faster than Katie had ever seen a boy run before. She truly believed that he would never use the word "nigger" again.

* * *

July 1964

"I think it's just wonderful that we have such a handsome, young minister in our congregation," said Betty Jackson while she scooped some potato salad onto her plate. She didn't even look down; her eyes were fixed on the young minister sitting at the head table of the Methodist Women's luncheon. She passed the bowl to Katie, who sat next to her.

"They said he did very well at Candler," said Ruth Lawson, past president of the Methodist Women's group at Springlake and former delegate to the Florida Conference of the Methodist Church.

Katie passed the potato salad along and accepted the plate of sliced ham. "If he can help our children, then I think we're very fortunate to have him."

"You know, he's single, too," Betty added.

"But we aren't," Katie cautioned her two friends.

"It's still nice to dream," Betty said. "Oh, dear," she added. "You have something on your pretty blouse."

Katie looked. It was just a bit of white thread.

"As my mother used to say, 'Everything is attracted to black except men and money,'" Ruth said, plucking the thread off Katie's black blouse. "That's much better."

Reverend Stephen Phillips, dressed in sport coat and turtleneck shirt, was talking to Gloria Smith, the current president of the Methodist Women's group. The women liked to stay current on what took place in their church, and on Reverend Phillips' first Sunday as associate minister at First Methodist, Gloria had cornered him to ask him to speak to their group.

Katie glanced down at the mimeographed sheet of paper beside her plate. It listed the agenda for the day's luncheon. At the bottom, a bio of Reverend Stephen Phillips described him as a native of Miami, Florida, and a recent graduate of Candler Theological Seminary in Atlanta. She moved her eyes up the sheet to his slot on the agenda. The title of his presentation was *The Times They Are a Changin'*.

Mary Lou Sommers sat down with her plate across from Katie. The elder woman pulled back the folding chair and plopped her rotund frame onto it. "Hrmph," she muttered. "I thought we were going to have a presentation on the Methodist Retirement Home today."

Betty leaned across the table and whispered, "I think since Reverend Phillips joined us a few weeks ago, Gloria wanted to give us a chance to see him."

"Well, I've seen him and I'm not impressed," Mary Lou snapped. "I think he's just too young."

"He could never be *too* young," Betty said.

"I think he will be good for the young people," Katie said.

"We don't *have* any young people in Springlake," Mary Lou argued. "We're a retirement community and we need a minister who understands the needs of retirees."

"Well, Dr. Strong, the senior minister, is almost retired himself," Katie said. "He can take care of the retirees."

Mary Lou glared across the top rim of her gem-studded glasses. "You just say that because you're so young yourself. When you get older, you'll understand." She shuffled in her metal chair, drew her hand to her back suddenly and made a painful grimace. "It's not easy getting old, you know."

"I'm not saying that it is easy, Mrs. Sommers," Katie said. "I'm just glad to have someone younger on staff here. I think he will be able to reach out to the teenagers in our community."

"What help do they need?" Mary Lou grumbled. "They just sit around in their cars all day listening to Elvis Presley."

"Well, mine prefer The Beatles and The Rolling Stones."

Mary Lou just glared some more.

"Would you like some potato salad?" Katie asked with a smile, sliding the large bowl to Mary Lou's side of the table.

"I really shouldn't," Mary Lou said, "But this looks so yummy." She dug into the bowl like a child digging in a sandbox, and plopped several helpings onto her plate. As she reached for the ham platter, Gloria Smith stood to call the meeting to order.

Katie glanced down at the title of Reverend Stephen's talk again. *The Times They Are a Changin'*, she thought. *Lord I hope so.*

* * *

August 1965

Boy Scouts, Little League Baseball, church socials, and more kept the Franklin family busy throughout the year. Katie did all she could to guarantee that her children would grow up with opportunities and experiences that she could never afford as a child. Irma was her helpmate, providing support and working to make sure that everything was done when it needed to be done.

Katie knew that growing boys needed time together

with people their own age, so she made every effort to help them build strong friendships. One afternoon, Sarah Palmer and her two sons were visiting at the Franklin home. Sipping afternoon coffee on the porch, Katie and Sarah smiled as they watched the four boys playing baseball in the backyard. The Franklins had grown a bit over the last couple of years, and were now sporting "dutch boy" haircuts, like the Beatles. The Palmer boys, on the other hand, still had short-cropped hair.

"Is Kenneth still planning to play baseball next year at Springlake High?" Katie asked.

Sarah paused and looked down at her coffee cup. "Ed and I decided to put Kenneth and John in the new private school over at St. Mary's in the fall."

"Oh," Katie said. "Whatever for? Didn't they do okay in junior high?"

"Yes. Their grades are fine. They get along with all the other children so well."

"Then why would you transfer them to Catholic school?"

"Well, Katie," Sarah said. "You know, things are really changing. High school isn't the same as it used to be."

"Sure it is," Katie protested.

"No, it's not. Ed doesn't like the direction that the public schools are heading. Everything is changing too fast. And I agree with him." Sarah paused, clearly hoping that the conversation might end with that.

Katie continued to stare at her.

Finally, exasperated, Sarah said, "Katie. Haven't you heard? They are going to allow n-i-g-g-e-r-s in the white schools this fall. I don't want my boys' educational experience to suffer. It's just not right."

And just like that, Katie knew her friendship with this woman would not last much longer. Katie felt in her soul that what Sarah had said was wrong. Her attitude, her assumptions, everything . . . all ignorant and wrong.

Katie also knew that many parents who chose to send their children to private school did so for much more noble reasons than to avoid "n-i-g-g-e-r-s," as Sarah had so carefully spelled out. Many just wanted their children to have an education grounded in faith and a belief system that they weren't getting in public school. The fact that Sarah had brought up the race issue disappointed Katie to the core.

Katie had no idea what to say, but she knew that something must be said. "Sarah, I don't understand what is wrong with black children and white children attending school together."

Sarah looked genuinely surprised. "Oh come now. You know they aren't as smart. I'm afraid that they will take the teachers' attention away from my children."

"I don't believe that for a second," Katie countered. "Given equal opportunities, blacks can learn as well as whites."

"You do know their schools are behind our schools academically, don't you?"

"Which is one of the main reasons for integration," Katie answered. "The old 'separate but equal' policy plainly failed."

"Why don't you just put Robby and Timmy in private school?" Sarah suggested. "I'm sure St. Mary's would allow a couple of good Methodists."

"No," Katie replied. "I don't think we could afford it." But of course that wasn't the real reason.

The rest of the day, Katie could feel the distance growing between her and Sarah. They talked about light things, like new laundry soap, the boys, and their husbands. Neither of them ever spoke of integration or private school again.

* * *

November 1965

"Have you ever found yourselves in total darkness, completely surrounded by the absence of light and the presence of . . . nothing? That's precisely what our friends and relatives faced this past week when the power went out all over the northeastern part of the United States."

Dr. Strong was opening his sermon on Sunday evening at First Methodist. The sanctuary was far from full, but Katie and her family sat in the pew beside the support column under the balcony, as they did every Sunday night that they were in town. It certainly wasn't the best seat in the house, but it was a tradition. For them, this was a social event, a chance to get out of the house and off to a good start before the week began. And, happily, it ended before Bonanza began on NBC-TV.

Katie knew exactly where this sermon was heading. The massive power outage, as long as twelve hours in some areas, affected twenty-five million people. The television news stations couldn't find anything else to cover. Surprisingly, very little looting or violence took place throughout the ordeal.

"There are those who walk in darkness all of their lives. But that doesn't have to be the case. You and I can help bear our neighbors' burdens and show them the light of the Gospel of Jesus Christ."

The service ended with a hymn and a prayer, and Katie and her family filed out the back, shaking hands with Dr. Strong and Reverend Phillips as they left. Stephen shared some friendly remarks with Tim and Rob, and Ray turned to speak to some guys he knew from work.

Katie paused and looked up into the dark night sky, thinking about the sermon and the blackout and the darkness in the world. It occurred to her that darkness was not always so bad. Tonight, for example, the dark sky seemed empty of all the clutter of clouds and stars and planets. It felt open and inviting.

Late that night, after the kids were tucked in bed and the television had been shut off, Katie was standing in front of the bathroom mirror removing her makeup before bed. Suddenly, the lights went out and the bathroom was pitch black. Katie gasped.

"Have you ever found yourself in total darkness, completely surrounded by the absence of light?" Ray asked in a deep voice.

She felt his strong arms wrap around her from behind. She sighed as he embraced her tight and pulled her into him, relaxing as he began to nibble on her neck.

"I'd be afraid that the boogeyman would get me," she said, turning to kiss him. "You're not the boogeyman, are you?"

Ray did his best to mimic a radio preacher. "No, my dear. I am the Right Reverend Doctor Graham Cracker Strong, at your service."

"Don't take this personally, Dr. Graham Cracker," Katie said, giggling, "but I think my husband preaches your sermons much better than you do."

"Why, thank you, ma'am," Ray said as he guided her toward the bedroom.

* * *

November 1967

Katie's worst fears nearly came true when she received a phone call one afternoon from Ray saying that Tim had been involved in a two-car accident on County Line Road. She met Ray at the Springlake hospital, and they waited together while the doctors worked to mend Tim's battered body.

Most of the events of that traumatic day were a blur to Katie. She remembered Reverend Stephen Phillips fetching Rob from basketball practice. She remembered spending hours in the waiting room and beside Tim's bed. She vaguely remembered talking with the doctor and finding out that Tim's legs had been badly crushed, but that, in time, he would be able to walk again.

Mostly, though, Katie remembered the people who came by to help. Reverend Phillips stayed at the hospital almost as long as she and Ray did. The Watsons came by on several occasions. Irma put in some extra days to help Katie manage the house, and the Wesley Guild from church brought half a dozen casseroles to keep the Franklin family well fed.

Whoever proclaimed that "time heals all wounds" couldn't have been a worried mother. Katie knew that it would take more than time for Tim to come around and for the family to get over the shock of his accident. But the truth was that time was the one thing that was most abundant, so she waited patiently. Eventually, Tim came home from the hospital and in time, he set aside the crutches for a cane. Soon enough, he would be able to set that aside, as well.

Irma Brown, ever the optimist, tried to find the silver lining around the terribly dark cloud over Katie's family. She gave Katie a pep talk one day while they were hanging the laundry to dry out back.

"Lawdy, Miss Katie," she said, clipping the corner of a sheet to the clothesline. "That poor Timmy seems to be in a mess o' pain."

"He's coming along," Katie said in a flat voice. "The doctor says he should be able to walk without the cane, eventually."

"You know," Irma continued. "My nephew was about Tim's age when he got hurt real bad on the farm."

Katie looked up. "What happened?"

"He fell off that old tractor they had while plowin' a field," Irma said.

"Oh . . . that's terrible," Katie said.

"Well, he had to hobble about wit' a cane, like Mr. Tim, for the longest time. When it came time to sign up for de draft, the army wouldn't take him, 'cause of his condition."

"Is that right?"

"Yes'm. They put him on the disqualification list, and he din't have to go over to Vietnam."

"Maybe that is good," Katie said. She thought for a moment. "You know, Ray and I did expect Tim to join up after he turned nineteen. Now, maybe he won't have to."

"Da Lawd works in mysterious ways, Miss Katie."

"Yes, He does." Katie smiled gratefully.

* * *

March 1969

Occasionally, Irma would call Katie to request a

ride to work, when their family car was not working or her husband needed it for work. One Thursday morning, Katie headed across the tracks to pick up Irma. Katie had heard the phrase "across the tracks" all her life. It referred to the poorer side of town. In Springlake, it meant Irma's neighborhood, which people once called Colored Town. It sat literally across the railroad tracks from the rest of the city. It was made up of about ten interwoven streets, which separated fifty or sixty run-down, shabby houses. Each house was little more than a shack with a yard, few of which with much grass growing in them.

Irma and her neighbors put a lot of effort into maintaining sizable gardens in their backyards to help supplement whatever foods they bought at the grocery store. Okra, corn, lima beans and all sorts of melons sprouted from the sandy soil all through the neighborhood. Gardening took a lot of work, and people took pride in their backyard gardens.

Irma had one of the nicest gardens in the neighborhood. She worked hard to keep it up, and often brought berries or pole beans to Katie's house to share.

As Katie drove up the street beside Irma's old house, she was shocked to see her friend, head down and shoulders hunched forward, standing in a mess of torn plants and squashed produce. Several other neighbors were standing nearby in gardens that had also been destroyed. It looked as if a small tornado had swept through the neighborhood, ripping up every vegetable and fruit in its path.

"Irma, what happened?" Katie called as she stepped out of her car.

"Oh, my, Miss Katie. Look what they done to my garden." Her voice broke and she shook her head. "Why would somebody do such a thing?"

"Who did this?"

"I'll tell you who did it," said an older gentleman with a huge walrus mustache from one yard over. "Them white boys in their pickup trucks did it."

Another neighbor added, "They calls it nigger-bogging. They get drunk and drive their huge trucks through our gardens and destroy all our fresh vegetables. And they shout and yell all kinds of terrible things while they do their mischief."

"Why would they do such a terrible thing?" Katie asked.

"They're mean, ma'am. They're just mean."

Throughout the neighborhood, Katie could see scores of backyard gardens, smashed and dug up by the high-speed tires of several trucks.

"That ain't all they done," said a beanpole of a man. "They caddy-scratched my car."

"What's that?"

"Well, ma'am," he explained, "I ain't got much money. But when I was able to get a loan from the car dealer, I bought me a nice Lincoln. I ain't got no garage, so I park it out in front of my porch every night."

Katie looked across the street to where the man pointed at a late-model Lincoln Continental.

"They took their car keys or some knives, I guess, and scratched the paint right down to the metal. They calls that caddy-scratching."

Even from fifty feet away, Katie could tell that the repairs would run hundreds of dollars. "Has anyone called the police?" she asked.

"It don't do no good," the man with the walrus mustache said. "They don't even come by to write up a report."

Katie picked her way through Irma's destroyed garden and made it to her friend just in time to hug her as she broke into tears.

"Why would they do sech a thing, Miss Katie?" Irma cried.

"I don't know, Irma, I just don't know."

Katie changed her plans and spent the day helping Irma salvage some of the collard greens and carrots that had survived.

It seemed to Katie as if Springlake was feeling the birth-pangs of change, and they hurt the innocent.

* * *

July 1969

Shaking the pot vigorously, Katie heard the popcorn kernels popping inside. She turned off the range, lifted the lid and poured the fluffy snack into a large bowl.

"Hurry up," Ray shouted from the other room. "He's getting ready to leave the lander."

"Coming," Katie shouted back. She shook some salt over the bowl and carried it into the living room. Finding her place in the middle of the sofa, she held the bowl in her lap while Ray and Rob started gorging themselves.

The ghostly images on their new color television set showed Apollo 11 astronaut Neil Armstrong descending the ladder of the lunar module and preparing to drop to the moon's surface.

"I wish Tim could be here with us," Katie said softly. "Something this important should be shared by the entire family."

"I'm sure they're watching this at camp," Ray said. Tim was spending the summer as a camp counselor at a youth camp in Leesburg, Florida.

No one took their eyes off the television set as the astronaut leapt backwards toward the surface of the moon. When he landed, the trio erupted in cheer. Katie hoped they were also cheering at camp, even all around the globe.

SANCTUARY TWO

Business

"In business be as able as you can, but do
not be cunning;
cunning is the dark sanctuary of incapacity."

— Philip Dormer Stanhope, 4th Earl
Chesterfield (1694–1773)

GEORGE ROBERTS

March 1958

No doubt, one of the finest days of my life was the day that I opened the hardware store on West Plant Street in March of 1958. I'm not a man who likes fanfare and hoopla, so the grand opening was anything but grand. To me, the spaciousness of the building, the incredible assortment of products and our top-notch service would be sufficient to appeal to one and all. Heck, if people wanted entertainment, they could go out to a movie.

I bought an 8x10 half-inch piece of plywood from Lakeland Lumber and hired Frank Landon to paint the words *Grand Opening* in bright red letters on a white background. My neighbor had called Landon the best painter in Springlake, at least when he was sober. I found out after the fact that his specialty was painting houses, not signs. I guess I got him on a good day though because he did a fairly decent job.

I also bought two eight-foot lengths of 2x4s and mounted the sign outside the front door, and went inside to wait for someone to drop by for a visit. It was a beautiful, sunny March day in Florida, the perfect day to buy some home improvement items.

Florida is full of funny folks. I think they have so many beautiful days in Florida that they tend to let them go to waste. Back in New Jersey, people would trample you to get building supplies on a nice day. No one trampled anyone on my Grand Opening morning.

It was the most exciting and the longest day of my 34-year-old life. Not one solitary soul ventured through the front door all morning. It was still exciting though, because this was *my* shop. I busied myself by cleaning the already spotless shelves and resorting nuts and bolts. I polished the already gleaming light fixtures. Every time a cloud passed overhead or a truck drove by or someone walked by on the sidewalk, I'd look up in anticipation of my first customer.

For lunch, I ate the ham sandwich that my wife, Betty, had made and washed it down with an RC Cola from the brand new cold drink machine standing in the back of the store. Already I was ten cents in the red.

Then, about 4:30 in the afternoon, the shiny glass front door finally swung open and a tall, distinguished gentleman strode confidently inside. Dressed in a white suit, beige shirt and a polka-dotted bowtie, he strolled straight to where I was—beside a display of Dupont paint cans that I had just finished restacking for the fourth time—and extended his hand.

"My name is Elmer Rawlings," he said. "As the mayor of Springlake, I would like to welcome you to our wonderful little community."

Elmer struck me as one of those "I'm in charge" types. He had a full head of silver hair, brushed back with a touch of Wild Root. He wore black-rimmed glasses that seemed to accentuate the movement of his eyes.

Surprised that the town mayor would drop by for an opening day visit, I swallowed my disappointment that he wasn't a paying customer and shook his hand. "I'm honored to meet you, Mr. Rawlings." Of course, I would have been honored to meet anyone on that long and lonely day.

"Call me El," he said, leaning in close with a big smile. "Everyone else in town does—that is, except the Republicans." He winked. He lifted a screwdriver from a display and twisted it in midair, pretending to tighten an invisible screw.

I smiled. "Hello, El."

He continued. "We're mighty happy to see your hardware store open its doors today. We see it as a real sign of growth and future prosperity." It sounded like he was reading a travel brochure from the Chamber of Commerce.

"Why, thank you," I said. "This is an exciting day for me and my family."

El surveyed the expansive, empty room from one end to the other. "I'm not sure I could take this much excitement for an extended period of time," he said with a drawl that used far more syllables than Webster would normally allocate.

I had to laugh, looking at the grand total of zero customers in my shop. He was obviously pulling my leg.

"Well, it's a start, a marvelous start," El said. "And, it will grow like a magnificent garden." He waved his arms as he spoke. With the screwdriver in one hand, it looked like he was conducting an orchestra.

"I'm counting on it," I said.

"As are we, my friend, as are we. We are ready to embark on a new expansion effort that will surely impact every businessman and every family in this wonderful little town. I believe quite confidently that your business will be one of those that will profit most from this exciting endeavor."

"What endeavor is that?" I had a sneaking suspicion I was being lured in for the kill.

El laid the screwdriver aside on the counter. "Why, a brand new hospital, filled with the latest scientific wonders to keep our citizens healthy and happy," he announced in his grandiose fashion. I could tell he was proud of the project. "We are in the final approval stages, and expect construction to begin within eighteen months." He lowered his voice confidentially. "You know how slow and inefficient committees can be."

I shrugged and smiled.

"Now then," El said, returning to his upbeat tone, "Can we count on you, as a businessman, for a donation to help get our new hospital off to a good start?" So that's what he'd been after.

"Oh," I stuttered, caught more off-guard than I should have been. "Well . . . I just opened, you know, and I haven't really gotten my feet on the ground, yet . . ."

"Perhaps a little seed money . . . say, fifty dollars?" This man was without shame. "You'll see multiple returns on your investment, I'm sure."

I wrote the check. I don't know *why* I wrote the check, but I did. Maybe I really was convinced that it would be good for my store, or maybe a part of me felt the hospital would really help the community. It did make sense for Springlake to have its own hospital. After all, the nearest hospital was thirty miles away. Honestly though, I think in the end I just wanted him to leave and I didn't think that he would do that without my money.

El thanked me for having the "vision and foresight" to help our community grow, so that in turn my business would grow as well, and then he walked toward the front door. With his hand on the door he turned and said, "You know, you really should consider advertising in our weekly newspaper, *The Springlake Tribune*. Everyone reads it." And then he was gone.

I felt a little down on myself when I realized that his fingerprints were the only ones on the door besides mine. It was to remain that way all day.

At the end of Day One, I closed the doors to my hardware store, realizing that I was fifty dollars and ten cents in the red.

Late that night, while getting ready for bed, I replayed my conversation with Elmer Rawlings and realized that I had never told him my name.

* * *

Over the next couple of days, a few customers began to trickle through my front door. By the end of the week, the trickle had become a steady stream. Word of mouth and a great deal of patience paid off, and I felt that I just might be able to make this work.

I found myself enjoying my work in ways that I hadn't expected. People would come to me with their problems, and ask how I might suggest they fix them. Bobby White had recently bought an old run-down house in the sticks and he was trying to install his first indoor bathroom. I showed him how to connect the pipes and what he needed to make it happen. Ron Ayers had a leaky roof and needed some roofing cement. A nice little old lady wanted a sprinkler for her front lawn. I helped her find the right one—actually, the only one we had in stock—along with twenty-five feet of hose. I wished it could just go on that way forever. People coming. People going. People buying hardware.

But I forced myself to keep things in perspective. Over the years I'd learned that just when you think things are going to settle into a meaningless rut, life has a way of coming along and changing it all. The problem is that we're never really ready for the change when it happens. Sure, some people say they like change. I've said that myself from time to time. But when it gets right down to it, the only thing good about change is the feeling we get when we drop a little into the offering plate.

* * *

Whenever Betty's parents came to Florida to visit, I felt like those funny British Royal Guards who wear those big black hats and stand watch outside the Palace in England. Bascially, I knew I was being put on display for Mr. and Mrs. Henson. But this time I was more than ready to deliver the grand tour.

We began the visit by sharing a delicious Sunday dinner at Morrison's Cafeteria in Ocala. The Hensons liked the variety of foods at the Cafeteria, and the fact that a crew of black waiters graciously helped out by bringing the trays of food to the table.

From there, I took the family to the hardware store. After Dorothy and Earl stepped out of the car, I escorted them to the front door.

"When we constructed the building," I explained, "I made sure we used the finest materials available. The outer shell is made of the very latest in corrugated steel and aluminum, and it's covered with a white enamel that's actually baked onto the metal." The walls of the building glimmered like sunlight on a lake.

"Tell me again why you chose a hardware store," Mr. Henson asked. He had a way of feigning casual interest when he was actually sizing me up to be sure that I could take care of his daughter.

"When I returned from the War, one of the first things I noticed was how run-down most of the houses were in my hometown. I figured people would need to repair their homes, and that they would need tools and supplies to do that."

He watched me closely as I spoke, ready to catch me if I misspoke.

"What I wanted to do," I continued, "was build the homeowner's dream shop, filled with everything anyone could possibly need for home maintenance."

I opened the front doors and switched on the overhead fluorescent lights. The store was immaculate thanks to the hours I had spent preparing the previous week. The metal on the saws, drills, chisels and hammers hanging from a display on the right shined in the light. A display of floor cleaning products stood out on the left. Shelves, filled with every imaginable hardware product, ran the length of the store, and large stacks of paint cans lined the back wall.

The Hensons, stunned, stared at the sight before them like tourists at a national monument. I looked at Betty. She was beaming.

"As you know, Betty and I chose Springlake because of her arthritis. We thought the warm Florida climate would be easier for her."

Mr. Henson grunted his approval.

The interior climate was a cool seventy-two degrees, thanks to a thermostatically controlled central air conditioning system. I pointed to the thermostat and Mr. Henderson seemed impressed.

"You'll get a lot of carpenters and retirees coming in just for the cool air," said Mrs. Henderson, pulling the fabric of her blouse back and forth to help circulate the cool air against her skin.

I felt like I was finally beginning to win their approval.

"Does it cost much to run?" Mr. Henderson asked.

"A few cents a day, Dad," I said, forgetting that he always tensed up when I called him that. "But worth every cent."

Mr. Henderson was even more impressed when I took them to the back office and showed them the meticulous maintenance schedule I had created. I reminded them that I had been a maintenance technician in the Navy, so I understood how important it was to take care of everything. I briefly showed them how I had tracked the inventory, making sure that everything was accounted for and everything was in its place.

Needless to say, I was proud of the store. I took the stewardship of my resources seriously and the store reflected my devotion. We concluded the tour and stepped back into the warm Florida sunlight.

"Let me ask you this, George," Mr. Henderson said, staring down the street. "Is it safe?"

"What do you mean?"

"Will Betty be coming down to the store very often, and if so, is this a safe neighborhood?" he clarified.

I followed his gaze and zeroed in on a shiny new Cadillac driving by. Through the open windows, I could see four Negro men inside.

Betty quickly answered for me. "I don't come down here that often, Daddy," she said.

I added, "I have been thinking about adding a burglar alarm bell soon. I just haven't gotten to it, yet."

"Might want to make that a priority," Mr. Henderson said.

I nodded my agreement.

As I turned to lock the front door, I got my first really big compliment from my father-in-law. "Well, good job, son. It's almost like a cathedral, so carefully cared for."

I smiled so big that my cheeks hurt.

* * *

Springlake had the Big Four: Kiwanis, Civitan, Optimist, and Rotary. I visited them all in the early days of my store. They received me with open arms and welcomed my "much-needed" business, as they put it, to the community. The programs were mildly entertaining but the baked chicken lunches were not.

I don't remember which club meeting I was at when a couple of gentlemen pulled me aside for one of those two-on-one talks that you just know have ulterior motives. One of them was older, with a high forehead dotted with freckles. His partner sported a neat and trim crew cut that reminded me of a freshly mowed lawn. Both were wearing plaid sport coats and striped ties.

"We were just talking," Freckles said, "and we thought you could clear something up for us."

What an opening line. He could go anywhere from there. Who do you think took the Lindbergh baby? Do you believe in UFOs? What would you say is the meaning of life?

In reality, their query was much less sensationalistic. But it was still somewhat ominous. "We were wondering why you chose that location for your store." It was really more of a statement than a question.

"You know," chimed in Buzz Cut, "everyone says it's all about location, location, location. How did you choose that particular . . . location?"

You can always tell when there's a "right" answer to a question someone is asking you. That had happened to me once when my drill sergeant shouted, "Are you a man or a little boy?" Another time was when my girlfriend asked, "What do you think is the best age to get married?" Here was another, and yet, for the life of me, I couldn't think of anything to say more profound than, "A friend of the family put the property up for sale, and the price seemed right."

Freckles and Buzz stared intently at me for several seconds. Then Freckles said, "You know you're pretty close to a rough part of town, don't you?"

"I guess I'm hoping they will need to replace a lot of windows and do a lot of painting," I replied, trying for humor.

"It's just that . . . things can get kinda dangerous down there. It gets a bit—*dark*—in that part of town, you know?" On the word "dark," he raised eyebrows meaningfully.

"We gotta look out for our own, you know?"

I took a moment before replying. "Well . . . Thank you for the warning. I may need to invest in a burglar alarm and spotlights for the parking lot. You know, we sell a nice, loud alarm bell that should do the trick."

Another pause. Then both men broke out laughing. I guess my alarm idea wasn't exactly what they had in mind.

"Look," said Buzz. "If you decide to expand or just move to another location, give me a call." He handed me his business card. "We've got the largest real estate office in the city. We've got connections to owners who don't even know they are about to sell, if you know what I mean." For the life of me, I had no idea what he meant. They both shook my hand, and wandered off to, I assumed, intimidate another visitor.

That afternoon, a little over a hundred years after Edwin T. Holmes installed the world's first electrical alarm system, I, George Roberts, installed an alarm bell outside my building. It had switches on both doors, which rang the bell if either one was opened after hours.

As I was wiring the back door switch, a colored man drove up in a rat-trap of a Ford pickup. He got out of the truck and eyed my work curiously. His skin was blacker than most coloreds and he had a large scar on his right arm. He was holding a five-dollar bill in his right hand.

"Looks like you're settin' some fancy alarm bell there, mistuh," he said. "You don't need to worry about people 'round here. They're all God-fearin' folk."

"You never know," I responded. "What can I do for you?"

"I don't mean to disturb you," he said. "I'm doing

some repairs on Mr. El's home and he said I needed a gallon of white paint. Mr. El said I should get it from you. I got the money." He held out the five-dollar bill.

I went in to get the paint, feeling uneasy. Something about the man bothered me. Maybe it was the scar or his interest in my alarm system. When I returned to the back door with his paint, I noticed that he was staring at the alarm bell like it was a gun pointed at him.

"Thank you, suh," he said. He took the paint and the change to his truck and drove away.

Maybe I should *consider relocating,* I thought. But I had invested too much in this property to just pick up and leave.

* * *

Eventually, I followed Mayor El's advice and wandered into *The Springlake Tribune*'s editorial office, a tiny little stand-alone building that housed several reporters all talking on telephones, a receptionist, who was also talking on a telephone, and a back office that I assumed was for the editor-in-chief—who was probably talking on yet another telephone.

It looked like they printed the paper elsewhere, because I couldn't see a printing press. Somewhere in Springlake, I imagined, a printing press was rolling off great sheets of newspaper. And the press operator was probably also talking on a telephone.

After watching the receptionist chatter away for what felt like ages, I finally saw her hang up the phone and smile my way. "May I help you?"

"Yes," I answered. "I'm interested in placing some advertisements in your paper."

She said nothing, but one of the men in the office hung up his phone and hustled to the front of the little building. He extended his hand. "I'm Jake Goodling. I handle advertising, this week," he said.

"George Roberts," I responded, shaking his hand firmly. "I recently opened a hardware store on Plant—"

"I know, George. We've heard of you," Jake said.

"C'mon back."

Jake cleared a small space on his desk and pulled a pad out of a drawer. He slid a sheet of carbon paper under the first page and positioned his pen at the top. Looking up from his desk, he asked, "What kind of ad are we talking about?"

I explained that I wanted to let local citizens know about our products. As I talked, Jake checked off various boxes on the form, checking several times to ensure that the marks were going through to the second page. At one point, he pulled a huge book from a shelf behind him, and opened it to a section of hardware clip art. I selected one or two for the ad, and he noted them on the form.

Within thirty minutes, we had designed three versions of a newspaper advertisement that would appear in the next six editions of the *Tribune*. I signed the bottom of the form, agreeing to the *Tribune's* staggered payment plan, and sat back, satisfied that my store would receive the publicity that it needed.

On the way out, we shook hands again, and I asked, "Say, Jake. How did you know about my store?"

"El told us to look for you," Jake said. "He owns the *Tribune*."

* * *

When you invest your finances, your energy, your time, and your life into something, it is of the utmost importance that you select your help carefully, making sure they're people you can count on.

The advertisements in *The Springlake Tribune* and the other ones I took out on the local country radio station—owned, incidentally, by El's brother—paid off. Within a couple of years, Springlake Hardware had grown large enough to warrant additional staff. I knew I had to hire the best in order to keep the high levels of service and professionalism I had established for my customers. I especially didn't want to have to keep a sharper eye on my employees than on my business.

In fact, the city itself was growing. New housing

communities, called subdivisions, were being built and people were buying hardware.

But Springlake Hardware wasn't just another store. I had worked hard to make it the ideal hardware store, with the right mix of products and the right atmosphere to fulfill any carpenter's needs. I knew my customers. I knew their needs. I invited them into my shop and made sure they got the tools and material they needed.

Over the course of three weeks, I interviewed at least twenty people for the position. I eventually settled on Ray Franklin, a tall, skinny man who had moved to Springlake from Georgia. He worked hard, was never sick, and treated the customers with respect. I couldn't ask for more.

Like most businesses in the South, Springlake had white customers and colored customers, and the coloreds would come to the back door to pay for their purchases. They seemed to like it that way since we dealt with them on a more personal level and they wouldn't be embarrassed if they couldn't read or do math.

I had also built colored restrooms for men and women out back. They didn't buy that much hardware, but from time to time they would drop in for some nails or paint or basic maintenance supplies.

Ray was good about taking care of their purchases, which freed me up to deal with the higher-paying customers inside the store. Ray would meet them at the back door, listen to their needs and then come inside to pull together a sack of products. He'd return to the back door to collect payment.

He also worked well with our part-time driver, Bubba White, whom I had hired when our lumber business picked up. There were a couple of lumberyards nearby, but I found that some folks liked the convenience of buying their hardware supplies and their lumber at the same time, so I put up some tin sheds out back and stored some common lumber items in them. Often customers didn't have a large enough vehicle to carry the lumber, so I'd have Bubba drive it over to their worksite, as a favor and a sign of good service.

After hiring Bubba, I was reminded that, unfortunately, you really can't always tell what you're getting when you hire an employee, even if you're real careful.

Like any businessman, I had my preferred customers. The Kinney brothers were among the best. Tom and Dan had dropped out of high school to take over their father's carpentry business when he was sent to Chattahoochee for alcoholism. The Kinneys ran a successful operation, building new upscale homes on the south side of town. They were hard-working, God-fearing boys who had managed to make it work in a tough industry.

One night, as I was locking up the store, Dan Kinney pulled up in the driveway. Figuring he was dropping in for some last-minute supplies, I unlocked the door and walked over to Dan's truck.

"Hi, Dan. How can I help you? Do you want to come inside?"

He seemed uncomfortable. "Naw," he said, looking out of his truck window at the parking lines in the asphalt. "George, I need to talk with you."

"Sure, Dan."

He cleared his throat and spat a wad of something out the window. "You know that last load of lumber your boy delivered yesterday?"

"Sure. Was the lumber all right? I can exchange it if you aren't happy."

"Naw," he said. "It ain't that. It's just . . . When your boy dropped off the lumber, he seemed to be driving kinda reckless. One of the other carpenters said he smelled liquor on his breath."

I was shocked. I had never known Bubba to drink, especially while on the job. I was furious to think that he might be making me look like a fool, not to mention endangering the reputation of my business. "I promise you, Dan, I don't tolerate that sort of thing from my employees. I'll talk with Bubba about this."

"Well, I didn't smell it myself," he said. "But I did

see him drive away. I thought that nigger was going to take out a big oak tree on the property."

"I sincerely apologize for this, Dan. I will handle it," I promised.

"Well," Dan said after a long pause, "I was hoping you'd say that, 'cause I ain't sure we can continue to get our lumber here otherwise," he said. "It would look pretty bad to our customers if there was a serious accident or something." He looked at me with one eyebrow raised.

Embarrassed by my poor choice of driver and livid at Bubba for almost costing me one of my biggest customers, all I managed to say was "I'll take care of it immediately."

Dan nodded. "I knew you'd do the right thing." He spat again and drove away.

The next day, I told Ray he would have to take over delivering the lumber.

"What happened to Bubba?" he asked.

"I had to let him go," I said. "I had reports that he was drinking on the job."

"Bubba? That can't be," he protested. "I thought he was a teetotaler."

"What can I say?"

"It's just that . . . he said his church wants to bring back prohibition. He talks about it all the time."

"You never know," I said.

"You never do."

* * *

January 1960

Sometimes you just don't make the best business decisions.

Just before the Christmas of '59, I had ordered an assortment of sporting goods. I thought people would snap up the footballs, basketballs and baseballs for Christmas gifts. At the time, I didn't think anyone else in town sold bats, gloves or helmets.

Unfortunately, a new Woolworth's Department

store opened up downtown in November and they sold the same stuff for less than I could buy it wholesale. I couldn't compete. In January, I had to drop my sporting goods line and put everything on sale. But I still couldn't move it.

One day, Ray suggested that we donate the balls, bats, helmets and the rest to one of the churches across the tracks.

"Those Negro boys and gals don't have much, you know. And, we could take a tax write-off for the donation."

Ray volunteered to deliver the stuff on his own time. It wasn't a bad suggestion, but I just couldn't bring myself to give those things to a bunch of colored kids. The inventory sat in the back room for years before I finally donated it to the new Springlake Goodwill Store.

I had paid a pretty penny for those items.

* * *

March 1960

One spring day, when I was in the back office balancing the books, Ray stuck his head in the door and said, "I've got kinda a strange request." He had pen and pad in hand and a deep frown on his face.

"Shoot," I said.

"Tom Kinney just called. He says he wants 75 sixteen-foot-long 6x6s of untreated lumber, and several gallons of kerosene. Seems like a strange order."

Nothing that the Kinneys ordered had ever surprised me. Their can-do attitude was the hallmark of their business. They often bragged that their success was based on the fact that they took the jobs that no one else wanted.

I once sold Tom Kinney several water pumps because his customer wanted to build his house on existing swamp. They had figured on bringing in some fill dirt and digging what they called a retention pond to catch the seeping swamp water.

On another occasion, they'd built an observation tower so a strawberry farmer could keep an eye on the migrant workers when they picked his crops. But this wasn't just your run-of-the-mill observation tower. This one was forty feet tall, completely glassed-in and air-conditioned. I thought it was a brilliant idea, because those pickers are like gypsies—they'll steal half of what they pick.

"Who knows what the Kinneys are doing," I shrugged. "Do we have those in stock?"

"Not enough, but we can special order it. It just seems strange. There's nothing else in the order. No plywood. No boards. Not even 2x4s," he said. "What are they building?"

"No idea," I said. "Take the order and move on."

* * *

September 1960

Hurricanes in Florida are more common than fleas on a stray dog. Some have been downright devastating. The Miami Hurricane of 1926 left over 25,000 people homeless. Hurricane Okeechobee killed over 4,000 people back in 1928. The Labor Day Hurricane of 1935 killed over 400 people, including many World War I veterans in Islamorada.

But until 1960, all of us in Springlake had dodged the bullet, so to speak, when it came to really facing a mean 'cane. Still, everyone prayed for another year like 1954, the only year in recent history when not a single hurricane struck Florida.

Then came Donna.

Hurricane Donna drove up through Cuba, the Keys and the west coast of Florida with winds above 100 miles per hour and drenching rains. She plowed her way northward just past Fort Myers and then turned east to soak the state on her way to the coast. She seemed to have homed in on our sleepy little town, and people started to panic.

The hardware business was booming.

Droves of customers came to the store to buy

lumber, plywood, tape, nails, flashlights, and anything else they could get their hands on to hold their homes together through the storm. They cleared the shelves of everything except flowerpots. Expensive little battery-powered television sets, slow-moving items considered a luxury purchase by most customers, were snapped up in no time. Transistor radios disappeared. Buckets, sponges, and batteries quickly sold out.

Ray and I worked at a furious pace, ringing up order after order. Betty had to put in a couple of hours a day to help us manage the load. Ray handled the colored people's orders out the back door, as usual. At one point I had to caution him that we needed to ration items going out the back door so our regular customers could get what they needed. We had to turn away more than one family who couldn't afford the supplies they wanted.

At around noon on Friday, September 9, we had to stop taking credit and lay-away orders. That made some of our customers with credit accounts angry, but for every angry customer, five more were standing in line with cash in hand. It was a retail businessman's dream come true.

At one point I stopped taking orders altogether and grabbed the supplies that I thought I'd need for my own house: masking tape, lumber, batteries, and flashlights. Then I directed Ray to take a break and do the same for his house.

By late afternoon, we had nothing left to sell and closed the shop doors. Customers continued to pull into the parking lot, so I had Ray take some of the remaining paint and make a sign on the outside wall of our store that said we were closed and out of stock. I figured we would just repaint the wall after the hurricane passed. Painting the sign was difficult because the storm had started and the wind was battering the wall with torrents of rain.

We spent three more hours that day taping the store windows, tying down items in the backyard and sealing up the place. Radio reports announced that this was "the big one" and we needed to be prepared for the worst. Customers kept coming, even in the rain.

I finally sent Ray home and started to lock up the

store, not sure what I'd find there after the storm passed. I paused before locking the back door and surveyed the empty store. I felt a mix of satisfaction and fear. It had been a soaring success in terms of sales, but what would happen when Donna came knocking? I locked the door and hoped for the best.

*   *   *

Donna was terrible. I heard the citrus crops were hit hard. The farmers were going to suffer and migrant workers would have to head out west for work. Houses were demolished. Trees were knocked down everywhere. Yards were flooded and over 350 people were killed.

I don't know when I was ever so scared as when that hurricane hit. Betty and I huddled together under the dining table, but honestly my greater fear was for the store. What would we do if it was destroyed? Our life savings were tied up in Springlake Hardware.

I heard on the radio that Donna was so devastating that the name would be retired as a possible name for future 'canes. I'd never heard of such a thing before.

As it turned out, we were among the lucky ones. The hardware store had suffered very little damage. Some metal siding was torn away by the harsh winds, and I didn't have anything in stock to repair the damage. I didn't even have canvas to cover the damaged areas. I had to tear some tin off the sheds in the back to put a temporary patch in place.

But all in all, our damage was relatively minor. Plus, sales were so good over the next month that I found myself wishing a couple more hurricanes would come through. I've never had a better month than that September.

We worked diligently to refill our inventory. Over time, as demand died down, we were able to rebuild properly. Hurricanes may be devastating to people, homes, and land, but they are a godsend to the hardware industry.

* * *

As time went by, we developed a fairly steady clientele of handymen, carpenters, and a few do-it-yourself family men. Very few women came to the store, despite our efforts to advertise kitchen appliances and pots and pans. Children, too, were pretty rare at Springlake Hardware. After the sporting goods debacle of '59, I didn't bother trying to give them a reason to stop by.

That's why I was surprised to see Ray's sons, Timmy and Robby, come strolling through with a colored boy one Wednesday morning. They all looked like they had been playing in the dirt. I shot a look at Ray, who quickly took the three boys to the back door to find out what they needed. Robby presented his father with a long list of supplies; they were building something in an old field on the east side of town and needed some nails, paint, and a few sticks of wood. Ray pulled their supplies together and helped them tie them to the backs of their bicycles.

* * *

March 1963

We celebrated our five-year anniversary with as much fanfare as our budget permitted. My wife helped decorate the store with banners, balloons, and crepe paper. It was a bit difficult for her because she was still struggling with painful arthritis, but she did what she could. Ray's height came in handy as he and Betty hung the decorations. He would stand on the ladder, with his head in the rafters, taking tape from Betty below who kept telling him to adjust whatever he was fixing to the ceiling.

Naturally, we advertised in *The Springlake Tribune*. We also posted catchy signs on telephone poles around the block and in the front window. We planned to have drawings for prizes throughout the day, with three grand prizes. One was a brand new refrigerator. It had a special new feature called frost-free. The manufacturer claimed it never needed defrosting. I was skeptical, but figured it would make a good raffle prize. Our second grand prize was for a set of plastic bowls with lids, called Tupperware. The third grand prize was a new bicycle.

Lots of people took a close look at that new refrigerator. No one cared much for the plastic bowls. But the bike? That really drew some attention. Children came by all week long to press their faces up against the window for a closer look. It really was a beauty—a bright red Schwinn Stingray with gleaming high-rise handlebars and a white banana seat. No one had anything like it in Springlake.

The bike was so popular we had to shoo the kids away from the window several times a day. We'd go out, chase them off, and they'd come back twenty minutes later. I considered taking the bike out of the display window because the constant parade of kids was getting to be a bit of a nuisance, but I decided to leave it. It was building hype, and it did turn the heads of our adult customers as well.

Some colored folks wanted to be in the drawing as well, and Ray went ahead and passed out registration cards and pencils to them. He gave them to me and I admit that I was a little surprised that those coloreds knew how to write. But I felt the drawing should be to reward our better-paying customers, so I left their cards out of the bucket. Besides, what would colored people do with a set of plastic food storage containers?

At about 4:00 p.m., we had everyone gather at the front of the store for the raffle. There was quite a crowd watching as Betty dug into the big paint bucket to select the winners. The *Tribune* had a photographer on hand to capture the event, and even the local radio station was there with a live broadcast.

Shirley Johnson won the refrigerator. She was overjoyed because she said their old Frigidaire was starting to make strange noises.

The plastic bowls went to Herb Stillwell, one of the only bachelors who had filled out a drawing card. Herb had a bewildered look on his face. "I don't know what I'm going to do with all those," he said doubtfully.

"Maybe you'll find a pretty lady who can put them to good use," El Rawlings shouted from the back of the room. Poor old Herb's face turned about as red as the lids on those plastic bowls.

But the big prizewinner was little Rodney Smith, Bill Smith's son. When Betty announced his name as the winner of the Stingray bike, he ran to the front of the store, jumping and shouting. Ray had to slow him down to keep him from driving the bike through the display window. Ray took the bike outside and set it on its kickstand. Rodney jumped on the bike and headed for the parking lot.

Apparently, riding a Stingray is slightly different from a regular bike because of the handlebars. Rodney rode straight into Dan Kinney's new work truck, scratching a long line through the *Kinney & Co.* logo. I caught Dan giving a hard look at Rodney's dad. I guess the bike wouldn't be completely without cost to the Smith family.

Rodney himself was all right in spite of this first little accident. I suspected that it wouldn't be his last. He jumped back on the Stingray and rode around the parking lot for an hour. Eventually, Ray had to chase him down to get him out of the parking lot so the customers could go home. The boy's father loaded the bike in the trunk and Ray tied the lid down with some twine from out back.

I closed the store that night pleased and proud after my first five years of business. The store was holding up pretty well for all the traffic she endured. I needed to patch up a bump here or there and maybe invest in a little paint, but the inside was still gleaming and the products were as popular as ever. I was looking forward to working toward our ten-year anniversary.

* * *

July 1964

Down the street, the counter at the local Springlake Diner was buzzing. The tiny restaurant had served the community for nearly twenty years. Binding business contracts had been signed over coffee there, and even more binding marriage agreements had been settled over dinner. But it was more than just a place to eat. It was a daily meeting place for the men of the town to discuss important issues and air their concerns.

The federal government had recently enacted some legislation that forced businesses to allow colored people into public places. Bill Grant, the theater owner, said he was going to have to let coloreds sit down in the main section of the theater, instead of just the balcony. He thought it would kill his business.

Frank Reynolds, a salesman at the Buick dealership, pointed out that they already accommodated colored people, even to the point of giving them their own separate restrooms, so what more could they want?

Ron Burton, the jeweler, said that they couldn't afford most of his merchandise anyway, but he did worry about someone breaking into his shop.

The owner of the diner, an old guy named Jimmy Jackson, half-heartedly said he didn't expect any trouble with his business. "Hell, I don't know how to cook anything they like to eat," he said. He also offered to pass out axe handles to keep the peace, so to speak, like Lester Maddox did up in Atlanta, but no one took him up on it.

A few locals—a barber, a mechanic, and an appliance repairman—didn't have a problem with the ruling. The barber had cut colored people's hair in the army, and the other two didn't think colored customers would be much trouble.

The person who seemed the most upset about the ruling was probably the one who was going to be affected the least: Reverend Daniel P. Kingston, the pastor of the Independent Church of Springlake.

"Listen up, citizens," he said. "Before you know it, they'll be stealing our wares right out from under our noses. They'll be moving in next door to you and they'll be dating our daughters."

"Beg your pardon, Rev," Frank Reynolds said, "but you ain't got no daughters."

"That's not the point," the minister shot back. "Bill does," he said, pointing toward the theater owner. "And Harry does," pointing toward the appliance repairman. "It ain't right. It's an abomination for the races to mix. We are witnessing the downfall of American society," he said.

"Well, what can we do about it?" Frank asked.

"We can stop it, now!" the minister shouted, his voice reaching a high pitch.

I gave some serious thought to slipping out the front door, worried that the minister might be about to pass an offering plate, but I decided to stay in case the old guy started making sense. He obviously had the attention of everyone else at the diner, so maybe he had something worth hearing. So I spoke up.

"Excuse me, Reverend Kingston. *How* do we stop it, exactly?"

Kingston jumped at the chance to answer my quesiton. "Well, it begins by understanding exactly what the government is doing to us regular citizens. They're telling us who we can sell to in our shops. They're telling us who our kids can go to school with. They're telling us what we have to do. That's not freedom. That's a dictatorship."

The Reverend Kingston was headed way off-topic, complaining rather planning, so I tried to reel him back in. "But what can we *do?*"

"Well, I think we have to protect our own," the jeweler cut in. "I've already ordered some metal bars for those plate glass windows in my shop."

"My kids are going to the Catholic school in the fall," Bill Grant said.

"From the fryin' pan into the fire," Reverend Kingston shot back. "You gotta watch them Catholics more than the coloreds."

"We have to be careful," Jimmy Jackson said, turning away from the grill and walking toward the counter. "If we make too much out of this, they'll get self-righteous, and it'll backfire on us. I don't want no riots on the streets of Springlake like they had in Mississippi and Massachusetts."

"So what do we do?" Bill Grant repeated my question, thinking in practical terms like me.

Jimmy raised a finger toward the ceiling. "This is the time to wait. We need to lay low and wait it out."

"No," Reverend Kingston shouted. "We've gotta act, and now."

"If we do," Jimmy said, lowering his voice so the people in the diner had to lean in to hear him, "we might fan the flames and give them more attention than they deserve. Right now, we need to work in the background."

I watched Jimmy closely. He talked like a man who knew what was what. He had a confidence about him.

"There are people," he continued, "there are people who are rallying together to counter this very threat. They know what's at risk. They know who's involved. They are very influential. And they know how to fix this mess we're in."

"Who are they?" I asked.

"In time, George," Jimmy said. "Right now, we need to follow the jeweler's advice. Let's make sure we protect our own. When the time's right, we'll know it." Jimmy turned back to his grill without another word.

Well, I was sold. It seemed pretty clear to me that Jimmy knew more about this situation than I did. I committed myself to taking his advice and looking out for what's mine.

I went back to my store and double-checked my security system. I tested the burglar alarm bell, scaring Ray so bad that he dropped a monkey wrench on his foot.

I drafted some new guidelines to limit the cash kept in the cash register.

I also ordered some large hanging mirrors for the corners of the store. With them in place, we could see whatever anyone was doing from anywhere in the store.

I had Ray paint over the word "Colored" on both of the restroom doors out back. That idea was a waste of paint though, because the whites continued to use the indoor restrooms and the coloreds used those out back anyway.

* * *

August 1964

The brochure looked appealing: four nights in Las Vegas, Nevada, for a hardware convention. The timing was perfect. Betty would be off visiting her sister in Indianapolis. The price . . . well . . . it was more than I wanted to spend. But, I thought it was time to see what was new out there. So I mailed in my registration form.

I was not prepared for the Vegas Strip. Up to that point, the gaudiest thing I had ever seen was the makeup that Betsy Harris wore to church every Sunday. But this was a whole other kind of extravagant. The days and nights were filled with loud noises, slot machines unloading coins into metal trays, screaming winners sitting on vinyl-topped stools, and a frenzy of flashing red lights. The sidewalks overflowed with people and the casinos were bursting at the seams. Bars and nightclubs promised all types of entertainment at all types of prices. Things that should not have shined, well, they shimmered.

The hardware convention tried to emulate the flash and flare of the city with glimmering lights, bright signs and attractive sales ladies on the display floor. Signs, surrounded with light bulbs, blazed from everywhere. Balloons floated above products to draw the eye. Blue drapes coated with spray-on glitter hung from pipes overhead. But no convention could hold a candle to the city itself.

I walked the convention floor several times a day, looking for product lines that I may have missed. I found some promising hardware items. New tools designed to make a carpenter's work easier and faster lined the aisles. New appliances, like a portable dishwasher that could be stored in the closet until needed, were everywhere. But what really caught my eye were the guns.

For some reason, I'd never sold guns at Springlake Hardware before. I spoke with several other hardware store owners and found that many were making quite a bit of money selling rifles and handguns. One, a guy from

Detroit, said guns were his best-selling products.

"I can't get enough of them," he said, scratching his shoulder through a bright yellow sport coat. "The market is as ripe as a Georgia peach in the springtime."

"What do you sell more of, handguns or rifles?"

"In my case, handguns are hot," he answered. "Now, someone who is in a more rural location, like yourself, might find that hunters are interested in the rifles. But I carry both. I'm thinking about expanding my store so I can sell more."

I didn't understand the sudden interest in guns.

"It's like this," he said, leaning in as if to tell me a secret that only he knew. "People are scared. You got Commies in Cuba, hippies in Houston, blacks in Boston and drugs in Detroit. My God, man. We've got junkies shooting up in the alley behind the store."

All of a sudden, I was grateful that I lived in the middle of nowhere.

"Nobody's safe anymore, including you and me," my new friend said. "I keep a loaded revolver beneath my cash register."

"That seems a little extreme, doesn't it?" I asked.

"Maybe today. But it's getting bad everywhere. We might as well make a bit of a profit while we help protect our neighbors."

His words stayed with me. I spent a lot of time talking with several manufacturing reps and ultimately placed an order for several rifles and handguns. Plus bullets, of course. Other accessories also made sense, like scopes for the rifles, cleaning products, that sort of thing.

Betty wasn't too excited about my decision to carry guns in the hardware store, but by the time she found out about it, the deed was done. The products were set to ship within a couple of weeks.

When they arrived, I spent the day modifying an old display cabinet to hold them. That week we ran an ad in the *Tribune*, and the floodgates opened. Customers came from as far away as Ocala to buy a gun. We had to quickly order additional supplies to keep the items in stock. I couldn't have anticipated that the demand would be so high if my life had depended on it. Of course, I had no way of knowing when I placed my order that race riots would break out in Harlem the week my advertisement ran in the *Tribune*.

The Harlem riots were all over television, with scenes of people throwing rocks and storefronts ablaze. Apparently, a colored teenager got himself shot by a white police officer, and then all hell broke loose. Hundreds were injured and arrested in New York City. The riots went on for six days. Riots in Chicago, New Jersey, and Philadelphia followed.

Back in Springlake, fathers became very concerned about what they had seen on TV. The fact that colored students would be allowed to voluntarily attend white schools in the fall only fueled the fire.

My only regret was not ordering ten times as many guns.

* * *

October 1966

We must have sold a good hundred beanbag chairs and over fifty gallons of day-glow paint in the mid-sixties. Hanging swag lights were popular and people couldn't buy enough of those bead dividers kids put over their doorways. Styles were changing, and attentive hardware storeowners like me drew a pretty profit.

Those who did suffer, in my opinion, were the barbers. In February, Ed Sullivan had that rock and roll band from England called The Beatles on his TV show, and American teenagers went wild. Boys started combing their hair down in their faces like girls. Girls would scream and cry whenever they heard their music. It was crazy, like some strange spirit had inhabited the minds of our youth.

The associate minister at the Methodist Church dropped by one day to ask if we had any carpet samples that we could donate to his church. I don't know what he planned to do with them. I had attended Fred Dalton's funeral there in the spring and the carpet runners in the aisles looked brand new.

We set up a display of new Stereo 8 music players for cars, and they sold better than hot cakes at the Springlake Diner. Kids called them 8-tracks and mounted them under the dashboards of their cars. They also bought speakers, which they wired in the front and back.

Although I enjoyed the new revenue stream, I felt the kids played their rock and roll music too loud. I wasn't alone. It became a regular topic of conversation at the diner. Officer Rawlings said the music was a distraction and caused an increase in the number of automobile accidents in Springlake. Dr. Thompson said the music was damaging eardrums, and he predicted that all of the teenagers would be deaf by the time they were thirty years old. Reverend Kingston proclaimed, again, that we were witnessing the downfall of American society.

* * *

May 1967

Just when you think the world can't get any stranger, something comes along to bring everything back into balance. In my little world, that happened one afternoon in May.

I had just sat down in one of the swivel chairs at the counter of Jimmy's Springlake Diner, as he had started calling it in 1966, and ordered a cup of coffee and a slice of pecan pie. The place was fairly empty, so Jimmy fetched the coffee and pie himself. Placing both in front of me, he leaned across the counter and said, in a half-whisper, "How are things over in your part of town?"

"Fine, I guess," I said. "Why, you know something I don't know?"

"Naw, George," he said. "It's just that you're so close to Colored Town, and all those black people are causing so much trouble all over the country. I was kinda concerned about you, you know?"

"I appreciate that, Jimmy," I said. "You're right.

These days we've gotta keep on our toes and watch out for our friends."

"Well said, my friend, well said." He nodded, swiping a sticky spot on the counter with a damp rag. "It's not just the niggers, you know. Those damn hippies and liberal politicians are about to run our country into the ground."

"Yeah. Things are getting pretty bad."

"Well, what are you gonna do about it?"

"Me?" I asked. "What *can* I do about it?" I was reminded of the conversation we'd all had here a few years back.

Jimmy paused and looked around the diner to see if anyone was listening to our conversation. The only other soul in the diner was Bob Neely, the postman, who was wasting time in one of the booths because he didn't want to go home to his nagging wife.

"There's gonna be a meeting," Jimmy said, pulling a flyer out from under the counter. He slid the sheet face down to me. "Hundreds of us are gonna meet in old Wagoner's Field next Saturday."

I turned the paper over and quickly read about the rally. It was called an All-America rally. The brochure said the meeting would talk about things like how to reinstate the traditional values that most Americans believed in, and would include information on how to keep America free and safe. A line at the bottom of the page indicated that the rally was sponsored by the Springlake Segregation Council.

"I don't know about this, Jimmy," I muttered.

"Listen, George," he said. "This group is exactly what we need right now. I went to a rally like this up in Macon, and it really helped me understand things. It cleared my head."

I didn't say anything, just stared at the paper.

"These are the only people who are standing up for business people like us," Jimmy continued. "If we don't support them, how can we expect them to support us?"

Jimmy did have a point. How could I expect support if I didn't offer any myself? Maybe these people were like me, frightened by the changes that were being forced on us.

"If you don't go, it's just like giving in to the niggers and the Commies," Jimmy said. Harsh words, but was he wrong?

I left the diner with a small stack of the flyers and passed them along to some of my more loyal customers. Three or four farmers, a handyman, and a plumber accepted the flyers and agreed to come. The Kinneys said they already knew about the event and would definitely be attending.

*   *   *

There were a lot more people at the All-America rally than I'd expected. The old field was full of cars of every make and model. Some looked so rusted out, I was amazed they were road-worthy. Others looked like they had just been driven off the dealership lot.

I pulled through the cattle gate into Wagoner's Field and was greeted by two men wearing white robes and white hoods. They looked me over real good, and then waved me through. At that point, my suspicions were confirmed: this was a Ku Klux Klan rally. The Klan had gotten some bad press recently, so I was a little concerned that someone might recognize me and assume that I was a member. But I was also curious, so I drove into the field.

Feeling a little hesitant, I stayed in my car and watched the people around me. I wasn't sure whether it would be good publicity or bad publicity to be recognized at an event like this.

After waiting fifteen minutes without recognizing a soul, I decided to leave the car. A crowd had gathered around the stage at one end of the field, so I made my way over there. A large cross had been erected behind the stage. The podium was flanked by an American flag on one side and the flag of the KKK on the other.

A man climbed the stairs to the stage and approached the podium. He introduced himself as the head of the Springlake Segregation Council and welcomed everyone to the Rally. He outlined the short agenda for the event and introduced the first speaker. One after another, prominent businessmen and local politicians stepped up to share their stories and vent their feelings of concern and frustration. The longer I listened, the more I found myself agreeing with their arguments, sharing their passion and outrage. They weren't a bunch of senseless hotheads just overreacting—what they were saying actually made sense to me.

The speaker I liked the most, and the one who sold me on this whole All-America thing, was a businessman, like me. He owned a medium-sized pharmacy in a community that was gradually changing from white to Negro. "I watched," he said, "as my neighborhood became run down by gangs of niggers and degenerate bums. I can't let my wife and daughter walk out in the streets no more. My property value's been cut in half." He paused for effect. "It happened to me. It's coming to you."

"NO," the crowd shouted.

"*Hell* no!"

He held up his hands to calm the crowd and said, "I wish I'd known the guy who's gonna talk next ten years ago. It may be too late for my neighborhood. But he can stop it from happening in yours."

The final speaker was eloquent and inspiring. The crowd hung on every word he said. Spontaneous applause and cheers echoed through the night.

I drove away after the rally believing to my core that our country was facing a peril greater than any since the Revolution. Now I understood how integration would corrupt the moral fiber of our cities and states. I realized that I had to be willing to take a stand in order to protect my family and my business. No one else would if I didn't.

That night, sitting at our dining table, I wrote out checks for $500 each to the Springlake Segregation Council and the Ku Klux Klan. I mailed them the next morning on my way to work. It felt good to be doing good.

* * *

March 1968

Ten years passed far more quickly than Betty and I had anticipated. Springlake Hardware had reached its ten-year anniversary. We were so wrapped up in the business that we almost forgot to plan a celebration. One afternoon in late January, Betty and I made time to sit down at the kitchen table and list several ways we wanted to mark the occasion.

First, we wanted more products. I felt confident that many of those who attended our five-year anniversary would have spent more if we'd had more to offer. So we started ordering special items that we didn't carry on a day-to-day basis. I found a wholesaler of kitchen and hunting knives, and bought a large display case from him. I also increased our stock of other hunting gear, including outdoor socks, boots, tents, and lots and lots of guns.

I remembered that the Stingray bicycle was a real hit at the last anniversary party, so this time I purchased a ten-speed bike to give away. But I didn't stop there—I bought several bikes to sell as well, hoping that those who didn't win the prize might still want a "cool bicycle" enough to shell out the cash.

Of course, I ordered lots of small appliances as well: blenders, toasters, toaster ovens, electric can openers, and electric carving knives. We stocked up on hair dryers, irons and do-it-yourself hair clippers, although I worried a bit that no one would buy them since long hair was so popular those days.

I really didn't care for the hippies and their way of life, but I wasn't above taking their money. Many of them had taken to "natural living," and some even lived in communes, with free sex and drugs and lots of natural homegrown foods. I'd heard a rumor that there was a commune over at Wagoner's Field, but I never saw any sign of hippies out there. I didn't like them, but customers are customers I guess. I sold them all the shovels, rakes, hoes, seed, and fertilizer they could afford. I even carried some copies of The Farmer's Almanac, which sold like hot cakes.

We arranged to have a large white tent set up in the parking lot to display all the items that we didn't usually carry. This turned out to be a smart idea, because I could put the stuff the hippies and blacks wanted out in the tent and not have to worry about them coming into the store.

The tent was kinda like a prelude to the real stuff inside the store. I remember a minister talking once about how the synagogue was divided into the common area where most people would go and the "Holy of Holies," where only the priests would go. Privately, I imagined that my store was like an inner sanctum for my regular customers, those who really supported my business.

I made it a point to give those special customers unique privileges. They received special coupons in the mail and they got special attention when they showed up at an event.

Ray, Betty and I worked extremely hard in a short amount of time to prepare the store for the anniversary celebration. We cleaned the place up so it looked like new, and polished every piece of chrome until it shined as bright as diamonds. I swear the store was cleaner than the day we opened in 1958.

The response to the ten-year anniversary bash was huge. The cash register rang nonstop. We ran out of paper sacks for the merchandise. People walked away with some great hardware products. My gun case was almost empty by the end of the day.

The best thing about the event was that I was able to reconnect with some of my best customers. I saw some former regulars, too, people I hadn't seen in three or four years, not since that new Western Auto store opened on the south side.

Naturally, El Rawlings stopped by to chat for a moment. He had a unique way of showing up when the crowds were at their largest, and hanging around until most had gone home. Sometimes I wondered if he chased them off. We shared a late afternoon cup of coffee when the crowd had died down a bit.

"Mr. Roberts," he boomed. "You have done quite

well for yourself."

"Thank you, El," I said. "You know, you were my first customer."

"I remember it well, my friend." he said. "Yes sir, this town has treated you quite well, wouldn't you say?"

"If you take care of the customer, the customer will take care of you."

"Well said, sir," El responded. "You know, we have another opportunity for you to show that you care about those customers."

I'd known *that* was coming.

El pressed on. "We are working to develop a little clinic over on the east side of town, out near Wagoner's Field. Do you know the area?"

"Yes, I'm familiar with it." I tried to change the direction of the conversation. "Do you think they'll ever do anything with that field?"

But it was no use trying to be the captain of a conversation with this man.

"That's a big heap of litigious balderdash," which sounded funny coming from a former lawyer. "We recognize that there is a certain element of the community that might be better served by their own clinic," he continued. "The African American citizens of Springlake might enjoy a health facility in their own neighborhood. Now, it wouldn't be nearly as large as the Springlake Hospital, but would still serve the community at large, if you know what I mean."

"I think it's a marvelous idea," I said, deciding to cut my losses and try to wrap up the conversation in time for dinner. "Do you think a two hundred dollar donation would help?"

"I think the community is hoping for something closer to a thousand, my friend."

"We've had a pretty good day," I said, thinking. "Let's say five hundred dollars, and you let me know later if you need more." At least I was getting better at bartering.

"That would be right nice of you, Mr. Roberts."

Someone once said to keep skunks, bankers, and

lawyers at a distance. I'd amend that to include former lawyers turned politicians. I wrote the check.

After the crowds had gone and the lights were off, I paused to look around the store. True, you could see signs here and there of the wear and tear of ten years of operation combined with the day's anniversary festivities. But by and large, the old store was holding up pretty well.

* * *

June 1969

Early in the summer of '69, I had an interesting conversation with Dan Kinney. He had slipped into the store without my knowing and was staring down into the handgun case by the cash register. His son, Cale, stood at his side, listening as his father described various features of the pistols in the case.

"How's it going, Dan?" I asked, moving behind the display case. I pulled out my keys and unlocked the case, knowing he would want to hold one of the guns.

"We're fine, I guess," Dan answered. "That is, considering the mess our world's in." He pointed to a black '38 with a pearl handle. "That, Cale, is a nice piece of equipment."

I took the gun from the display, checked to make sure the barrel was empty, and laid it on top of a piece of felt cloth we kept behind the counter to keep guns from scratching the glass.

Dan picked up the gun like a priest might pick up the Holy Sacraments. He pointed it at a display of paint cans and aimed down the barrel. "Man, that's nice."

Then he turned to me. "I'm telling you, George. "This country is messed up. These kids are listening to music that is awful and destructive. That bastard, Johnson, he's giving out handouts to anybody and everybody, and those hippies are selling drugs right here in our schools. Ain't that right, Cale?"

His son had picked up the gun and was aiming it at the display of cans. "That's right, Dad."

"It's getting pretty bad," I agreed.

"Citizens need to take their safety into their own hands," he added. "We can't count on the government to defend our families anymore."

"We never should have. This handgun can make you feel pretty secure," I said, hoping for the sale.

"That it would," he answered, "that it would." After a pause, he added, "I may come back later and put it on layaway."

"Just let me know, Dan."

Carefully, I replaced the gun in the display case.

* * *

September 1969

One thing many people didn't know about the hippies was that some of them had money to spend.

Not all, of course. Many just lived off the teat of the community; they all knew how to get their hands on food stamps, and when those ran out they begged for money on street corners. Somehow, they found the money to buy stuff like kerosene and black light bulbs at my store. I think the ones who used kerosene lived out in the woods and used it for their kerosene lamps. But for all I knew, they could have been getting high off the stuff. I think the ones with the black light bulbs lived at home and used the bulbs to give their rooms a "funky" atmosphere.

Personally, I didn't get it. I was raised to be a responsible citizen, to contribute to society and to make a name for myself. As far as I was concerned, kids who dropped out of school, hitchhiked around the country and smoked dope were throwing their lives away. I guess it goes back to their parents. If they had used a little more discipline now and then, maybe their kids would be more responsible and maybe our country wouldn't be in such a mess.

But I was a businessman, so I stocked the light bulbs and the cans of kerosene. I kept them with the 8-track tape players at the back of the store where I could keep an eye on them and the customers buying them.

I also kept a close eye on the black people who shopped in my store. Since Springlake Hardware was so close to Colored Town, I had more Negro customers than I would if I had built on the other side of town. I didn't have much trouble with them though, because I was careful when they came into the store.

One thing I hated was how little respect they paid me and my store. At least twice a week, this one black fella with an Afro hairdo the size of a beach ball would come into the store "picking" his hair with a big long-toothed brush. He'd stand around in the air conditioning for a while, look at the tape players and then leave without buying a thing. And then I'd have to get out the broom and sweep up the tiny little kinky black hairs he left behind from all his picking. It was just plain irritating.

All of the hippies bothered me. The worst thing about them was the smell. They never bathed and reeked like a putrid, rotting pile of garbage. I don't know how they could stand it, themselves. After they left, I'd have to break out a can of air freshener and spray down the whole store. It was a crying shame.

* * *

January 1970

The last day I worked in my store was one of the coldest days of the year.

The weatherman had predicted another severe freeze that night, so I had the heaters turned up high. The warm air combined with the bright glow of overhead fluorescent lights gave the place a welcoming feel. I remember taking a good long pause after finishing accepting a shipment of kerosene cans and just admiring the store. Light still glittered on the edges of the shelves, and the products still gleamed.

I had quite a few customers that day, so Ray and I stacked the boxes of kerosene cans in the corner of the office by the back door. They made it a little difficult to move around, but we were busy so we'd have to wait to stock the shelves until later.

But later never came—more and more customers flocked to the store to buy space heaters and electric blankets, and the day flew by. In the afternoon, a bunch of hippies came in out of the damp Florida cold. Mostly, they just stood near the heating vents. After about twenty minutes, I told Ray to see what he could do to get rid of them. I listened in to their conversation while attending to some paying customers.

Ray approached the tallest hippie in the group, a big black man. "How are y'all doing today?"

"We're cool," the man said. He pulled out his pick and proceeded, complete unaware of my irritation, to pick his hair. I watched as hundreds of curly black hairs fell on the clean linoleum.

"Is there anything I can do to help you?" Ray asked.

"Naw, man. We're just hangin'."

Another hippie piped up. "Could you make it warmer outside, man?"

"I wish I could," Ray said. "You guys got a place to stay tonight?"

"We're cool, man," the black man answered. "I figure we'll find some place around here to crash in the next few, bro."

"It's awfully cold out there," Ray said.

A pretty, slender blonde came over and hugged the black guy, smiling at Ray.

"We keep each other warm, ya dig?"

I felt my stomach turn. Some mother or father somewhere must have been very sad that their daughter had turned to this.

"Look, guys," Ray said. "It's supposed to freeze tonight, so you might want to be extra careful. My church opens up a shelter on nights like this. You stay warm and you get a good breakfast in the morning."

"Cool, man," the other hippie said.

"They do separate the guys and the girls," Ray noted.

"Bummer."

Ray gave them directions to the church and wished them well. With the promise of warmth and free food in the morning, the little troop shuffled toward the door and out into the cold.

I got out my can of air freshener.

The rest of the day was busy, but it went by without incident. We made good sales and I prepared the cash statement for the bank. We locked up the front doors and I collected the money in a bank bag. Ray said he would drop it in the after-hours drop box. I locked the back door and headed home, where Betty had prepared a delicious meatloaf.

Turns out that was the last time I would ever lock the doors after a day of work at Springlake Hardware.

SANCTUARY THREE

Nature

"When one loses the deep intimate
relationship with nature, then temples and
mosques and churches become important."

— Krishnamurti

WAGONER'S FIELD

October 1959

A few years ago, The Field was just rugged swampland. The Seminole Nation hunted for rabbit and squirrel among majestic cypress trees and expansive grasslands and fished for catfish and bass in the shallow ponds and swamps. Alligators hunted there too—sometimes, they both wanted the same thing and other times, they wanted each other.

More recently, white farmers had claimed the land. Tall, slender pines and massive cypress trees were cut down to make way for rich farmland and pastures. The swamp areas dried up and the sandy soil was treated and tilled so it would grow crops and grass. At some point, someone tried planting an orange grove, but the chilly winter frosts came along and killed all the citrus trees north of Lake Wales.

Old Man Wagoner bought the land before the Second World War. After clearing away the old citrus trees, he turned The Field into a beautiful pasture and set up a successful dairy farm, selling milk throughout the state. Cattle grazed where gators had once sunned. Barns rose up where pine trees used to stretch toward the sky.

Unfortunately, his two sons, Wayne and Grant, fought bitterly over the land after his death. Even put together, the two of them weren't half the businessman their father was, and the dairy farm fell apart. The land lapsed into a rugged meadow, overgrown with wild briar bushes and prairie grass. The squirrels and rabbits and even a few alligators came back, and The Field returned to its roots.

For Springlake's teenagers, Wagoner's Field was the place to be on weekend nights. Their souped-up hot rods and their parents' family cars could be found nestled in the bushes, with their occupants nestled in each other's arms, music from car radios floating through the night.

In 1959, the court system stepped in between the bickering brothers, tying up the farm in legal red tape and guaranteeing many more years of inactivity for The Field. But Wayne and Grant weren't unresponsive. They responded loudly and bitterly every time they met. They were uncooperative and unwilling to work together to resolve their differences. They were also up to their eyeballs in back taxes. Times were tough.

* * *

Pastor Wright of the fledgling Springlake Community Church asked Wayne and Grant Wagoner for permission to use their field for their upcoming evangelistic crusade with The Evangelist Chase Andrews. The brothers gladly agreed, hoping to use the event as a tax deductable donation and perhaps to earn some good will with the community and its court system.

The crusade was no small event. Just preparing Wagoner's Field took more manpower than it had seen in years. The Kinney brothers' construction company donated some of the labor and a bulldozer for half a week, and the crew leveled the land and wood-chipped 20,000 square feet for the tent floor.

The tent, tucked away inside a semi-trailer, arrived two days before the revival was scheduled to begin. A professional team had it raised in half a day's time. It was magnificent—a yellow-orangish structure with pinnacles that were almost spires, reaching upward into the night sky. When the interior lights were lit, the tent glowed. For the citizens of Springlake, the massive tent had a magical, make-believe look, like a castle in a children's book or one of the old cathedrals in Europe.

The first thing people noticed when they walked up to the enormous tent was the smell. The citrus and pine sawdust and wood chips gave off a rustic and welcoming scent. The sight of the huge structure, standing resolute and mighty, was certainly eye-catching, and it drew people to The Field like a neon, flashing Vacancy sign might draw a weary traveler to a roadside motel.

In addition, music from a Hammond organ and Baldwin grand piano, ranging from extravagant to mediocre to cute, emanated from the large, orange tent.

The Range Riders Gospel Quartet looked every bit as elaborate as they sounded, with bouffant hairstyles and glistening jewel-studded jackets to complement their perfect four-part harmony.

On the mediocre side of things, Mary-Beth Johnson's off-key rendition of *Nearer My God To Thee* made audience members (and even a few animals in the nearby woods) wish they were farther away from her. But, Mary-Beth had donated a hundred dollars to the evangelistic campaign, so the planning committee was happy to include her solo in the worship experience.

The darling of the show was definitely Little Bobby Lyle, the hymn-singing, guitar-strumming, Bible-quoting child prodigy from Turkey Creek. When Bobby sang *Onward Christian Soldiers* dressed in a World War I soldier's outfit, everyone rose to their feet and cheered. Other musically talented notables included Little Bobby's father Robert Lyle, also known as the Amazing One Man Band, The Shannon Sisters, and Reverend and Mrs. Delmos Jackson. A critic from *The Springlake Tribune* wrote, *I may not have been saved or sanctified, but I sure was entertained.*

A careful study of the makeup of the audience on any given night would reveal that most of the attendees were already active members of other nearby Springlake churches: the Baptists, Methodists and Presbyterians made up easily ninety percent of the crowd. On Wednesday night, though, most of the Baptists stayed away to attend their own prayer meeting. The Assembly of God church members chose not to attend the event at all because they were planning their own tent revival early the following year. And, of course, the Episcopalians and Catholics were absent because, according to them, tent evangelism "wasn't their thing" (although some members of the Evangelistic Tent Meeting Steering Committee had suggested that a bingo game or two might bring out some of the Catholics).

Conspicuously absent were members of the Beulah Missionary Baptist Church, the Springlake African-Episcopal Church and the Bethel Gospel Tabernacle. These were very active and very crowded houses of worship on the outskirts of Springlake that mysteriously did not receive an invitation to the evangelistic tent revival.

Some uninvited guests did appear at the revival, however, but they were not of the human variety. A nest of pesky fire ants attacked the entire fourth row on the first night of the crusade. Fortunately, Mel Smith of Mel's Pest Control Service took care of the situation the next day with some extra-potent pesticide. Those sitting anywhere near the fourth row on subsequent evenings reported a spiritual high unlike any they'd ever had before.

On Thursday night, a blacksnake slid in under the flowing robes of one of the choir members, who obviously didn't buy into the promises of Mark 16 on snake handling. She let out a scream that was so off-key that some thought she'd lost her mind. Then she dashed out of the tent with the snake clinging by its fangs to the bottom of her robe. She never returned to the choir loft. Neither did the snake.

The Evangelist Chase Andrews was a devout man who took his mission seriously. He stood straight and tall, like a lighthouse. His eyes were like twin searchlights that could burn a hole deep into an unrepentant man's soul. To some, his voice was like a blaring horn, ceaseless and demanding. To others, it was like a soft lullaby that could calm a crying baby. A very few even described it as a bubbling creek that could lull a tired old man to sleep.

On the fourth night of the Springlake Evangelistic Crusade, The Evangelist Chase Andrews stood before the audience and announced, "This is a holy place, adorned with majestic stars and glorious fields. It is good to be in the Lord's Temple. While in prayerful consideration of tonight's service, I felt compelled to share my personal faith journey with you."

All eyes were on him. All ears, too. The lights were down, and the cool breeze was gentle and calming.

"I was born in a place far different from this beautiful, lush pasture; it was the very antithesis of this natural retreat. I grew up in the heart of New York City, in a one-bedroom apartment down a dingy little alley where prostitutes and alcoholics used to hang out. My daddy was one of those alcoholics. He drank like a fish— no, like the very fish that swallowed Jonah. When I was seven years old, he couldn't fight against the demons of drink anymore. He pointed a Colt 45 pistol to his skull and blew his brains across the kitchen table. BANG!"

Every person in the crowd jumped. One of the ushers, holding an offering bucket in his lap, leapt up and dumped seven dollars and fifty-three cents into the sawdust at his feet. Half a dozen small children woke up suddenly and started crying. Betty Anderson, a plumpish woman who sat on the front row every night fanning herself, started fanning her fan so fast it looked sure to snap in two.

"But my dear saintly mother," The Evangelist Chase Andrews continued, looking up to the top of the tent cathedral, "she saw to it that I was raised according to the Scriptures. She prayed with me every night and prayed for me every day."

A man in the crowd yelled, "Amen." Others echoed him.

"When Uncle Sam called me into the army to fight the Germans," The Evangelist Chase Andrews continued, "I answered the call and was sent into the very heart of battle. My brothers-in-arms were dying all around me and I stood my ground against the evils of Nazi Germany." Several of the young boys raised their heads and stopped doodling in the sawdust with their shoes when he talked about the war. "I know . . . I know that I survived that horrible ordeal because my Momma was praying for me back home." He turned his gaze skyward again.

Amens floated through the night once more.

"But that wasn't enough. I was critically wounded in battle and brought back to the States. I was near death when they carried my body into the VA Medical Center in Lexington, Kentucky. At that fine military hospital, I met a man of God, a chaplain in the army." He was speaking more passionately now, and the crowd responded enthusiastically.

"This man saw my plight and heard my story." It sounded like "stow-ree" when he said it. "He spoke with me about the Lord and my lost situation." He was shouting into the microphone, enunciating his words slowly for emphasis. His voice boomed across The Field.

"I tried to fight Him, I must admit in all honesty. I tried to dee-ny the offerings of my blessed Lord. I wanted to shout NO. But Jee-sus had other plans. He turned a deaf ear to my dee-nials. He refused to stop. He pursued me like a hound after a rabbit. He would not let go."

Suddenly, the volume of his voice dropped and his eyes lowered, as well. "And then, Friends, Jee-sus came into my life. Yes, He became real to me. The living Savior transformed my sinful and wicked life and washed me whiter than the whitest snow. And he can become real to you tonight. Yes, my friends. The Lord of this beautiful cathedral of stars and lights and moons is ready to meet with you in a real and personal way. Since knowing Him, I look at a beautiful sunrise, or a majestic scene or the mighty ocean in a new way; because I know the Creator. I know the One who formed this land on which we're meeting tonight, He who knew that one day we'd be here to share in His glory, He who made this all possible, even for a poor boy born in a one-room apartment down a dirty alley in the inner city of New York."

Instead of an eruption of cheers, there was a hushed, trancelike silence in the tent. The Evangelist Chase Andrews had hit a home run.

The music played softly for what seemed like an eternity as men, women and children filed down the aisle during the invitation. At the makeshift altar, some cried softly, while others wailed uncontrollably.

Night after night, the Springlake Evangelistic Crusade continued. It warmed hearts and changed lives. And then, it was over. The professional tent movers came back and pulled the mighty canvas structure down, packed it up in a semi-truck and took it away.

The Field was quiet once more. Animals made their way out into the night air again. Down the old wagon paths, high school students parked in the moonlight. Gradually things returned to normal.

* * *

March 1960

On most nights, The Field sat dark and empty, only interrupted by the occasional car every now and then. On one January night, however, a flatbed pickup truck pulled up the driveway and onto the field. The truck stopped abruptly about fifty feet from the entrance and two men got out.

"C'mon, Jake," one man said. "We've got eight more of these things to deliver."

"I'm coming as fast as I can," the other said. "I can't move as fast as I used to."

The two men dragged a sixteen-foot 6x6 out of the back of the truck and dropped it to the ground. Then the first man grabbed an eight-foot piece of lumber and started pounding long nails into the middle of the smaller piece of wood. Hammering was difficult in the dim light, but his handiwork didn't need to be carpenter-grade. He placed the smaller plank against the larger one and nailed the two pieces together.

The other man used post-hole diggers to create a three-foot hole in the ground. "Looks exactly like the cross in the Presbyterian Church," he said, inspecting the completed structure. He reached into the back of the truck, grabbed a five-gallon jug of kerosene and began soaking the cross with the flammable liquid.

"How would you know?" the other man asked. "You ain't been in the Presbyterian Church in years."

When the cross was thoroughly soaked, the two men mounted it in the freshly dug hole and let it slide into place. They shored up the sides of the hole with leftover dirt.

"Light 'er up," the first man said as he headed for the driver's seat.

The second man struck a match and held it up to the kerosene-soaked cross. Within seconds, the wood came alive with fire, burning and crackling. The man jumped into the passenger side of the truck and the vehicle roared off toward the edge of the property.

Looking back, the second man said, "Ain't that a pretty sight?"

"Sends the right message," replied the driver. He spat something nasty out of his window.

With that they sped out onto the highway, wheels squealing, and headed for another pasture.

The two men weren't wearing the traditional robe and hood of the Ku Klux Klan. They didn't need to. Tonight's event wasn't a Klan meeting, but rather a massive demonstration of the Klan's power.

Tonight, hundreds of similar crosses would be erected and burned throughout the southern states to highlight the fact that some people didn't want colored people mixing with white people. They liked things the way they were and didn't want to fix what they thought wasn't broken in the first place.

"Just wait until tomorrow morning," the second man said as he consulted the map to their next destination. "People are going to think twice about this integration business."

"That's right, Henry," the other man said. "Tonight, we make history."

The truck drove on into the darkness, bringing fire and hatred with it. They did indeed make history.

* * *

September 1960

Hurricanes are a part of the give and take of life in Florida. The rains nurture growth. The winds clear away death. Life carries on.

The Field was calm as it awaited the mighty Hurricane Donna. And then the battering came. Old trees, nearing death anyway, were yanked from their roots and laid to rest in large pools of water. Branches were snapped from their bases and young trees were bent over backwards.

In time, the storm passed, moving farther up the coast to attack elsewhere. The Field returned to calm—wet and renewed and ready for another day.

* * *

October 1961

Three boys dragged a wagonful of wood and supplies behind their bikes to the edge of The Field. They pulled off the road onto the dirt path and through the gate toward the northwest corner of the property. They had chosen this place because the terrain was generally higher and a bit less even here. They had found a depression in the little hill—if you could call anything in Florida a hill—into which they would dig their foundation.

Laying the wood aside, the boys began to dig a hole. They sank the foundation about two feet into the shallow depression. This, combined with the mounds of dirt around the hole, gave them an area that would be large enough for a young boy to stand upright.

They sank old 2x4s into the sand and shored them up with planks of plywood. They nailed more old 2x4s to the corner pieces and secured some plywood on top for a roof. They even had a roll of old tar paper that they stretched over the plywood to keep the rain out.

At the end of the day, the dirty and sweaty boys

inspected their creation with pride.

"Bring on the Russians," one yelled at the top of his lungs. "We're ready."

"Okay, Mr. Castro," another yelled. "We ain't afraid of you."

Finally, the boys sat down on the roof of their fallout shelter and inspected the area around them.

"Do you remember this place, Robby?" Tim asked his younger brother, in between chaws on a long piece of prairie grass.

The younger boy looked around. "Naw. Should I?"

Tim stood up tall and straight on top of the homemade fallout shelter. "That revival thing we went to was held here."

"What revival thing?" asked the third boy, Larry.

"Are you sure?" Robby asked.

"Yep. It was right here," Tim said.

"What revival thing?" Larry repeated.

Tim turned to his friend. "About two years ago, Mama dragged us all out to a tent revival with . . . what was his name? Chase Alexander?"

Robby snapped his fingers and smiled. "The Evangelist Chase Andrews."

"That's right. The Evangelist Chase Andrews," Tim said in a booming voice that echoed through The Field. "So you do remember. It was held right here in this pasture. They had a huge circus tent, and singers and speakers and tons of people. I ain't never seen so many people in one place before."

"What happened?" Larry asked.

Tim sat back down on the makeshift roof. "It was the scariest thing I ever seen in my life. People were singing and shouting and screaming and crying and all get-out."

"Yeah," Robby said.

Tim pointed at Robby and gently teased, "He grabbed my hand halfway through the thing." Looking at Robby, he added, "You were so scared."

Robby laughed good-naturedly and replied, "And you squeezed my hand so hard I had bruises for a week."

"So you two little girls were holding hands in church?" Larry said with a grin.

"I'm telling ya, Larry," Tim said. "I don't ever wanna go through nuthin' like that again in my life. I thought it would never end."

As the setting sun began to dim the light in their fallout shelter, the boys knew it was time to return home. They tied the wagon to their bikes again, and rode down the little trail to the street and then home.

* * *

The boys returned the next weekend, loaded with more lumber and supplies for their homemade fallout shelter. They spent the day digging and hammering and sawing until they were sure it could withstand the most powerful atom bomb the Russians had in their arsenal.

Eventually, they explored the terrain around their shelter. To the north, they found a large canal that ran along the perimeter of The Field. The upper banks of the canal were at least eight feet wide and the water was almost black, a sign of just how deep it was. They tried throwing rocks and sticks into the murky water to see if they could find the bottom, but they didn't come close.

The boys found a huge oak tree anchored close to the canal with limbs that extended across the water. Tim scaled the tree while Robby ran back to the shelter to retrieve a thick length of rope. He tossed it up to his brother, who tied it securely to the branch using the best Boy Scout knot he could remember.

Tim was the first to try the rope swing. He fearlessly surveyed the chasm before him, leapt into the air and grasped the rope as high up as he could reach. The swing carried him easily to the other side, but he chose to hang on and return where his friends were waiting. The other two boys cheered and shouted as he dropped safely to the ground.

"I'm next," announced Larry.

"You sure?" Tim asked. "I heard that you people can't swim that well. If you fall in, I ain't going to jump in after you."

"What's this 'you people' shit? I can outswim your white ass any day." With that, he followed Tim's example and swung across to the other side. He dropped safely on the bank.

Robby crossed the canal with equal ease, and landed with both arms up in the air like a gymnast. The boys continued to swing across the canal for the rest of the day. A rope swing, a wide canal, and a hot afternoon—the perfect recipe for a blissful day for three boys.

* * *

August 1964

Early in the morning, not long after sunup, a short, somewhat chubby figure carrying a dark object entered The Field from the west. It was a boy, no more than 12 years old, sporting the once-popular crew cut hairstyle. In his arms, he was carrying a burlap bag as if it were full of heavy bars of gold. About 100 feet into The Field, under an old oak tree overlooking a nearby pool of water, he placed the bag down gently.

Between sniffs and hasty rubs against the moisture in his eyes, he knelt down and dug into the sandy soil with his hands. The deeper he dug, the more audible his sniffs became, and eventually, they turned to shouts of anger, tinged with grief of a kind no boy should have to experience.

"Why did you hit him?" he shouted into the silence. "Why? He didn't know no better. You didn't have to beat him."

He dug deeper. "Now he's gone," he yelled. "He's dead! He's dead and he'll never come back."

His voice broke and his whole body tensed as he fought hard for control. He stopped digging and wiped his grimy hands on his shorts. Grabbing the burlap bag, he dragged it into the hole. The bag fell open slightly and a tiny black paw peeked through the opening. The sight of the paw, so fuzzy and small, pushed him over the edge.

"He wasn't a bad dog," he sobbed. "He was just a puppy. A puppy! He couldn't help it if he crapped in the garage. He was just a puppy."

He took a deep, shaky breath and then continued his strange eulogy. "You said he was a nigger dog. You said he was no good. He weren't no nigger dog. He was just a stray."

The boy scowled at the area around him, then his expression softened as he looked down at the paw again.

"You'll like it here," he whispered. "You're out here in the woods, near a pond. It's real peaceful."

He gently tucked the little paw back into the bag and started pushing the loose sandy soil on top of it.

He kept whispering as he worked. "He was just a stray. Didn't have no mama. Just like me. Didn't have no friends. Just like me. We were both just strays."

The breeze blew in over the pond, cooling the shady area beneath the oak tree.

A sudden, violent yell erupted from him. "He weren't no nigger dog, Daddy."

Exhausted and heartbroken, the boy sat back on his butt, shoulders hunched forward. Barely audible, he said, "He was my friend. My best friend."

The boy cried long and low until he couldn't cry any more. He wiped his grimy hand across his face once more, pulled himself up and turned away from the tiny grave. His face was dirty and his eyes were red and his short-cropped crew cut was full of dirt from the soil on his hands.

Slowly, he turned and walked home alone.

* * *

April 1967

The Field remained empty, except for one or two weekends out of the year when Boy Scout Troop 732 visited the property, with the Wagoners' permission of course, for a weekend camp out. The Scouts pitched tents, built bonfires, played Capture the Flag and enjoyed the land as much as they possibly could during the short weekends.

Then, another group was granted permission to use The Field. Some members of this group were familiar with the property, having visited it before. It was located in an ideal spot: out of town and away from nosey neighbors, but close enough for people to know that someone had been there. This group had struggled with societal change for over a decade. Its members witnessed things that they disagreed with and, in many cases, felt unable to influence. They saw others gaining freedoms, and they somehow interpreted these as encroachments upon their own rights. These radical and drastic changes were viewed through a lens of fear. That fear caused them to act in irresponsible and irrational ways.

In fact, many of those fears were trumped up by some members in the group who had selfish or power-hungry ulterior motives. These influential members used fear tactics and falsehoods to frighten others into action. And they were very effective.

Some local building contractors arranged to have a stage built deep within The Field. They found the ideal spot, a large open area that backed up to a stand of tall pine trees. There would be plenty of room for parking and lots of space for people to stand facing the stage.

People with inside connections arranged to hook up the power lines that had once run the dairy farm, so the stage area would have lights and sound. A temporary arrangement was made with the Tampa Electric Company, and the power was turned on. A local DJ from the country radio station was lined up to install and operate a powerful sound system.

A small print shop was commissioned to create brochures that could be discreetly handed out to the right people at the right time. Hundreds of the black and white leaflets were created.

But the real work went on well behind the scenes. People were contacted in secret. Phone calls were placed and personal visits were made. Influential people were invited. Confidentiality was stressed.

Late in the afternoon, carloads of people began to flow onto The Field. One after another they drove toward the parking area in front of the stage. The occupants remained in their cars until dusk. Then, patriotic music began playing on the loudspeakers.

As if beckoned by the music, one by one, people dressed in long white robes and pointed hoods stepped out of their cars and approached the stage. Someone threw a switch and the stage was illuminated with bright, harsh lights. Someone else brought a blazing torch and set a huge cross behind the stage aflame.

The stage was empty, except for a single podium and two flags, one of which was American.

In turn, various men stepped up to the microphone and implored the crowd to take responsibility for their communities, to take a stand for their beliefs and to take back America from the enemies that were trying to lead her down the path to ultimate destruction. The speeches dragged on through the night, never relenting and never straying from their core message.

Then, late in the evening, one of the cloaked figures announced the final speaker of the night. He had come to the meeting from the organizational headquarters in Georgia, and the crowd was in for a special treat, they were told.

Dressed in a long white robe like his predecessors, but this time with no hood, the man approached the microphone. He stood tall, like a tower. His eyes flashed fire, like bullets from a rifle. He spoke with authority. This was one who knew what he was talking about and who would confidently convey his message to those hungry to hear it.

"There are forces in our country working against our traditional beliefs and values to make us weaker," he proclaimed. "They want to water down our school systems, our faith systems, and our bloodlines. They want to cater to the lowest common denominator and to make America a weak, socialist nation, not unlike Cuba or Russia. There is legislation passing through the halls of Congress right now that will force your children to attend school with those who we know to be inferior. We're already having to share our transportation system, our infrastructure, and our entertainment with people that we know are different from us. Our forefathers never expected anything like this when they founded this great land. It's time to put a stop to this insanity," he said, almost shouting into the microphone. "For our children. For our families. For our mighty nation. If we fail, we will fail Almighty God Himself!"

The crowd applauded wildly. The man held up his arms to calm them. He paused while the crowd grew silent.

"We are in serious times, my friends. There are those who want to see America fail. They want to see us weakened and diluted. They know that they are too weak and ignorant to reach the potential that others have achieved, so they seek to bring everyone down to their level. But we *cannot* let them succeed. We *cannot* let them win. Join me and this august body of soldiers to make a difference in our communities, our country and our world. The time is now. *Your* time is now."

He stepped back from the podium and basked in the moment—the light of the burning cross behind him, the spotlights overhead and the adoration of the crowd before him.

One young man stood in the midst of the white-robed audience and cheered and whistled in support of the message he had just heard. He wore his hair in a tight crew cut, like they used to wear in the 1950s. His face was pockmarked with acne, the result of poor diet, poor genes and poor hygiene.

With a sudden sharp pang of sadness, the man flashed back to when he'd been here three years before. He took a deep breath to fight back the coming tears. This place brought back an intense mix of emotions—pain, grief, anger. This was where he'd said goodbye to his best friend.

But on this day, he vowed to be a hero. He would be a soldier for a cause that was as just and pure as any cause could possibly be. He felt could help make the difference between failure and success for his country. He felt the call of destiny, and he answered yes.

* * *

September 1968

The three boys continued to visit The Field throughout their early adolescence. Often, they came in a group, as a part of a scout troop on a camping trip or on a church picnic. But sometimes they came on their own.

Gradually, though, Tim and Larry ceased their visits. They became busy with other things and could find little time to visit The Field anymore.

But for Robby, The Field remained his special place. It served to remind him of simpler times when kids built fallout shelters in the dirt and played baseball in the grass. Visiting there brought him peace and comfort when the rest of the world was anthing but peaceful.

He would sit on an old fallen tree and stare off into the sunset, and the view would give him a sense of peace and calm. He marveled at the splendor and glory of the celestial canopy that hung overhead in the late afternoon. He relished the cool morning breezes that reminded him of things that were simple and real and reverent. To him, The Field represented peace and calm and hope.

SANCTUARY FOUR

School

"The library is the temple of learning, and
learning has liberated more people than all the
wars in history."

— Carl T. Rowan

ROBBY FRANKLIN

September 1965

Rob Franklin entered the seventh grade with just the right amount of fear and trepidation. Junior high school was a new experience. No longer would he be able to sit in front of the same chalkboard with the same teacher. Instead, he'd have multiple teachers and different classrooms and schedules that changed every hour, like high school, where Tim went. As if that weren't enough, the seventh grade at Springlake was scary for another reason—the building itself.

A plaque bolted into the foundation of the building said that the school had been constructed more than fifty years ago. Rob didn't doubt it. The school showed every day of its age and smelled like crap. Like fifty years of screwed-up biology experiments.

His next door neighbor had said that the four-story red brick structure had originally been a high school, but when a new high school building was constructed, junior high students got the hand-me-down.

For Rob and his friends, the seventh grade was new and different in other ways too. Somebody in some government office had decided that black students could voluntarily enroll in white schools. Before 1965, black kids went to black schools and white kids went to white schools. They were supposed to be equal in quality. Some said they weren't.

On his first day, Rob felt tense. Students were standing in small groups outside the building, talking quietly. He could overhear other kids whispering about integration. Some of them seemed to be attempting to speak in some sort of code, as if openly discussing that subject was against the rules. It was on everyone's minds.

Rob had arrived early. He was standing next to three other seventh graders at the top of the front steps, listening to their comments on the new school and the new situation.

"Somebody said that half of the school will be made up of them," a boy named Jeff said.

"I ain't seen any yet," replied a short boy with tons of freckles.

"I guess we'll have to 'extend the right hand of friendship,'" a chubby kid called Meat said, pounding his right fist into his left hand and laughing at his own joke.

For Rob, voluntary integration meant he and his friend Larry would be attending school together for the first time. Larry's father pulled up to the front of Springlake Junior High and scanned the crowd. When his eyes met Rob's, he nodded toward his son. Larry climbed out of the car and waved goodbye. As he climbed the steps leading up to the massive front doors, Rob was acutely aware of the angry glares and stares that many kids gave the black boy. Rob ignored them as much as he could.

He greeted Larry with the "soul handshake," where they interlocked their thumbs rather than clasping each other's fingers like a traditional handshake. It pulled them closer together and kinda looked like they were getting ready to arm wrestle rather than shake hands.

Rob and Larry turned and walked through the big white school doors and headed toward their first period class. Meat, Jeff and Freckles (whatever his real name was) stared after them, open-mouthed. On the way in, they passed a kid Rob recognized as Cale Kinney, who he didn't really know very well. Cale was leaning against the wall watching them. He was wearing a plaid shirt, an old-fashioned crew cut and a look of sheer disgust.

"Nigger lover," he said, low enough for only Rob to

hear.

Rob had never seen such open hatred directed at himself. It reminded him of the looks his mother had received when they flew into Tallahassee a long time ago.

He held up two fingers and said to Cale, "Peace, brother."

"Yeah, well peace on you, you little piece of shit," Cale snapped back.

Rob tried to just ignore the insult, but it lingered in the back of his mind, like an infected sore that would fester and grow into a real problem. The rest of the day, he kept looking over his shoulder for Kinney. Fortunately, they didn't have any classes together.

The impact of voluntary integration was quite small. Like most of his peers, Rob had two or three classes that were "integrated" with one or two black students. The other classes were all white. It seemed like most of the black students all stayed together and most of the white students avoided them.

When he got home and his mother started grilling him about his relatively uneventful first day of school, he just replied, "It was fine."

* * *

October 1965

Rob's American history class was held in the school auditorium. This class used a new teaching method called "broadcast video." Every day, the class would gather, roll would be called, announcements made and assignments given. Then, precisely at 10:00 a.m., six 19-inch televisions lining the sides of the auditorium would come alive so the class could watch that morning's lesson.

The students were told that all over the state other seventh graders were watching the same television shows about American history. It was "a thrilling achievement in educational milestones" and boring as hell at the same time.

Broadcast video was sold to the students and their

parents as a wonderful innovation, but even young Rob could tell that it wasn't all it was cracked up to be. On some days, the televisions only showed some aging teacher sitting at his desk, reading a lecture to the students. Once, the teacher actually used flannelgraphs to explain the structure of Congress.

On the rare occasions when the televised classes included panel discussions, movie clips or other creative methods, Rob did enjoy the class. But, like several of the other boys in the large class, most of the time he took advantage of the "thrilling achievement in educational milestones" by catching up on sleep.

One day when he couldn't doze off and he was tired of drawing pictures of cars on the back pages of his notebook, Rob spent a little time discreetly watching the classmates around him. Jolene Smith, one of the black students, was sitting a few seats in front of him, one row over. She clearly took her educational experience seriously. She was staring fixedly at the television screen, possibly in part because of the thick silver-rimmed glasses she was wearing, but she appeared to be genuinely interested. She took notes—real notes. Her folder was full of words and outlines, not scribbles and drawings like Rob's.

I wonder why she's here, Rob thought. *Why would she go to a school made up almost entirely of students who are not like her?* He imagined that her parents must have insisted that she take advantage of this opportunity. After all, some said that the black schools were not as good as the white schools, and parents are always saying kids should take their schooling seriously. *I wouldn't be here if I didn't have to,* he thought, looking at the old walls surrounding the auditorium.

In a few moments, the television class was over, and Rob gathered his books and joined the exodus of students flowing into the hallway. He looked over his shoulder and noticed Jolene coming up beside him. He smiled at her and said hello, but she was scurrying off to her next class and didn't hear him.

"Can you believe she's here, stirring up trouble?"

Jack Dickson asked.

"Huh?"

"Her. The colored girl. I saw you staring at her."

Jack had almost white blond hair that he combed into a wave at the top of his forehead. An avid Beach Boys fan, he claimed to know everything about surfing, but Rob was pretty sure he'd never been on a board in his life.

"Yeah. So?"

"People like her just want to make trouble," he declared all-knowingly. "My dad says their schools are fine. They don't need to come over here." They waded side by side into the mob of students.

Rob didn't know Jack very well. They only had the American history class together. "I heard that their schools are in pretty sad shape," Rob said.

"The colored junior high school is a hell of a lot better than this dump," Jack said.

"Every other school in the state is better than this dump," Rob said.

"Well, I wish they'd all just stay in their own school."

"Right . . ." Rob said. But something deep inside wasn't so sure.

* * *

The bad thing about current events was that they were so current. Every Tuesday, Rob and his classmates were required to submit a newspaper or magazine article about some recent event that was newsworthy.

That was fine for the first week or two of school, but later, finding the right article was enough to drive a kid wild. The article had to be interesting, but could not be from the sports or comic pages. It had to be short, so Rob could read and summarize it quickly because he usually put off doing his current events assignment until the morning before school—to get the most up-to-date articles, of course.

The article had to be cool, too. Mr. Westbrook chose two or three to discuss each week, projecting the article's image on the big screen behind the podium using an opaque projector. It would be a bummer if Westbrook projected Rob's assignment and it was about some lame fashion event.

He finished gluing his article to a sheet of lined paper, on which he had written the article summary in math class, and hustled off to history. As he walked in, he placed his assignment on the top of the stack on the table at the front of the class and headed to his seat, halfway toward the back of the old auditorium. The good thing about current events class was that it meant they didn't have to go to TV history class on Tuesdays.

After attendance was taken, Mr. Westbrook addressed the class. "Most of you are doing a fine job with your current events articles. However, I sense that some of you are waiting until the last minute to do this assignment and I assume that you are rushing to finish. Please take your time with these. You may find something that is very interesting in your newspaper or magazine."

"Like your hair, Chrome Dome?" someone behind Rob quipped, too low to be heard at the front of class. The teacher *was* pretty thin on top.

"I want to share one particular article with you that was turned in last week. The student who submitted it not only intelligently summarized the chosen article, but also referred to other events leading up to it and offered a personal commentary on the situation."

He turned on the opaque projector.

The same guy behind Rob yelled, "Can't see."

Mr. Westbrook turned around and saw that the projection screen had not been pulled down. It took him a moment to locate the long hooked pole and even longer for him to connect the hook to the latch at the bottom of the screen. After several attempts, he finally managed it and slowly pulled the screen into place. The fuzzy unfocused image shown dimly on the screen.

"Still can't see it."

Mr. Westbrook fiddled unsuccessfully with the focus. Then he said, "I'll just have to read it to you."

He retrieved the original copy from his desk and

began reading.

"Can't hear you," the voice yelled.

Mr. Westbrook sighed again, and started over in a louder voice.

"*Six months ago, Jimmie Lee Jackson was shot to death by Alabama police and State Troopers while trying to protect his mother and his eighty-year old grandfather during a peaceful march in Marion City. Jimmie was black. Two weeks later, a white minister, Reverend James Reeb, was beaten to death by a white mob during a peace march in Selma, Alabama. Both deaths were useless, but not meaningless. Both men were protesting discriminatory voting practices that had been used to keep black people from exercising their constitutional right to vote.*"

At first, Rob had been listening only half-heartedly. But slowly, he and the other students had become more interested. Mr. Westbrook paused long enough to swallow once or twice.

"*Last week, President Lyndon Johnson signed the Voting Rights Act into law that prevents the types of discriminatory practices that these two martyrs were fighting against, from happening. Jimmie Lee Jackson was twenty seven years old when he died. Reverend James Reeb was only ten years older than that.*"

Mr. Westbrook turned to his now-attentive class. "This current event," he said, "comes to us from Jolene Smith." Rob looked over at her, but she was just looking straight at the teacher. "So, what do you think? What effect will the Voting Rights Act have? Was it necessary? Will it make a difference?"

At first, no one said anything. Rob thought about the black man and the white preacher and their fight for the right to vote. He thought about other ways black people had been treated badly by whites. *Would I be willing to give up my life so someone else was treated fairly?* he asked himself.

"Well?" Mr. Westbrook prompted.

"It *should* make a difference," a boy toward the front said, shrugging his shoulders. "Otherwise, why would they pass a law?"

"A little naive, Ralph," Mr. Westbrook said. "Anyone else?"

A red-haired boy sitting in the middle of the room raised his hand. "I don't understand what the big deal is. I thought everybody had the right to vote."

So did I, Rob thought, relieved he wasn't alone.

"Good point," Mr. Westbrook interrupted. "You are right. Every American has the right to vote—with exceptions."

The class waited.

"Literacy, for one. Some states want only the literate citizens to vote. And how can somebody vote if they can't read the ballot?"

So if everyone could read, that wouldn't be an issue? Rob wasn't confident enough to ask that out loud though. He thought about Jolene Smith and her decision to attend a school that would give her a better education, despite the obvious challenges of going to a mostly white school.

"Excuse me," said Maria, who had recently arrived from Cuba and spoke with a thick accent. "Does that include those who cannot speak English?"

"Well, yeah," said some guy on the far right. "After all, English is the official language, isn't it?"

Mr. Westbrook broke into the conversation. "You might want to re-read your constitution, Mr. Wright. You'll find that there is no *official* language."

Rob wanted to ask whether there were laws that kept black people from voting. At that point, Jolene spoke up.

"Those restrictions were added to keep black people from voting," she said.

"Those *restrictions*, as you call them, might also prevent someone from buying votes from people who didn't plan to vote in the first place," someone said from the other side of the room.

Buying votes? Rob had never thought of someone getting paid to vote a certain way. *How would someone know if I voted the way he paid me to vote? That argument doesn't make a lot of sense.*

"That's the whole point," Jolene replied calmly.

"These laws affect poor people, and blacks are often a part of that group. They were implemented to keep black people from voting."

"Doesn't seem that important to me," said Red in the middle of the room. "I mean with so many people voting, your vote doesn't even count, anyway."

A few students nodded.

"Tell that to Reverend Reeb or Jimmie Lee Jackson," Jolene muttered.

Like most of his classmates, Rob listened to the class discussion that the few bolder and more opinionated students were having. Rob felt a pang of guilt, like he should have somehow contributed to the conversation.

* * *

"Basketball is for pussies," Randy Hall said as he pulled his gym shorts over his jock strap. The other boys in the locker room were also dressing out for physical education class.

"What are you talking about?" Rob asked.

"It's simple," Randy said, pulling a T-shirt over his head. "Basketball is a no-contact sport. Only pussies play no-contact sports."

"Maybe you just never played it right."

A loud whistle sounded and the boys rushed out of the locker room and into the aging gymnasium. Coach Bridges was standing at center court holding a basketball against his hip with one hand. "Take a seat, boys," he yelled, and they all headed for the bleachers.

"The game of basketball was invented by James Naismith in 1891," he said, marching back and forth in front of the seventh graders. "Basketball is a game of skill and endurance and control. During the next few weeks, we will learn the fundamentals of this exciting game so you can compete with your friends or on the Springlake Seahawks team against other schools."

Physical education class, sometimes called PE, was a chance for junior high boys to become acquainted with sports, like basketball. For most of the boys, this was their first exposure to basketball. Not so for Larry and Rob.

Larry had learned basketball from his friends and at a much earlier age than most of the kids at Springlake Junior High. At the apartment complex where Larry and his family had moved after Hurricane Donna, one of the few recreational activities available was playing basketball in the parking lot. He spent hours on that court, practicing layups and jump shots, and basically learning about life through the game.

Growing up on the other side of town in a single-family house, Rob didn't have a hoop installed in his driveway until Christmas of his brother's freshman year in high school, so he learned how to play basketball elsewhere.

What he did learn, he learned in bits and pieces from Larry. They would meet at Larry's apartment, and Rob, the only white boy, would play ball with him and his friends. When they weren't playing the game, Larry would take time to explain concepts like man-to-man defense, full-court presses, and pick and rolls. They even walked through plays while hanging out at local playgrounds that didn't have a basketball court.

Other kids in their school thought they understood basketball, but compared to Larry and his friends from the apartment complex, they were rookies.

* * *

In October, an announcement was made on the school public address system that tryouts for the basketball team would be held the following week. Rob grinned at Larry, who shot back a quick wink. Basketball was *their* game.

Coach Bridges, who coached the seventh- and eighth-grade Springlake Seahawks basketball teams, stood about six feet, three inches tall. His dark eyebrows rose up and down when he spoke, like a pair of dancing caterpillars mirroring each other. When he got excited, they practically did circus tricks. More than once, Rob tried to get Coach fired up just to watch those eyebrows dance. But when he was running up and down the basketball court in the heat of the afternoon, Rob didn't give a shit about the coach's funny eyebrows.

About twenty-five boys gathered in the old gym on the first afternoon of tryouts. As the boys arrived, they grabbed nearby basketballs and warmed up. Watching from the sidelines, Coach Bridges jotted down notes on an old clipboard.

Rob also made mental notes about the talent around him. He could quickly tell which boys knew the game and which had never picked up a ball before. He found it amusing if not humbling to watch the other boys bounce the ball off their feet, throw up one-handed set shots that missed rim and backboard, and stumble while trying to chase a loose ball.

A few of the guys had definitely played before, even though their fundamentals were lacking a bit. Rob thought that Tom Bowden favored his right hand way too much; he needed some practice dribbling with his left. Dennis Young, easily the tallest on the team, apparently hadn't yet learned the valuable skill of rebounding, which should have been his biggest strength. It was also clear that Keith Rainer had a consistent jumper, but his follow-through sucked.

Coach Bridges spent the first week of practice on fundamentals. Rob had heard from his brother that the high school coach played a no-nonsense type of command-and-control ball, and would be looking for a pool of boys who knew the basics when they became high school students. Practicing basic ball handling was a bit boring for Rob and Larry, but they knew that they would eventually work up to layups and hook shots, and maybe even some offensive plays.

At the end of practice, it was time for suicides. The suicide drill was the quintessential basketball get-in-shape exercise. Everybody hated suicides. They were tough, and they always led to three predictable results: 1) kids got in better shape, 2) coaches found out who had a tendency to wimp out, and 3) some boys threw up.

Coach Bridges had developed his own variation of

the suicide drill. The entire team lined up at one end of the court. On the whistle, everyone ran to the first foul line, reached down and touched the court, and then turned around to run back to the edge of the court. There, they touched the floor and turned to run to the half-court line. They would turn around and run back to the sidelines, Then run to the foul line on the other end, and run back to the sidelines, touching the floor at every stop. Finally, everybody would sprint all the way to the opposite end of the court where they'd touch the floor and then sprint all the way back.

Suicides were brutal and highly effective. By the end of practice, three boys had walked off the court swearing they would never touch a basketball again. Five boys were leaning over with their hands on their knees, hurling their last bit of lunch. Everyone else was walking around in circles sucking in gasps of oxygen.

"Now *that*," Rob heard Coach Bridges say, "is what basketball is all about. Take it in, boys."

* * *

"He ain't gonna stay on our team, is he?" Cale Kinney confronted Rob as he stepped outside of the locker room and into the gym.

"Who?"

"Your nigger friend," Cale said.

"Why not?" Rob asked. "He's a good ball player."

Rob tried to walk past, but Cale grabbed his arm and pulled him around so the two boys were facing each other again. "White boys wear these uniforms. After we're gone more white boys are going to wear these uniforms. Whites don't want to wear the same uniforms that niggers have worn."

Cale was staring him down, and he felt like he had to say something. He wanted to support Larry, but at the same time, Cale was not the sort of guy you'd want as your enemy. Finally, he blurted out, "Cale. I wash my uniform after every game. Don't you? Use some detergent." He turned and ran onto the court, wondering why he'd come up with *that* line of all things, and why he couldn't have said something cooler.

Larry ran onto the court, took one look at Rob and said, "Hey, man. What's goin' on?"

"Nothin'," Rob said, passing him the ball. They took shots to warm up until they heard a loud, shrill whistle.

"All right," Coach Bridges yelled. "Today, we're going to have a scrimmage. Young, Wells, Thompson, Franklin, and Watson, take off your shirts. Griffen, Watkins, Kinney, Rainer and Bowden leave your shirts on." Bridges walked over to the sidelines to watch the game. "Skins, take it in."

Young inbounded the ball to Rob, who brought it up the court. He fed it to Larry, and Kinney was on him like white on rice. Kinney wasn't just playing man-to-man. He was playing aggressively, and he was playing poorly. Larry gave him a shoulder fake, dribbled left and spun around to the right, leaving Kinney stumbling over himself in the dust. Larry drove toward the basket for an easy layup. This made Cale even angrier, and he insisted on bringing the ball up the floor, even though he was supposed to play forward.

Larry, keeping his voice low, said to Rob, "Let's show this boy how we play ball." He picked Kinney up at half-court.

"Pass the ball, Cale," Bowden yelled, but Kinney ignored him.

Larry slid quickly into Kinney's path, forcing him to pivot around and head in the opposite direction. To Kinney's surprise, Rob had dropped off his man and was double-teaming him. Larry reached around Kinney and tapped the ball toward Rob, who scooped it up and headed down court. Kinney, frustrated and embarrassed, dashed after him. Larry paralleled the pair, and Rob bounce-passed the ball to him for another easy layup. Cale tried desperately to block Larry's shot, but he was so far behind him that his efforts just looked silly.

Bowden brought the ball back down the floor and ignored Cale's pleas to pass him the ball. The shirts scored a goal. Before the shirts could return down the floor, Larry and Rob had brought the ball in and were feeding their big center for a hook shot.

The ass-whipping continued for twenty more minutes. One after another, the Watson and Franklin duo would snatch the ball away or sneak in a bounce pass, resulting in a layup or a jump shot. They made a great team.

The others, though, had a whole lot of work to do. Foremost for Kinney was learning to control his temper. The more mistakes he made, the angrier he got. He started muttering under his breath, "C'mon, nigger," and "Let's go, Sambo." Rob and Larry switched positions and Rob covered Kinney instead.

Bridges blew the whistle and told Kinney to grab a seat on the sidelines. It should have been a good opportunity for him to cool down, but it wasn't working. Kinney started shouting from the bench. "He fouled him!" "You can't do that!" "Double dribble!"

After practice, Coach Bridges pulled the troublemaker aside for some one-on-one coaching. Rob walked by the pair and Cale gave him a look that could melt steel. The coach's lecture lasted for fifteen minutes. Rob was grateful for the chance to grab a quick shower and head home without facing Crew Cut Kinney in the locker room.

* * *

November 1965

As the semester dragged on, teachers began to pile on the homework like they took some sort of sick pleasure in making sure Rob had no free time. One of their most popular trauma-inducing techniques was the term paper. Rob had three due before Christmas break. Luckily for Rob, that forced him to seek out the library, which ended up making all the hard work worthwhile.

The library at Springlake Junior High was much better than the one at his elementary school. Here, he could find all the classics and many of the latest in fiction and nonfiction. With its shelves towering to the ceiling, Rob could find books about basketball, cars, dragons, and virtually everything else.

Books weren't all that was available. Rob could read newspapers from faraway cities like Atlanta, New York, Chicago and Los Angeles. He could grab the latest editions of Look Magazine, Life, Sports Illustrated, and Newsweek. He could stay in touch with the world without leaving school.

The library represented what Rob liked most about school: the chance to really *learn* things. Of course, writing term papers was still a pain, and doing research on photosynthesis did get a little tedious. But finding out what others had discovered, or what was really happening in other states or countries, or why one chemical works better than another was really fascinating stuff.

Plus, there was another bonus, and her name was Carolyn Gardner, the nicest-looking library assistant in the world. Whenever he saw Carolyn, he thought of the song *Cherish* by The Association. She had bouncy blond hair that was always held back with a bow or hairpins or whatever girls used to hold back their hair.

She was shaped just right: not too chunky and not too skinny. And she had a smile that would knock you out. She had helped Rob the first time he'd needed to check out books and she had stolen his heart almost at first sight.

Rob did some research and was disappointed to discover that she was an eighth grader—he knew most eighth graders wanted nothing to do with seventh graders. But Carolyn was different. She seemed to enjoy helping Rob find unusual books. One day, as he walked through the double doors, she waved him over to the reference desk.

Pulling a book out from behind the desk, she said, "This just came in. I thought you might like it." The title was *A Sense of Where You Are*, and it was about Bill Bradley, a basketball great from Princeton.

"My uncle is a sports nut. He says Bill Bradley is going to make an impact on the game."

"Gee. Thanks. Uh, this looks good." Rob was

surprised Carolyn knew about his love of basketball. He was even more surprised she knew he was alive.

He took the book home that night and read it cover to cover.

With so much to offer, the library became Rob's indoor haven when things got too crazy in the real world. He'd fake sickness, get a pass to the nurse's office and head for the library instead. Of course, he had to drop by the nurse's office to get the pass signed, but he managed to make his ruse work. On days when he had basketball practice, Rob would tell his mom to pick him up at 5:30 p.m. instead of right after practice. Usually, the library was open until then, so he'd hang out in the magazine section until she arrived.

* * *

February 1966

The basketball season in junior high school was short. They played only eight games, and eight games wasn't enough to really get started. By the end of the season, Springlake Junior High had won five, lost three. Rob and Larry led the team with the most points and the most steals per game. They made a good team, and the hours they played together at Larry's apartment complex had paid off.

Rob could tell that Coach Bridges had leaned on Cale Kinney all season. Cale was a hothead, and hotheads couldn't control their temper, much less the basketball. More than once a week, Coach Bridges would have to pull him aside for some a one-on-one chat. The coach played him whenever possible and seemed to make every effort to help the boy learn to deal with his issues.

At the last practice of the season, the coach called for a simple pick and roll, with Larry running off the pick that Young set at the foul line. They were playing at half speed to get the play right, and things went smoothly until Cale, who was playing forward, dropped off his man and attempted to stuff Larry's easy jumper. Larry was the more agile of the two, and Kinney missed the block completely, falling to the floor below the backboard.

Rob taunted, "Faked you out, Cale."

Cale was up and in Larry's face in a heartbeat. Rob grabbed him from behind and locked his arms around his chest. He started dragging him away from Larry.

"No, Rob," Larry yelled. "Let him go. This sucker's been asking for it all season."

Rob loosened his grip and Cale wrestled free and lunged at the black boy. Larry planted his feet and popped Cale in the nose with his left fist. Bone and cartilage crumbled under the force of Larry's fist, compounded by Cale's forward motion, and Cale fell to the floor screaming. Blood gushed everywhere. Amazingly, Coach Bridges let Larry off without more than a warning.

Cale sat out the rest of practice, holding a blood-drenched sport towel against his nose. Rob watched him carefully for the rest of the day. When he looked into Cale's eyes, he only saw revenge and hatred staring back.

* * *

March 1966

Larry and Rob rounded the corner from the cafeteria and headed off to third period. On their daily march to and from class, they passed by a bank of gray lockers, each with its own locker number and padlock. Larry stopped at number 511 and began to turn the dial on his lock. Rob walked on down to number 639.

"What the hell?" Larry said as he pulled a folded piece of paper from his locker.

"Must be from your girlfriend, Lar, you old dog," Rob teased.

Larry stood stone still and read the paper in his hand. When he turned the note around, Rob's jaw dropped.

"Give me that," he said, snatching the paper.

Most of the page contained a hand-drawn picture of a body hanging from a tree. The words *Die, NIGGER!*

headlined the page. Further down, someone had scrawled, *You think you're hot shit. Well, we're going to burn your house down, Jigaboo. We'll see how hot you are then.*

"This is sick," Rob muttered. "We've gotta take this to the office."

"No, just . . . just let it go," Larry said, snatching back the paper. He crumpled it up and stuffed it in a nearby garbage can.

"I'll bet it was that asshole Cale," Rob said.

"He ain't even in school today."

"Maybe he had one of his idiot buddies deliver it."

Suddenly, Larry spun around. He was at least three inches taller than Rob, and he stared down on him. "Don't you get it, man? There are lots of people in this school that don't want me here. Cale Kinney is just one of 'em. There are lots of people in this po-dunk little town who don't want me here either. There are lots of people all over this country that don't want me here. They don't like the black man. Got it?"

Rob backed away, holding both hands up. "I'm cool. I understand, bro. You black boys got it tough."

"No, man," Larry yelled. "You don't understand shit. Blacks got it tough, because to some people we are niggers and we will always be niggers." He slammed his locker shut and stalked off.

Rob let him go. He knew instinctively not to chase him. He also knew then that the road home for blacks and whites was going to be long and rough. Lyrics from the Rascals song *People Got to Be Free* floated into his mind on the way to biology class.

* * *

May 1966

Everyone was looking forward to summer. Some kids had plans to travel out west to Disneyland for vacation. Others were going to summer camp. But many, like Rob, had nothing planned at all. That bothered him and he was trying to think of something he could do that would be fun and exciting as he rounded the corner to the cafeteria. Suddenly, a blur flashed through the warm afternoon air, and he felt a stinging pain in his jaw. Someone threw him violently to the ground. He tasted blood. Pushing up onto his hands, he felt his stomach cave in as Cale Kinney drop-kicked him three or four feet down the hall.

"You stupid, nigger lovin' faggot," he said, landing a second kick to Rob's gut.

"What is your problem?" Rob managed to gasp between kicks.

A small circle of onlookers formed around the two boys.

"My problem?"—*kick*—"People like you messin' up this school and our country—"

Rob rolled twice sideways and dodged the next kick. "I ain't doin' nothing," he said. Adrenaline rushed to his brain and he jumped to his feet to defend himself.

"You're a coon lover," Cale screamed as he rushed forward and tackled Rob. News spread fast, and more students came running to see the fight. In a matter of seconds, the small circle had become a proper crowd. Some students cheered for Rob, others cheered for Cale, and most just yelled, "Fight! Fight!"

Rob threw Cale off and jumped back up to his feet to take the best fighting stance he could. He hadn't been in any real fights, just a few skirmishes with his brother, but they'd never used their fists. He had to rely on his instincts and did what came natural.

Cale came at him with a right, and Rob managed to dodge it and plant his own right fist in his Cale's soft, sponge-like stomach. Cale doubled up and made a noise kind of like a bark. Rob backed away to see what Cale would try next.

"Listen, dickhead," Rob said. "You leave Larry and all the other black kids in this school alone."

And then, from out of nowhere, Coach Bridges and Mr. Wiley, the science teacher, stepped in to break up the fight. Each teacher grabbed one of the boys, although Mr. Wiley really wasn't much of a restrainer. Stragetically, Coach Bridges had been the one to grab

Kinney. The crowd was dismissed, but the fight was all anyone could talk about for the rest of the day.

Rob and Cale were taken down to the office—Rob went willingly, but Kinney fought the whole way—and both boys were suspended for the remainder of the week. That night, the Franklin phone rang off the hook as friends called to find out what had really happened.

Since Rob was grounded, he couldn't talk on the phone. His mother screened all the calls. On the eighth one, she knocked on his bedroom door. "It's Larry," she said. "I'll let you take this one."

Rob went into the kitchen where the telephone hung on the wall. Holding the receiver, he slid down to the floor with his back against the wall.

"Hey, man. You okay?" Larry asked.

"I'm fine, bro."

"So Cale just jumped you?"

"Yeah. What an asshole, right?" He looked up to see if his mother had heard, but if she had, she didn't show it.

"Damn," Larry said. "I gotta tell you. The rumor mill has it that you sent Cale to the hospital with three broken ribs and a concussion."

"Naw," Rob answered. "I wish I had."

"Billy said Cale might not get out of the hospital for a week."

Rob laughed.

There was a pause.

"Rob?"

"Yeah?"

"I heard that he jumped you because we're friends."

Rob shrugged, even though Larry couldn't see him. "Who knows why Cale did it. The guy's wacked out."

"Well," Larry said. "I owe you one, man."

There wasn't much more to say, even though Rob didn't want to go back to the boredom of his room. "Well, I'd better go. Thanks for the call."

"Cool, man," Larry said. "I'll call you back tomorrow."

Rob hung up. He was glad that he had stood up for Larry. He thought back to the fight. Cale had told him that he was going to beat him up just because he was friends with a black person. Rob was sure there was nothing he could have said or done to prevent the fight.

Looking up from his crouch, he saw his mom was watching him from across the kitchen. She was obviously no longer angry; if anything, she had a strange look of almost admiration on her face. It embarrassed him a little. She turned her attention back to what she'd been doing.

Rob slipped back into his bedroom, wondering why people got so upset just because a person looked different.

* * *

July 1966

The summer of 1966 was the most boring summer of Rob's life. Nothing. Happened.

The highlights? He discovered the public library, and rode his bike there several times a week. He played basketball at the junior high school gym. He watched television.

Otherwise, the summer was a void.

All around him, however, exciting things were taking place. Tim had started working at an auto parts supply shop and was saving up his money to buy his first car in the fall. He seemed to enjoy the work. He'd come home each evening, exhausted and about as grimy as a guy could get, but satisfied.

Tim had also started dating one of his classmates and was spending more and more time with her every day. If he wasn't at work, he was either on a date with Becky or talking on the phone with her.

For lack of anything else to do, Rob kept up with current events. Actually, he'd been doing that off and on anyway since his class with Mr. Westbrook. The rest of the world, it seemed, was busier than he was.

The American Football League and the National Football League agreed to merge into one football organization.

A couple of astronauts circled the earth in another

Gemini capsule.

Another Civil Rights leader, James Meredith, was wounded by a sniper in Jackson, Mississippi.

Some crazy guy murdered eight nurses in Chicago.

Another shot and killed thirteen students from a tower on the University of Texas campus.

John Lennon said The Beatles were more popular than Jesus, and then apologized, explaining, "I never meant it as a lousy anti-religious thing."

Rob realized that he genuinely missed school. He missed his friends. He missed the school library and Carolyn. He even missed the classes and the term papers and the exams. There was something about school that gave him a purpose, a challenge. He enjoyed that. Without it, in the summer, he felt empty.

Larry had spent the summer with an uncle in Chicago, returning only a few days before school started in August. He called Rob as soon as he arrived in Springlake, and Rob twisted Tim's arm into driving him to Larry's apartment for some round-ball.

When Rob climbed out of Tim's Camaro, he couldn't recognize Larry in the small crowd of black kids playing basketball. Then a tall, thin black kid stepped out of the crowd and waved him over. "Hey, white boy."

Larry looked entirely different. He had grown his hair longer, for one thing. Rob had never seen a black person with long hair, and Larry's made his head look like he was wearing some sort of helmet.

"What *is* this?" Rob asked, patting Larry's hair suspiciously.

"Don't mess with the 'fro, man," Larry said, backing away. "Everybody wears their hair this way in Chicago."

"Everybody?" Rob asked.

"Well, not you crackers," he said, grinning. "Y'all ain't got what it takes, you know?"

Rob looked Larry up and down. In addition to the 'fro, as Larry called it, he had on a tank top shirt and bell-bottom blue jeans. But in his eyes, Rob could still see his best friend. Larry tossed him the ball and they started playing.

Larry had become even more aggressive on the basketball court. His one-on-one play was no longer just an opportunity to demonstrate skill—he played like he was on a mission to prove something. If a shot missed, he blocked out aggressively. He rebounded with arms and knees and elbows, causing pain and bruises without restraint. It was like Larry had gone to Chicago as one person and come home another.

Rob, on the other hand, felt like he'd changed very little. His summer had taken him nowhere and the world around him had passed him by.

One evening, about the time the court lights were scheduled to go out and Rob would normally head home, he stuck around to ask his friend about his experience in "the big city."

"It was cool, man. My cousins, whoa, they are way more connected than we are down here in this hick town." He wiped a sweaty wristband across his forehead to keep the sweat from dripping into his eyes.

"Yeah?" Rob asked.

"Hell yeah, man," Larry said. "They are so far out, we aren't even in the same galaxy down here." He paused, as if lost in thought. "You remember how in history class Westbrook used to tell us blacks and whites were coming together? Well, they're really doing it in Chi-town. Blacks and whites hang out together all the time. There is no separation up there. Black dudes are dating white chicks and nobody freaks out."

"God," Rob responded. "Half the town would shit a brick if that happened here."

"Yeah, man. And things are happening all night long up there. People party in the streets. That town is really bad, man."

"Groovy," Rob said, not sure if it was the right word to use. He picked up the ball and dribbled it as they walked away from the court.

"We could use a good dose of that down here," Larry said. "Heavy stuff."

"I don't know if Springlake is ready."

"I don't care, man," Larry said. "It's coming."

* * *

September 1966

Entering the eighth grade was supposed to be exciting. After all, Rob was now one of the top dogs. Instead, the first few days of school were no different than the rest of the summer. The weather was still hot and clammy. None of the teachers and none of the students were interested in being there.

The most entertaining part of the first week was the new batch of seventh graders. To Rob, they were way more lost than he had been. They were scared to dress out for PE, or at least embarrassed. They couldn't figure out how to open their lockers without help. No way had he been like that. But in reality, they weren't so different.

Well, except for Doug. He was the only seventh grader who carried a briefcase. He claimed it was a great way to keep his books and papers together. It made him look like some sort of junior lawyer or something. Doug was different.

So it wasn't a huge surprise when Doug came to school one morning in early September more excited than ever. Completely oblivious to the rules of junior high hierarchy and his place in the world as a seventh grader, he jumped right into a conversation Rob and some of the other eighth grade boys were having.

"Hey," he beamed, unable to contain his excitement. "Did you guys see Star Trek last night?"

Most of the boys rolled their eyes and ignored him, but one asked, "What's a Star Trek?"

"It's only the neatest new show on TV," Doug explained. "It's all about this crew of astronauts on this starship that is way into the future. It's really neat."

"Yeah, kid, we know," Rob said. "You said that already."

"I saw the show," Larry said.

"So, what did you think," Doug asked.

"What I want to know," Larry said, moving up close to the kid, towering over him, "is why there ain't no black people in the future."

"Huh?" Doug said. The color drained from his face and he stepped backwards.

"They got Japs. They got Scottish boys. They got Ruskies. Why ain't there no black men in the future?"

"Uh, ah, oh," Doug sputtered, clearly spazzing out.

"Did all the whities kill off all the blacks?" Larry demanded.

"Take it easy, Lar," Rob cautioned. He figured Larry was just teasing the poor kid, but he didn't want him getting worked up for real.

"I, uh, I . . . it's only the first show," Doug managed.

"Here's what I want you to do," Larry instructed.

"Yes—uh—sir?" It was really bizarre to watch a black boy tell a white boy what to do. All of the boys in the group were just standing there silent.

"I want you to write a letter to the president of NBC and tell him to put a black man or two on that spaceship."

Doug actually pulled out a notepad and jotted that down.

"Now get to work," Larry said. He pushed the stunned kid out of the group.

Doug ran off. One of the other eighth-grade boys, scratching the back of his neck, said, "I saw that show last night. Hey, Larry—wasn't Uhura, the communications officer, black?"

Larry laughed. "I know," he said. "I was just messin' with him.

* * *

February 1967

The Springlake Seahawks had a winning season in 1967. The team had snagged a couple of tall seventh graders and lost out-of-control forward Cale Kinney. The maturing eighth graders showed a great deal of improvement, and they carried the Seahawks to a five game winning streak that ended when they faced

Lakeland Junior High.

After their final game, a win against Lake Wales Junior High, Larry and Rob were chatting while getting dressed in the locker room. "Man, I love basketball season," Larry said.

"You should," Rob answered. "You're good at it, bro."

"It's not just that. During basketball season I feel like the school, the community even, gives me respect. Those nigger notes in the locker go away. Those looks in the hall too. It's like I'm in a different world. I'm respected, not hated."

"Yeah, you're probably right," Rob said. "But I wouldn't know for sure. I hate you in and out of basketball season."

Larry threw his towel at Rob. "Typical white boy response."

Then Rob got serious. "It's weird, man. I think our school is coming along. It takes time, you know?"

"So what's weird about that?" Larry asked.

Rob frowned as he tried to explain himself. "It's just that I know students can accept people from other races, at least during round-ball season, when they need them. I don't understand why they can't do the same at other times of the year. Hell, I do."

"It makes you miss it when it's gone," Larry answered.

"Get out of here, boys," Coach Bridges yelled. "The bus leaves in five minutes."

"There's something I won't miss," Rob.

They threw their wet jerseys and shorts into their gym bags and dashed through the door.

* * *

The last week of school was an emotional roller coaster for Rob. When he wasn't cramming for final exams he was signing yearbooks and saying goodbye to his friends. Rob was tired, and he wanted to be out of school.

"It's kinda sad that they're closing this school," said

Tammie, a sweet but overly thin fellow eighth grader. The bell had just rung, announcing that the last Tuesday of the year was over. Only three more days of school were left in the school year. Rob had decided to drop by the library to study for Wednesday's exams. He was packing up his bag to head over there when Tammie came over to his desk to chat.

"True," Rob said. "But that new high school should be nice. This place is about to fall down, anyway."

"It's cool we were the last class here."

"Our little place in history," Rob added, teasing her but agreeing with her at the same time.

"Take care, Rob. See you later."

Rob headed for the library as swarms of classmates marched toward the exit doors. He passed by the auditorium, where he had endured those dry, televised American history classes. A lone figure, sitting on the front row, caught his eye. Rob stopped and walked through the open auditorium door.

"Mr. Westbrook?"

His former American history teacher was sitting quietly, staring at the stage. After a moment, he said, "Yes?"

"Are you okay?" Rob asked.

A sigh. "I'm fine."

Rob walked to the front row and sat down.

"This was my last year teaching here," Mr. Westbrook said. "Did you know that I've taught in this school for thirty-three years?"

"I had no idea."

"I've taught one governor, two state congressmen, one actor, a couple dozen small business owners, twelve criminals, and over forty students who are now teachers themselves."

"Wow. That's far out." The two sat in silence for a while. Rob, not knowing what else to say, added, "That's gotta make you proud."

"All except the criminals," Mr. Westbrook said with a small smile. "I wonder if I could have said something that could have made them . . ." his voice trailed off.

Another long silence. Then Mr. Westbrook stood and said, "Well, you'd better be heading home. Don't you have exams tomorrow?"

"Yeah, English and math. I'm going to study in the library."

"Good luck, Mr. Franklin."

The two of them headed toward the exit and Mr. Westbrook turned off the lights.

Probably for the last time, Rob thought.

* * *

May 1967

Some of the best-kept secret treasures of Florida are the numerous natural springs dotting the state. With the exception of the story of Spanish explorer Ponce de León and his failed quest to find the fountain of youth, most visitors to the state were unaware of the beautiful underwater playgrounds that burst through the Florida limestone. The frigid water was as clean and clear as water could be.

Florida's visitors didn't know much about the springs, but the locals sure did. In the northern part of the state, Blue Springs had once been a popular vacation spot for the well-to-do in the area. Down the road from Blue Springs was Naked Springs, where, at one time, those who couldn't afford swimsuits would go to cool off in the nude on hot summer days. A little further south, in the Ocala National Forest, thousands of gallons of water flowed through underground channels filled with salt deposits and exited as a salty mixture at Salt Springs.

Most of the springs featured clear water, which burst out of the ground at seventy-two degrees Fahrenheit year round. Many of these natural, God-made wonders were owned by the state. Beautiful state parks with camping and picnic facilities were built around the springs and thousands of vacationers enjoyed them every year.

Less than twenty miles from Springlake, one of the most gorgeous springs in the state rested in a beautiful oasis of cypress trees, sand dunes and fresh flowing rivers. Narváez Spring, named after Spanish explorer Pánfilo de Narváez, was a popular spot for day visitors. It had sandy beaches, lifeguard stations, and a well-stocked snack bar.

Springlake Junior High held an annual visit to Narváez Spring for eighth graders every May. It was a special treat for those who survived the building and the teachers and all the terrible things that the junior high school had forced upon its students.

The day was perfect. Blue skies matched the cool blue waters of the spring. Rob grabbed his beach bag— filled with beach towel, snacks, suntan lotion, and a library book—and was making his way from the parking lot to the middle of the blazing white sand beach when he walked by a couple of middle-aged ladies lying in the sun on a blanket. They were drenched in suntan lotion. One lady had raised her sunglasses to watch the hordes of junior high students swarm out from the school buses and make a beeline for the swimming area where she and her friend had been enjoying their heretofore-secluded spot.

Rob overheard her sigh and complain to her friend, "Oh my, Lorraine. Looks like we picked the same day as the junior high school."

The other lady pulled herself up to a sitting position, saying, "I remember our eighth grade field trip here. That was the first time Billy Wiggins kissed me, over there in the palmetto bushes."

"Look," the first woman said. "They brought some Negro children with them. I heard they had allowed them in the white school." She paused for a moment. "You know, colored people can't swim. I don't know why they brought them here. Everyone knows coloreds' bodies don't float as well as ours."

As if on cue, Larry ran by, throwing his beach towel at Robby. "Race you," he yelled, and was off toward the water, kicking up sand as he ran. He dove into the glassy water and swam out toward the boil, where the spring water rushed out of the ground at a rate of forty million gallons per day.

"Oh, my." Lorraine shrugged. "I guess he must

have a lot of white blood in him."

Rob dropped his gear and followed Larry into the water.

* * *

September 1968

Rob's freshman year was a blur. New classmates, new concepts, new courses, and new challenges all came together in a fuzzy haze of work and fun.

High school was unmistakably different from junior high. The teachers were more demanding. Competition for grades was tougher. Extracurricular opportunities were more plentiful. By the end of the year, Rob was exhausted, but finally into the rhythm of high school.

That summer, his rhythm was disrupted once again as the government enforced integration. Rob's mother said that over thirty percent of the students in the high school would be black, according to an article she'd read in *The Springlake Tribune*. The article also claimed that enrollment in local private schools had swelled.

As he advanced from ninth grade to tenth, Rob could feel the coming change like a man smelling salt water from the shores of the ocean.

* * *

February 1969

Rob was leaning against the wall across the hall from his fourth period class when Larry came marching straight to him.

"Hey, man. What's happening?" Rob asked.

"They're back," Larry said, handing Rob a piece of lined notebook paper.

"Who's back . . . Oh shit," Rob said as read the note.

The words *we're gonna get you nigger* screamed at the top of the page. Further down the page the writer had scrawled *we know where you live.*

"Man, this is so wrong," Rob said, fuming. "What are you going to do about it?"

"I'm gonna find out who wrote it and kill the motherfucker."

"I think you should turn it in."

"She-it. They wouldn't do nothin'," Larry said.

The bell rang and the two friends had to part ways.

The notes kept coming, sometimes twice a day. Larry refused to take them to the office, but Rob could tell that he was boiling beneath the surface.

"You can bank on this," Larry said one day. "I will find this asshole and he won't ever write anything else again."

Rob had never seen Larry so angry, and pitied whoever was writing the obscene notes.

Larry always kept his word.

* * *

March 1969

The spring thaw came and brought with it chilling acts of violence. Students began to face off against one another physically. The larger population of African American students could no longer be ignored by certain groups of white students, and when March temperatures rose, tempers flared.

The first fight started as soon as school was out one Tuesday afternoon. A crowd gathered and two boys tore into each other like rabid dogs. School administrators pulled them apart, but not before blood had been spilt.

Rob overheard a disturbing conversation one day in the hall among some white boys he seldom hung out with. "We went nigger-bogging last night. It was so fucking far out."

Rob stopped in his tracks. "What's nigger-bogging?"

"It's so much fun. You take your pickup truck and run through the backyard gardens they've got over in Nigger Town," he said. "I ain't never seen so much smashed watermelon in my life, man."

"That's sick, man," Rob said, staring the boy in the eyes. "Those people need that food to survive. You're killing them."

"Aw, c'mon. They're all on food stamps. They don't need that shit."

Rob walked away, shaking his head.

"Get the hell out of here, you fuckin' nigger lover," they called after him.

* * *

"Get the hell out of here," Larry yelled. He was sprinting down the hall. Following him were about fifty white high school students, all screaming, crying, running.

Rob, who'd been on his way to homeroom, was startled and confused.

"Run," Larry managed between breaths.

Rob instantly fell in beside Larry and they sprinted down the hall away from the approaching mob. "What did you do?" he asked.

"Not me," Larry panted. "They're not chasing me."

"Who are they chasing?"

"They're not *chasing*," Larry said, glancing back over his shoulder. "They're running."

The two boys dashed into a side hallway and hid behind some lockers. "What's happening?" Rob asked.

"Do you remember how that white kid jumped on Leroy Johnson 'cause he was talking to his girlfriend?"

"Yeah. They knocked each other around a bit, but that was all."

"No, it wasn't." Larry peered around the corner to be sure they were safe. "Leroy and some other blacks jumped a white sophomore after PE last Tuesday. Then a bunch of white boys punched out a couple of blacks who were in on that fight."

"Oh shit."

"You got that right, man. Now the brothers are out for blood."

"So why were you running from them? You're a brother."

"I wasn't running from them," Larry said. "I was making sure *you* did."

Noises in the hallway got louder as the angry black mob marched closer. Rob found a heavy metal door leading out the back past the lockers, so he and Larry slipped outside. Several police cars and an ambulance sped noisily by on the street in front of the high school.

That afternoon, Rob and all of his classmates were moved into the auditorium for a school assembly. The principal addressed the students. "We know that students are frustrated and tensions are high. We know a few individuals' behavior has gotten out of hand. Therefore, to protect those of you who are not causing problems, we are instituting a curfew to limit the amount of time students can spend in school hallways."

Rob glanced around at the faces of his peers. He saw anger and fear. Many of them booed the news. Others shouted threats and complaints.

The principal continued, "The school has hired several off-duty policemen to patrol the hallways during school hours. Also, after-hours activities, except for formal sports activities, are hereby suspended until further notice."

More moans and disgruntled sounds.

"We will have order," the principal said. He added that his office was open for suggestions about dealing with this situation.

As they left the auditorium, a student handed Rob a sheet of paper announcing a 24-hour prayer vigil for peace, sponsored by several local churches.

Two weeks after the school assembly, someone snuck onto school grounds late at night and painted racist comments on the outside walls of the school building. When Rob entered the school grounds the next morning, the walls outside of biology were covered: *Die Niggers, Niggers Git Out Of Springlake,* and *Fuck You, Blackie.* The mystery artist had a big mouth and was soon caught. Rob heard that he spent the weekend scrubbing the walls with kerosene and paint thinner.

Surprinsingly, word got out that the junior/senior

prom would be held as scheduled. Most people thought it would be canceled due to the racial tension. "Did you get an invite?" Rob asked Larry one Tuesday morning between classes.

"Are you kidding?" Larry said. "Even white boys like you don't get to go to the prom until junior year. What makes you think a brother is gonna get an invite?"

"I thought you'd get a date on your charm alone."

"If I got a date, it would be to the black dance over at the Days Inn by the interstate. You know, my people are having our own dance that night."

"But you aren't going to it, right?"

"What can I say. Their loss," Larry said with a sigh.

Rob discovered that Springlake High wasn't alone in its violent spring. Some students told him that other schools throughout the South were struggling to adjust to forced integration as well. He wished that everyone could work through their issues and prejudices, so things could return to relative calm.

* * *

October 1969

At practice, the suicide drills were getting tougher and tougher. Rob leaned against the block wall of the gym, gasping for breath. Most of the other varsity players did the same. Coach Bridges walked out the exit door on his way to his office. Practice was over.

Exhausted and a bit nauseated, Rob stumbled into the locker room. Stripping off his practice sweats, he made his way to the showers and quickly washed off. After putting on his street clothes and splashing on a little Brut, he grabbed his duffle bag and headed outside.

Glancing at his watch, he saw that he had thirty minutes until his mom would pick him up. Usually, he would talk with Larry for a while before heading over to the library to read some magazines while he waited. Today, however, Larry was not around. Rob glanced into the parking lot and saw that his Chevy II was still parked in his usual spot.

Shrugging, he headed up the brick hallway toward the library. He strolled past the band room and turned down an adjacent hallway, where he stumbled upon Larry painting the words *Die White Boy* on the brick wall with a can of fluorescent paint.

"What the hell are you doing?" Rob demanded.

Larry stood stock still, frozen in time, searching for an answer.

Then Rob noticed several other black students painting similar slogans on nearby walls. "What the fuck do you want?" one of them asked. He came at Rob, ready to fight.

"Hold on. He's all right," Larry said.

"What are you doing?" Rob demanded again, turning to face Larry.

Larry didn't say anything.

"Get out of here, white boy," another black student said. "And forget what you saw."

Rob ignored the remark and grabbed Larry in a bear hug, pulling him down the hall away from the rebel artists. "Come on, man," he said. "You're leaving." Larry dropped the aerosol spray can. The other kids shook their heads and returned to their graffiti.

Rob dragged Larry through closed doors to another hallway, and then Larry shrugged him off. "You don't understand," he shouted.

"You're right," Rob answered. "I don't understand what my friend is doing painting racist sayings on the school walls."

"You don't know how it is to get notes in your locker, to be watched wherever you go, to be called nigger."

"You're right, again. I don't know what that's like." The two boys squared off, face to face. "But this ain't gonna solve anything."

"This is the only thing we've got to fight back with."

"That's bullshit, Larry."

"People need to know how it feels . . ."

Rob took a breath. "You're right. They do. But painting shit on the walls isn't gonna make that happen."

Larry stared down at the bright linoleum floor. "You know, this floor was probably shined by a black janitor. And white people stomp on it every day."

"Yeah," Rob answered. "And that same black janitor will probably be scrubbing the shit off the walls back there tomorrow morning."

Larry began to shake. He rubbed his palm across his eyes, fighting back tears. "They can't treat us this way."

"Only if you let them, man. Only if you let them," Rob answered, placing a hand on Larry's shoulder.

They stood in the empty hallway for a bit. Then, Larry said, "Let's get out of here, man."

They headed down another hall and through double-doors to a sidewalk outside. They doubled back to the gym parking lot where Larry's Chevy II sat waiting. After Larry drove off, Rob walked back to the library using a different path, so he wouldn't pass by the black students who were vandalizing the school. His mother was waiting for him when he arrived.

* * *

November 1969

World History Assignment:
Look 30 years into the future and describe how you think the world will be different in 1999.

"Wonderful Advances"
By Rob Franklin

Thirty years from now, our country will have realized so many wonderful scientific advances and improvements. This paper is an effort to list a few that I predict will occur.

America will have colonized the moon and will be planning colonial expeditions to Mars. People will be able to vacation in outer space hotels featuring weightlessness and beautiful "out of this world" scenery.

Back on the earth, world hunger will have been almost completely obliterated through the establishment of thousands of giant hydroponic gardens. World peace will exist because leaders will seek negotiation and mutual compromise, instead of war. Most diseases will be eradicated by scientific breakthroughs and advances in medicine.

Our cars will take flight, allowing drivers to fly from one location to another. They will also feature automatic controls, on-board television and sophisticated rotary engines.

Telephones will evolve into viewphones, allowing callers around the world to actually see the person that they are talking to in the privacy of their homes. This will enhance all aspects of life, from how we buy and sell products to how we learn and teach.

"A Real Melting Pot"
By Larry Watson

In the next few years, America will elect its first African American President. He'll bring pride to the black people around the country and will pave the way for others to enter the Oval Office and other positions in government. Major companies will follow the example and place African Americans in their highest positions.

Blacks and whites will mingle together socially, and interracial marriage will be common long before 1999. As they mingle, so will their music, arts, and literature. America will become a real melting pot, once again.

"The Next American Revolution"
By Cale Kinney

Revolution is coming. Long before 1999 those in this country who have lost freedoms to others, who have watched their tax dollars go to pay the lazy people in this land, who have seen our country become weak militarily, will bring about a revolution destined to set this country on the road to greatness again.

By 1999, America will once again be seen as a great world power. People in communist countries around the world will follow our great example and overthrow their governments for democracies. The Berlin Wall will be taken down in Germany, and the Soviet Union will elect their first president.

The good, hard-working people who have made America successful in the past will come to power again and put the country back on track to greatness.

SANCTUARY FIVE

Church

"Praise the Lord! Praise God in his
sanctuary;
praise him in his mighty heavens!"

— Psalm 150:1

REVEREND STEPHEN PHILLIPS

June 1964

To say that things were quiet in Springlake, Florida, would be to grossly overstate the obvious. The little town was quiet by design. There was one theater: *The Spring.* White people sat downstairs and blacks sat in the balcony. The town had one diner, one family restaurant, and one drive-in restaurant. People didn't go out, except on weekends, when the restaurants and theaters were packed.

Back in seminary, some sociologist claimed that the real entertainment source for small-town America was the church. If that were accurate, then Springlake was an entertainment Mecca, because she had about fifteen of them. There were probably more church members per capita in Springlake than in any other city in the United States.

I received my appointment as associate minister of First Methodist Church of Springlake in June of 1965, having recently completed my Master of Divinity degree at Candler Seminary in Atlanta. The eighty-year-old red brick Methodist church was right smack in the middle of town, within eyesight of First Baptist Church and earshot of the chimes of First Presbyterian Church, which played every day at noon.

If Florida was a retirement state, then Springlake was its capital. With its quiet two-lane roads, stately old oak trees covered in Spanish moss, and countless shuffleboard courts, it was the perfect place to enjoy the sunshine years.

Consequently, First Methodist of Springlake was the church many older Methodist ministers served before they retired. The standard joke among ministers was that my church was the place older ministers went to cram for final exams. There was no conflict, little change and nothing to do except visit old blue-haired ladies in the hospitals and play golf. Preaching was easy; just pull out a sermon you wrote for some other church a few years previously, and no one's the wiser and everyone's happy.

The senior minister, Dr. Graham Strong, followed traditions like a good soldier of the cross. He was going on his second year at First Methodist, and expected to serve there until he retired in three or four more.

But something was happening in Springlake, just like it was happening all over America. Record numbers of children had been born not too long after thousands of soldiers returned from World War II. Those kids were now reaching their teens. The presence of all these hormally charged youngsters, who'd been dubbed the Baby Boomers, frightened the adults.

It wasn't just that there were so many of them. It was also a bunch of other things that people had never faced before. Kids were mobile. They had cars. They had time. They spent a lot of that time driving around, cruising up and down Main Street until way past midnight. Sometimes, they drove too fast. All those cars driven by all those irresponsible teenagers was enough to produce a few more gray hairs on any sexagenarian.

Young people also had rock and roll, and many older people couldn't understand that. Sure, in the early '60s, there was folk music, but that had morphed into rock, and then The Beatles and The Rolling Stones came along, and everything went to hell, or at least that's what many adults thought.

There were also rumors of drug abuse. A strange new substance called marijuana, which actually wasn't that new, was causing young men and women to go crazy.

As the years went on, fears of marijuana addiction expanded to include LSD, heroine and cocaine.

These kids also seemed so outspoken. They didn't keep quiet, like kids used to. Instead, they insisted on having a say in whatever went on in the school, or in the government or in the church.

Some said that the time was coming when black students would be integrated into white schools, and that scared the already-frightened adults even more.

That's why I was hired.

I was the "Radical Preach," fresh out of seminary and able to "speak their language" and relate to the young generation. My classmates and I enjoyed that designation. We used to boast that, at our graduation, instead of a cap and gown, we'd wear turtlenecks and smoke pipes. We welcomed the chance to be "real" with kids, to be relevant. We were expected to be like Moses, but for youth— marching through the wilderness of adolescence and leading teenagers to the promised land of adulthood.

Bullshit.

We really didn't know what we were doing. Sure, we wanted to be relevant. We wanted to be real. But no one ever wrote a manual on being relevant. No one ever taught a seminary class on how to be real.

We literally made it up as we went along. But somehow, even despite our cluelessness, I think God used our little successes to make a real difference. After all, isn't that what He does?

* * *

August 1964

Purpose. All I wanted was a little tires-meet-the-road purpose. All around the world a revolution was taking place, and I was stuck in Nowhere U.S.A. visiting little old ladies and nursery classes. I felt like a bedpan changer in a M.A.S.H. ward.

Only a few hundred miles northwest of me, in Mississippi, thousands of activists were working throughout the Freedom Summer to register black voters. In Washington, President Johnson had signed the Civil Rights Act of 1964, signaling the beginning of the end of racial discrimination. A few hundred miles northeast of me, Lester Maddox chose to close his diner instead of following the law and serving black and white people together. Race riots were breaking out in the summer heat of Harlem.

One stormy Sunday morning, I was sitting in the front of the Methodist sanctuary and silently stewing while I listened to Dr. Graham Strong make another lame attempt at a joke in his sermon. The members of the congregation, scattered about in the half-filled room, chuckled more at the effort than the joke.

First Methodist Church had an ornately royal feel. Dark, rich oak pews and altar rails were set against deep maroon carpeting and wooden floors. A large, lighted cross hung above the choir loft immediately behind the central podium, where the minister delivered God's Word, or rather, his interpretation of it. Two large, stately chairs occupied the stage behind the podium for the select few, the ministers, to sit during worship.

Along the walls, beautiful stained glass pictures depicting the life of Christ looked in on the faithful worshipers. The back rows of the sanctuary were cast in shadow by a balcony, seldom used since the olden days when the church was packed every Sunday morning and night.

I hadn't even gotten a chance to preach yet. I had struggled through four years of college and three years of seminary, learning Greek, expository preaching, and communication only to be stuck in this little church where the senior minister refused to give up the pulpit. I had been promised Wednesday evening prayer meetings and Sunday night services, but Graham had yet to let me preach once.

He kept saying that my days of working behind the scenes, like Martha serving Jesus, would prove fruitful one day.

* * *

September 1964

One of my duties was to visit members of the congregation. Graham had suggested that I go to the homes of those who had dropped out of church as well as those who were regular attendees.

From my vantage point in one of the stately chairs behind the podium at First Methodist, I could quickly look out through the crowd and determine who was in attendance and who was probably on vacation or skipping. Church members tended to sit in the same pews week after week. I once read an article that said that people tend to sit in the same place at a church, in meeting rooms and board rooms, and especially around the meal table, because the decision about where to sit was one less decision they had to make every day. The author said that we have too much to decide, so we just go back to where we sat last time.

I wondered if that was true. After all, even the early settlers had preferred pews. Some paid a pew tax to reserve theirs from year to year. But I seriously doubt that Josiah Settler had that many decisions to make, besides which crops to weed and where to hunt. After all, how many decisions did they make back then? So why the preference?

At any rate, I knew who to visit by scoping out the empty pews on Sunday.

The first group, the drop-outs, was the toughest to visit, but also the most predictable. They were always embarrassed that a minister had dropped by to visit. It was like they were caught playing hooky from school. They were always saying things like, "We're sorry we haven't been back to church lately," but they were a bit defensive too.

They also seemed to want to get rid of me as quickly as they could. Those visits seldom lasted more than twenty minutes. I felt like the king of the twenty-minute visit. But it left me hollow and empty. I went home feeling lonely rather than accomplished.

The other group was more receptive, even if they were a little concerned about why the minister would drop by their house. Their typical response was "Aren't there others who are more in need of a visit from the minister than us?" But every now and then, I would drop in on a family that really made me feel at home. Like the Franklins.

As a single young man and a lousy cook, I tried to plan my visits to active church homes around dinnertime, in the hopes that they might ask me to stay and have a bite to eat. And yes, the stereotype of Southern cooking is as real as the day is long. I dropped by the Franklin house one evening about five o'clock, and Mrs. Franklin insisted that I join them for fried chicken and mashed potatoes. She neglected to mention that supper wouldn't actually start for at least an hour, since they had to wait for her husband, Ray, to come home from work. But I was perfectly happy to wait for a good meal.

So I sat in the kitchen and chatted with her for thirty minutes as she battered the chicken, dropped it in a skillet full of lard and started cooking up the best dinner I had smelled in a long time. We talked about the town and the church and schools.

Then she suggested I might want to look in on her sons, Tim and Rob, while they did their homework. I did, and we spent the next thirty minutes doing English and "new math" homework together.

When Ray came home, Mrs. Franklin announced, "Reverend Phillips dropped by for a visit this afternoon. I've insisted that he join us for dinner."

"Sounds fine to me," Ray said. "As long as he doesn't eat all the chicken." Then he turned to me with a grin. "Hi, Stephen," he said, shaking my hand warmly.

We found our seats at the table, and Ray asked me to say grace. I prayed a fast blessing because my mouth was watering so much from the smell of good Southern cooking that I was afraid I might start drooling into the mashed potatoes.

As the food was passed around the table, everyone

quizzed me on everything from seminary studies to how I liked Springlake. Mrs. Franklin wanted to know if I'd met any special ladies in town, and I told her I hadn't had the time. Rob latched onto that topic immediately.

"I thought ministers didn't get married," he said.

"That's priests, you idiot," his brother corrected him.

"What's the difference?"

"Priests are ministers at Catholic churches," Tim said. "And they don't get married." He looked at me. "Right, Reverend?"

"There are also priests in the Episcopalian church, and some of them do get married," I said.

"The Pope allows that?" Tim asked.

"Well, they don't answer to the Pope, and neither do I."

The conversation with the Franklin family went like that, back and forth, for close to two hours. When Rob asked why I didn't preach in church on Sundays, I glanced down at my watch. "Oh my. It looks like I'm making up for not preaching in the pulpit by preaching here at your dinner table. I had no idea I've been talking so long," I said apologetically.

"Nonsense," Mrs. Franklin said. "We've all been talking. It's been fun."

I liked the way she used two syllables for one-syllable words like "fun."

"Thanks. I really should be heading out though," I said. "The boys have school in the morning and Mr. Franklin has to go to work."

Mr. Franklin replied, "Now don't forget. If you ever need anything, let us know. And Springlake Hardware gives a ten percent discount to church pastors."

We shook hands at the door, and I felt like I was bidding good night to lifelong best friends. I may have been doing just that. I told them that I would really like to visit again, and they invited me wholeheartedly to do so. I intended to take them up on that invitation.

* * *

March 1965

I became an activist.

The newspapers really drove me to it. Another civil rights activist was killed in Mississippi. A couple of weeks earlier it had been a black kid trying to protect his grandfather and his mother. The State Troopers shot him.

This time, it was closer to home for me. The victim was James Reeb, a white man and a minister. I was stunned. Reeb was beaten to death by other white people for trying to help black people obtain the right to vote. It made absolutely no sense.

I stared at the newspaper for a long, long time. *What could possibly scare people enough to cause them to commit such a hideous crime?*

I strongly empathized with James Reeb, even though I'd never met the man. He was older than me, almost twice as old. I wondered how his family was dealing with the loss. I wondered how his church would manage. I wondered if it was all worth it.

Throughout the morning, a verse from the Bible came back to me again and again: *Greater love hath no man than this, that a man lay down his life for his friends.* There was a time when I thought Jesus was only talking about himself in that passage. Now I understood how easily the verse could be applied to people like James Reeb.

I left my office around lunchtime, feeling like I needed the company of other people. I didn't want to eat alone, but I had no one to call. So I grabbed the newspaper and went to the Springlake Diner.

I slid onto the vinyl seat of the counter stool and spun around to face the grill, feeling a bit like a six-year-old boy, but relishing the presence of others. The cook, a guy with the name Jimmy embroidered on his grease-stained white shirt, dropped an order pad on the counter and asked, "Whatta ya have?" Before I could answer, his eyes glanced down at my folded newspaper. "Whatta waste," he muttered.

"I beg your pardon?"

He pointed to the headline. "That poor, dumb preacher. Whatta waste that he died for that."

"For what?"

"You know. He died for such a stupid reason. Registering niggers to vote? Jesus Christ. Niggers don't really want to vote. They're just causing trouble."

I found myself in a tough spot. I didn't know this guy, Jimmy, because I never ate at this diner. As a minister, I felt like I was always in a fishbowl. Anything I said or did might reflect poorly on our church. But also as a minister, and more importantly as a human being, I felt an intense need to honor the fellow preacher I had never known who had fought for his beliefs with his life.

I opened the paper to display the entire article. "Do you think Reverend James Reeb would agree with you?"

"What's it matter? He's dead."

"Yes he is. But the question is, do you think he thought helping blacks achieve the right to vote was a cause worth dying for?"

"He ain't doin' nobody no good, now."

"I'm not so sure," I said. "A lot of people are upset about this. It may have tilted the scales in favor of the Civil Rights activists."

"Jesus. I hope not."

Jesus might disagree with you, I thought.

"So anyway, whatta ya have?" Jimmy asked, obviously trying to change the subject.

"Cheeseburger, fries and a Coke," I said.

Jimmy turned toward the grill.

Speaking to his back, I asked, "What cause would *you* consider worth dying for?"

Jimmy turned back around, still uncomfortable and perhaps now a little annoyed that I hadn't dropped the subject. "I don't know. My family, I guess."

"Would you be willing to die so your family could have the right to vote?"

"They already have that right," he said curtly.

"Right," I replied, "but imagine they didn't. Imagine that powerful political people were trying to keep people from a certain neighborhood or certain income bracket from voting."

For a moment, I swear I saw a flicker of understanding in his eyes, so I asked him again, "Would you be willing to die so they could vote?"

He was frowning at me, as if I had forced him to go back and rework a difficult math equation that he'd never understood and never cared to use. Then he obviously gave up trying. "I'll get your burger."

After that, Jimmy kept his distance. He also kept his back to me nearly the entire time I ate my lunch and read the rest of the paper. He had to face me when I paid my bill at the cash register. He hesitated, then asked, "They couldn't do that, could they? Take away our right to vote?"

I took my change and replied softly, "That's what's happening to the black community."

His frown came back, and as I left the diner, I prayed that he would try harder to solve that math equation this time around. I prayed that he could.

* * *

September 1965

Seminary can be a real bonding experience. The relationships I built at Candler were strong enough to last for several years and survive thousands of miles of separation.

One such friendship was with Warren Jackson, a big, burly guy who looked like a lumberjack. His last year at seminary, Warren had let his beard grow long. That, combined with overly thick eyebrows and dull brown eyes, made him look more like the abominable snowman than a minister.

Warren's father had been in the Air Force, so they moved around a lot when he was a kid. Unlike most of us, who returned to our home states when we graduated from seminary, Warren had the whole country to choose from. His mobility, plus his exceptional grade average, especially in Greek and New Testament, made him a very attractive candidate to the ministry.

With the world at his fingertips, Warren chose California. He had lived there for a year or two as a teenager, and looked forward to surfing the Southern California beaches once again. He joined the staff of a Methodist Church in San Diego as their associate minister.

I received a letter from Warren saying he was planning a visit to his sister in South Florida and asking if he could stay with me one night. It sounded like a great time for two former seminarians to catch up. But at the bottom of his letter was a note I was less than thrilled to read: *P.S. Let's get together with Kevin.*

Kevin Morris had been Warren's roommate in seminary. He was traditionalist's traditionalist. His father was a Methodist minister, just like his grandfather. I'd heard that his great grandfather was a circuit rider in the 1800s.

I have no idea how Warren lived with Kevin for three long years. Warren and I loved to challenge everything, from theology to politics. We always asked if there was a better way or another view. Kevin, on the other hand, was content with everything as it was. He liked the services, the music, the structure, the schedule, and everything about the church.

But Warren was the visitor, and he wanted us all to get together, so I made the arrangements.

Warren parked his white VW van in front of the house and rang my doorbell. We hugged like brothers and brought his duffle bag inside. After a few minutes of chat, we headed to Orlando to meet up with Kevin. We met at a little pizza restaurant on the west side of town. Kevin was already there, seated at a little table in the back.

"Hey, man," Warren said, giving the skinny minister a huge bear hug.

"Steve," Kevin said, extending a hand to me. "Good to see you." I grabbed his hand in a soul handshake, which I could tell by the look on his face surprised him.

"What are you having?" I asked, pointing to his drink.

"I've got a Tab," Kevin said, sitting back down and sipping the dark liquid through a straw.

The waitress had arrived during our greeting, and Warren and I ordered beer. Radical, relevant, hip ministers like us *had* to have beer with pizza. Besides, odds were that forty-five minutes away in Orlando, I wouldn't run into one of the members of my own church, who might question my alcohol consumption practices.

We talked about where we lived and what we'd been up to. We asked each other how our churches were doing. We all lied freely about our churches—there are some things that ministers have no problem lying about, and church growth is one of them. My church was "growing by leaps and bounds." Warren's congregation was "thinking about enlarging the sanctuary." Kevin's church was "considering adding more staff." We talked about old seminary acquaintances and caught up on old stories. It was great fun.

Eventually, the conversation slowed. That was when Warren took a swig of beer, leaned forward on his two large forearms, and said, "Guys, I was in Watts."

"Watts? Los Angeles? The riots? No way!" I said.

"Why would you go there?" Kevin asked, disapproval clear in his voice.

"To help a friend," Warren said. "Last June, I met this Reverend William Wright at Annual Conference. We became friends, shared a couple of meals. Willie told me about an inner city ministry he had for poor people in Los Angeles."

The waitress brought our pizza, and Warren paused long enough to take a huge bite out of his slice. The cheese dripped down into his beard. He wiped it with the back of his hand and kept talking.

"In the fall, we had a coat and blanket collection campaign to help Willie's outreach program. I drove the donated items up to Los Angeles and he showed me around. His ministry was housed in an old warehouse right up next to the Projects. He named it the Reach Out Center."

I glanced at Kevin. He was already shoveling down

his third slice of pizza like it was his last meal. I couldn't figure out how he stayed so thin; he'd always been a big and fast eater.

I turned my attention back to Warren's story.

"Well, last August, when reports started coming in that there was trouble in Watts, the first thing I did was call Willie. The phone service was out, so I got worried sick." He took another gulp of beer. "I called another Methodist pastor, and he told me that things were pretty rough in the Watts neighborhood, but that he had spoken with Willie Wright, and he was holding out okay."

I jumped in. "We heard all sorts of rumors about what started all that, but never got the final word. What happened?"

Warren was thoughtful for a moment. "There has been this tension there for years, according to Willie. Most of the white people and the industry had moved out to the suburbs long ago. That left poor black people in the projects."

I nodded. "What I heard was the police were giving preferential treatment to certain people, especially any whites who still had businesses in the area. Naturally, the blacks resented this. It got to be a real mess."

Kevin paused mid-bite into his fourth slice. "That doesn't make sense. Why would the police favor the whites? Weren't there black people on the police force? Wouldn't they support the blacks?"

"I don't know," Warren said. "But the incident that started it all wasn't between black residents and black cops. The way the story went, a white cop pulled a couple of blacks over for drunk driving. He arrested the driver and had the car impounded, instead of letting the other guy drive the car home. That guy went home and told his friends about it, and they got pissed off. It was the straw that broke the camel's back, so to speak. A huge mob gathered downtown and people started throwing rocks and bricks. It didn't help when the police chief said they were all acting 'like monkeys in a zoo.'"

"Jeez."

"Yeah. Pretty dumb," Warren said. "Willie and

some of his friends called a community meeting at one of the churches, but it failed. People were too angry. Someone called in the National Guard, and all hell broke loose. They started fire-bombing some of the white-owned businesses."

Kevin said, "I saw on the news that blacks lost their homes, as well. They bombed their own homes?"

"It turns out that some of the crowd had torched the businesses that were getting the good treatment. They actually tried to avoid people's homes, but some of the fires spread, and many people were run out of their apartments and houses."

"Did Willie make it?" I asked.

"I'm getting there," Warren said. "I didn't know what to do, but I felt like I had to do something. So, I drove up to L.A. to see if I could help him."

"You *what?*" Kevin asked, incredulous. "You drove *into* a riot?"

Warren shrugged. "I had to do something. You would have done the same thing," he said, pointing to me.

"I hope so," I said.

"The city was burning. You could see smoke from the fires five miles away."

"I can't even imagine," I said.

"This is crazy," Kevin interrupted. "You had no business in L.A. You had work to do in San Diego, and yet you drove into a burning city. What is *wrong* with you?"

Warren ignored him. "I had to snake my way through some back streets because the police and National Guard were keeping people out, mainly to prevent looting. The place looked like a war zone, man. Trash was everywhere. There wasn't a glass window that wasn't broken. People were wandering the streets looking for action."

"And so were you," Kevin snapped. He took another sip from his Tab and shook his head. He was annoying me.

Warren stared into his beer thoughtfully. "You know. Nothing at seminary prepared me for what I saw."

"How could it?" I asked.

At the same time, Kevin asked, "Why should it?

You shouldn't have been there in the first place."

"Look, Kevin. I know you don't approve, but this was something I felt I had to do. I was *supposed* to be there. I just had to do it. Okay?"

Kevin sighed, raising one hand. "Fine, fine. I'll back off."

Warren nodded and continued. "I managed to find the Reach Out Center, parked my van around back, and went inside looking for Willie. The place was packed. He had over a hundred women and children sleeping on blankets on the floor. They'd been run out of their own apartments and he'd offered them temporary shelter." Warren reached into his pocket and pulled out a newspaper clipping. It showed a proud black man standing in front of the doorway of an old warehouse. A hand-painted sign above his head read *Reach Out Center*. "That's Willie," he said.

Kevin and I read the article and looked at the photo while Warren kept talking.

"I found Willie and he looked just plain exhausted. He said he hadn't slept since the whole thing began. I asked him if he thought he was safe, and he started laughing. Laughing! We were standing in this fifty-year-old warehouse full of poor women and children in a city that was burning around us. 'Of course I don't feel safe,' he said. Later, he told me that his center had a kind of protection around it. It was like most of the rioters knew he was helping the helpless, and they respected that. They steered clear of him."

"Did *you* feel safe?" I asked. I was loving Warren's story. Kevin had taken to sulking into his soda.

"Only when I was with Willie," Warren said. "The next morning, after we had fed breakfast to everyone who was staying there, I went out looking for supplies. Dumb move. Man, nothing was open and there was nothing to buy."

"Couldn't you have gone out of town?"

"Yeah, but I wasn't sure I would be able to get back in. I was pretty lucky the first time."

We ordered refills of beer and Tab.

"I was cruising back downtown when I turned a corner and ran smack into a mob of about a hundred people. It was bad news. They took one look through my windshield, saw a big white guy in a van, and started running toward me. I backed the van down the street as fast as I could go. They started throwing bricks and rocks. My van's still got the scars to prove it."

Kevin muttered. "That would have been enough to convince me to head home."

Now it was my turn to ask, "What were you thinking?"

"That's the point, man. You get into a situation like that, where you've never been before, and you don't know how to think. I was mad at myself for not wearing my clerical collar. If I'd done that, they might have let me go."

Then, to Kevin, he said, "I couldn't just bail, man. I felt like I had to help them out."

Kevin returned to his sulking.

"Then it got really scary," Warren said. "I turned a corner about three blocks from the Reach Out Center and ran into a crowd of cops, heading toward me. They pointed guns my way, and when the crowd of blacks rounded the corner after me, they turned them on the crowd." Warren looked down into his beer. "I've never been so scared in my life. The blacks started throwing stuff—bricks, rocks, pieces of furniture. Naturally, the cops fought back. Someone shot some tear gas canisters into the crowd. By then, I'd jumped out of my van, figuring it was about to be totaled. I thought it would be easier to run the rest of the way on foot."

I shook my head in disbelief.

Kevin asked, "Do you have a death wish, Warren? You jumped *out* of your van in the middle of a riot in a burning city?"

I decided then that Warren and Kevin were like an old married couple, arguing and complaining constantly, but living for the debate, loving it. That was how they had survived seminary together. That was why they enjoyed each other's company.

"I'm telling you," Warren said. "You don't think in

situations like that. You just react."

Warren's words made me think of Reverend James Reeb. If powerful crises dull the senses, maybe that was what happened to the white mob that killed him—they just stopped thinking.

"No sooner had I gotten out of the van than this little black kid, couldn't have been more than seven, stepped out of the tear gas smoke. He was crying and in pain. I mean, the stuff really burns your eyes, man. So, he was walking over to me, looking for help, and I felt about as lost and helpless as could be. I put my hand on his shoulder and started heading over to the Reach Out Center when three black guys came out of the crowd. They started asking what I was doing and where I was taking the kid. But they weren't listening to me. I tried to say I was taking him to a shelter for protection and they just kept pushing me. "

"I can't believe this. You are such an idiot," Kevin said. "Leave the kid and go home."

"I couldn't," Kevin said slowly, emphasizing each syllable.

"And then, the most amazing thing happened. I felt a strong hand grab my shoulder, turned around, and there was Willie Wright, larger than life. He had come looking for me, saw the crowds and figured I was in trouble."

"You are a lucky son of a gun," I said.

"You know it," Warren answered. "Willie stared down the three black guys and said, 'It's all right, boys. He's with me,' and that was all it took. They turned away and disappeared. We took the kid back to the shelter and washed his eyes and gave him some food. The rest of the weekend, I didn't leave Willie's side. He wouldn't let me."

"I should hope not," Kevin said.

"Wow. What a story," I said.

"It was tough, man," Warren answered. "What worries me is this: I think Watts is a sign of things to come. There's so much pent-up anger in the black community—here, Mississippi, Alabama, Texas, every state I drove through to get here. It's a ticking time bomb."

"Which reinforces what I said," Kevin exclaimed. "You've got enough to do in San Diego. Don't go sticking your head where it doesn't belong."

We spent the rest of the night talking about what we should and should not do about the situation our country was in. When they closed the pizza shop, Warren and I said goodbye to Kevin, and we returned home and talked until the wee hours of the morning.

After Warren bedded down in the spare bedroom, I went to bed, but couldn't sleep. I was in awe of my friend and the difference he was making with his life. He had been there. He lived and breathed it. Incarnational freaking ministry! This was what we had talked about in seminary.

When I finally dozed off, I had dreams about seminary professors dressed in cap and gown and throwing bricks and rocks at Kevin Morris.

* * *

April 1966

Time Magazine asked this potent question on its cover: *Is God Dead?* With that, almost everyone in Springlake who had a subscription canceled it.

I kept a copy of the article in the bottom drawer of my desk as sermon fodder, even though I didn't think anyone except me would bother to actually read it.

I found out I was wrong when Tim Franklin stepped into my office late one afternoon. I'd always had a special place for him since having dinner in his home the year that I came to First Methodist. We'd shared a lot of dinners since then. Tim was a deep thinker, more philosophical than most.

"Reverend Phillips?" Tim asked, sticking his head inside my office. "Got a moment?"

I stood to greet him and we shook hands. "Absolutely, Tim. Come on in."

I sat back down in one of the chairs that faced my desk and motioned for him to take the other. He sat down, looking uncomfortable. I assumed we were about to have a sex talk. When he reached into his back pocket and drew out a rolled-up magazine, I was even more convinced of it. Then he unrolled the rag and showed me the cover. I almost burst out laughing.

"Have you seen this?" Tim asked, not noticing my struggle for composure.

Without a word, I got up and walked behind my desk. Reaching into the bottom drawer, I pulled out my identical copy and tossed it on the desk in front of him. "Yep," I said.

We both relaxed.

"Well, what do you think?" he asked.

With most people, I would have danced around the issues in the article. I was prepared to give my "God is not dead—I talked with Him this morning" speech. But I sensed that this eleventh grader would be all right with a little ambiguity. "We studied most of that in seminary," I said. "Those concepts have been around for decades. Some of it, I find challenging, even intriguing."

Tim nodded slowly, waiting for me to continue.

"But what's more important to me," I said, "is what *you* think of the article." I paused. "Well?"

Tim took a deep breath. "First, I recognize that this stuff," he held up the magazine, "is not saying that God was killed, in the way we normally talk about living and dying."

"A lot of people are hung up on that."

"In some ways, what the article says about God being irrelevant . . ." he hesitated. "You could make that point."

I waited, giving him time to talk it out.

"I mean, in some ways that would make God nonexistent, if people no longer saw Him as relevant. In that sense, you could say He is dead."

"Do you think a part of it," I prompted, "is that man has evolved to such a point that some might feel we no longer *need* God?"

Tim thought about that for a moment. "I could see some people feeling that way," he said. "I mean, we're launching people into space, we've harnessed the atom, we've explored every inch of dry land in our world. We understand the sciences, like physics and biology, and no longer have to automatically give credit to God when something happens."

"Or blame," I added.

"Yeah. That too."

I went on to stir the pot some more. "Some theologians," I said, "suggest that people today have lost a sense of the Sacred. The sacraments are meaningless. There's no evidence of God's transcendence, His presence with us. In that sense, they say He is dead."

"But doesn't that imply that we need to find other ways to make Him meaningful? I mean, if lighting a candle doesn't mean anything to me, maybe I need to search for another way to find meaning in God."

I nodded. "Well said. Some say that when Nietzsche first coined the phrase 'God is Dead' in the 1800s, he was challenging the traditional morality of the time that gave so much power to religious leaders who used religion to control people who didn't think critically about their beliefs."

"Uh huh . . ." Tim said skeptically.

I sensed that he didn't entirely agree with this perspective. "What do you think?"

The young man sitting in my office was sharp. He thought for a few moments. "People around here talk a lot about 'believing in God.' They say if anyone believes in Him, they will not perish . . ." He took a breath. "It seems to me that someone may have gotten it wrong. I don't think it's as important to believe *in* Him. The important thing is to *believe Him*. Jesus said we should be peacemakers, we should help the poor, we should accept people who are different, we should serve others. That's what's important."

To me, Tim's tentatively expressed thoughts were as profound as anything any of my seminary professors had ever said. It was all the more uplifting to hear it from someone so young. I didn't say anything. There was nothing left to say.

* * *

October 1966

The more the world changed, the more frightened my church members became and the harder I worked to be relevant. I played my acoustic guitar in church. I took phone calls from parents who were afraid that their children were "smoking LSD." I met with the church board to defend the right for a teenager to attend church on Sunday nights wearing blue jeans.

One Wednesday morning around 10:00 a.m., I sat in silent meditatation in the sanctuary. It was peaceful. The light was streaming through the east-facing stained glass windows and I suddenly realized how unnatural—ancient, tinged with gawdy—the church decoration was. The windows were pretty, but very few homes, even in the '60s, had stained glass in them. The gold candelabras. And that cross! It was too glitzy. It occurred to me then that it was no wonder church sanctuaries failed to appeal to the younger generation. In fact, by design they tended to repel them. The decor screamed "behind the times," "irrelevant," and "out of touch."

That Wednesday morning, I set myself a mission. I was going to create a hip, "with-it" space that would bring the younger generation into contact with God.

I brought it up to some of the kids, and they loved the idea. We chose the location: the old parsonage across the street from the church. For years, ministers had lived there when they served at First Methodist. But when Dr. Graham Strong had come to Springlake, the church board found him a new house in a nice upper-middle class neighborhood. So the old parsonage had been empty for about three years.

I met with the Board of Trustees and got permission to let the youth use the old wooden house, at least the first floor. It was a traditional two-story Florida home. The bottom floor contained the living room, dining room and kitchen. The upper floor contained bedrooms. Naturally, young people were prevented from going anywhere near the bedrooms.

We scheduled a special Saturday to meet together to paint the inside of the parsonage. We used psychedelic colors and wild patterns on the walls. We let the kids paint hip sayings, like *Feelin' Groovy* and *Jesus is Just All Right With Me* and *Power to the People.*

We painted clouds on the ceilings in one room. Someone went down to Springlake Hardware and found some blacklight bulbs, which we put in all the lamps in one room. One family donated an old pool table. We got some old shag carpet sample patterns and glued them to the floor in one room and threw down some beanbag chairs for intimate conversations.

Then we had to choose a name for the place. Someone suggested *The Place.* Someone else wanted *Crossville*, but that sounded too much like Cross Creek and Florida already had a city and a novel by that name. We finally settled on *His Place* and announced that it would be open on Friday nights for kids to come and hang out.

The first Friday night, no one came because Springlake High had a home football game. We had forgotten to check the schedule, and I ended up sitting in His Place all evening by myself, feeling like it was just My Place. I did, however, read the first couple of essays from James Baldwin's *The Fire Next Time,* and then went home.

We opened His Place again the following Friday night. A few of the kids in the youth group brought some friends. Most of them attended other churches in Springlake. Rob Franklin introduced his black friend, Larry Watson.

"This is cool," Larry said, admiring the work Rob and his friends had done on the old house.

"Thanks, man," I said, sinking into a beanbag chair. "You go to Springlake Junior High, right?"

"Yeah," he said.

"How do you like it?"

"It's far out, you know. But some of the kids and most of the teaches aren't down with the times."

"How's that?" I asked.

"Man, those flat tops don't get it. They're just trying to keep the black man down. It ain't gonna happen."

"Rob's not like that," I said, nodding toward the kitchen where Rob was getting a soft drink and trying to impress a cute girl in a mini-skirt.

"He's good. But not everyone is as cool as my man Robby."

Someone had turned on the tape player and The Doors were singing *Light My Fire.*

"You know," Larry said. "They got things like this happening in Chi-Town all the time."

"Yeah?"

"I spent the summer there with my uncle, and that town is rockin'."

"Cool," I said.

He crawled out of his beanbag chair and went into the kitchen to join Rob.

The evening went by without incident, and I locked the doors to His Place at about 11:30 p.m.

The next week, Larry returned with a couple of friends from his apartment complex. They brought some albums by Aretha Franklin and Stevie Wonder, and seemed to get along well with everyone.

* * *

Churches are notorious for committees. Most focused on certain responsibilities of the church, like staffing, or managing buildings and grounds, or coordinating education. Our church even had committees designed to create committees.

Having been in Springlake for a couple of years, I had developed a feel for the committees, and I knew what to expect at each one.

But one Tuesday night in October, I got caught off-guard. The Board of Trustees had just finished rattling through the usual concerns and reports about various church facilities, when the chairman announced, "That brings us to the next item. Reverend Phillips, it has come to our attention that we might have an unsavory element in the old church parsonage."

I looked at Reverend Strong, but he just stared at his notebook. "I don't understand," I said.

The chairman took off his glasses and stared hard at me. "These are unsettling times," he said. "We're concerned about our children getting caught up with the wrong crowd and becoming involved with, uh . . . dopers and addicts."

Another member of the board added, "We understand what you're trying to do with your Friday night activities. It's just that we think they're drawing in the wrong crowd. What is going on in that building on Friday nights, anyway?"

The chairman added, "There has to be another way to keep our own children involved in the church, Reverend Phillips. Maybe if they served as accolytes."

When people use formal titles like "Reverend Phillips," I tend to cringe. Formalities are never used without motive. I quickly thought about what might cause this sudden concern, and the only thing that was really different in our Friday night program was that some black students attended. I thought about what the Board was asking me to do. I also thought about what I should say. In the church, everybody donates money to pay the bills, so everybody feels like they pay your salary. In a sense, I was talking with my bosses in this meeting.

I felt like standing to make my defense statement, but I remained seated. "When the youth of this church decided to name their meeting area His Place, they deliberately chose that name for what it said as much as what it didn't say. The name shows who is in charge and who isn't. His Place isn't an exclusive hangout for white church members. It isn't a whites-only recreation center. It isn't even our place at all. It's His."

The room was silent.

"Please be assured," I continued, "that the facility will be properly chaperoned by volunteers and by myself whenever it is open. In fact, if any of you would like to volunteer to join us on Friday, we'd love to have you."

Still no response.

Finally, the chairman spoke up. "We have shared our concern with you, Reverend Phillips. It now falls on you to to look out for the best interests of our children. I hope you understand the weight of that responsibility."

I left the meeting knowing that I had lost points with the Board, but feeling that I'd done right by members of His Place.

The ironic thing was that His Place died a natural death within a couple of months anyway. Football games, holidays and other activities conflicted with our Friday night gatherings, and attendance dropped off altogether.

* * *

April 1967

The world seemed hell-bent on destruction, in the worst way possible.

A few months earlier, India had faced a terrible famine, a sniper had killed and wounded scores of students at the University of Texas, and another civil rights activist was shot in Mississippi.

In spite of several promises, agreements, pacts, and councils, no one seemed to be able to bring peace to Southeast Asia.

Martin Luther King, Jr. spoke out against the United States' involvement in Vietnam.

I longed to leave the safe haven of this tiny Florida town to make a really significant impact. I made some phone calls to a couple of my professors at Candler, who put me in touch with some politically active people in Washington, and they in turn gave me some names of people in other states. The Mobes—loosely connected mobilization organizations—planned several peace marches and meetings to protest the Vietnam War, the draft and Civil Rights issues. I contacted one group, a division of the Quakers, that was part of the Mobes. The Quakers, known for their denomination's strong pacifistic stance, were glad to share information about upcoming events.

Apparently, a major antiwar parade called the Spring Motivation for Peace was being planned in New York and San Francisco in mid-April. My fingers were actually tingling when I dialed the phone. I was able to find out where and when the meetings would be held.

I had to make special arrangements to attend the protest. I requested time off with the proper church committees and with Dr. Strong. I checked the bus schedules, since I didn't want to drive in the traffic that would surely come to New York City for the event.

What gave me the strongest feeling of cognitive dissonance was paying my income tax. Like many Americans, I usually waited until the last minute. But since the event was to be held on April 18, I had to mail my tax forms before heading to the bus station. It was such a strange feeling to be paying the government, knowing that I was about to embark on a journey to protest what the government was doing. But, that's what America is all about, right?

Every bus ride I've ever taken took too long, but this one was by far the longest. I read books, napped and stared at the scenery. The closer I came to New York, the more people who climbed on my bus appeared to be there for the same reason I was. Outside of Atlanta, I tapped one guy on the shoulder who was wearing an old army jacket with a peace sign drawn on the back.

"Are you going to New York for the protests?" I asked. It was a safe assumption.

"Right on," he said.

"My name's Stephen Phillips," I said, offering my hand.

He grabbed it in a soul handshake and said, "I'm Mark Richardson, but everybody calls me Maverick."

A black guy sitting across the aisle from us leaned in. "I'm Earl Knight. Headin' to the Big Apple myself."

"Have either of you guys been to one of these before?" I asked.

"It's the greatest thing since primo weed," Maverick said.

"My first time," I said.

"Mine too," Knight added.

"Virgins," Maverick exclaimed. "Boy are you guys in for some fun. Let me tell you what's happenin'." It was apparent that he'd been here before. He was a pro. "First, you've got to recognize your purpose. The New York and San Francisco events are demonstrations of massive force. We're not coming to confront anyone other than the American public. With a show of large numbers of protestors, we'll state our message to get out of Vietnam."

I felt like taking notes.

"This ain't like the protest at the Democratic National Convention. We went there to disrupt the fuckin' Dems' big, bad show. We wanted trouble. We wanted to stop what they were doing, and by God we did."

"You were in Chicago?" I asked.

"Fer sure," Maverick said. "There won't be many arrests in NYC if everybody stays calm. They can't arrest a quarter of a million people. Where would they put us? That's the beauty of this. That and the fact that some very important people will be there to witness it. Martin Luther King, Jr. and Dr. Benjamin Spock will be speaking and witnessing everything that goes on."

"What if there is trouble?"

"Well, first of all, don't fight back. The pigs will win."

He pulled his stringy hair to one side of his face to reveal a two inch long, thin scar just short of his hairline. "I got that when I tried to argue with some pigs in Madison, Wisconsin, where we were protesting the draft. One sucker punched me and his partner clubbed me three times." The scar looked grotesque in the pale light of passing street lamps.

"She-it," Knight said.

"Really, man. All you can do is cover your head with your arms and hope they're too busy to get mean."

"So, what is our role?" I asked.

"Enjoy," Maverick said. "Enjoy the moment. Take a little walk a couple of miles from Central Park to the UN, but that's about it. Shout. Sing. Let President Johnson know that his warin' days are over."

Knight said passionately, "Johnson lied to us all. He said the war was going well, and, let me tell you, the brothers know that it's all gone to hell over there."

"They're all crooked as snakes," Maverick said. "As long as they can keep us tied up over there, we'll have to listen to them over here."

"Well," Knight said. "The people aren't going to put up with it any more. There's talk of a revolution coming."

We talked big throughout the night. Every major city we stopped in added more to our bus. As we neared New York, some of the riders began shouting protest chants. "Hey, hey, LBJ. How many kids have you killed today?" and "Hell, no, we won't go!" and "End the war, NOW!" all rang out through the night.

New York was like a circus. It was more crowded than I ever thought possible. I could tell that thousands of first-timers were "protest-virgins" like me. Reports were that over 400,000 people were there for the march. And the people were bizarre and beautiful at the same time: long hair, strange outfits, makeup, and more.

Like everyone else, I spent much of the day before the event taking in the sights, like the Statue of Liberty and the Empire State Building. Also like everyone else, I was excited about what was happening all around me and ready to get things going.

I found my way to one of the church basements where pre-march preparations were taking place. I introduced myself and asked if there was anything I could do to help. A pretty girl with her blond hair braided around her crown took me to a back room and showed me how to run an antiquated mimeograph machine. I spent a couple of hours printing up thousands of flyers on blue sheets of copy paper.

That evening, several of us took the flyers to the streets and began giving them to anyone who would take them. Most of the people welcomed them, but a few were openly hostile to the whole idea. "Go home, hippie," someone yelled. "Communist," another shouted.

I ran out of flyers and headed back to the church

basement to get another stack. I found the pretty girl who had introduced me to the wonderful world of print earlier, and she gave me another couple of reams of flyers to hand out. I worked up the courage to ask her if she wanted to join me.

She took a long hard look at me, then looked around the busy room and said, "Sure. I need a break."

We walked out into the New York City night and toward the public library on 5th Avenue and 42nd Street. People were everywhere. Some carried guitars and sang. Others gave out flowers. We passed out the flyers as we walked.

She told me her name was Sunni, and I wondered if it was her real name or just a nickname. She was a journalism student at Columbia. The evenings were still a little chilly, and she wore a suede coat and blue jeans. After an hour, I suggested we grab some coffee at a corner diner.

"So, what brings a preacher boy from Florida to a peace march in New York City?" she asked while prepping her coffee with lots of sugar and cream. It sounded more like a challenge than a question.

"Are you kidding? This is the culmination of everything I have studied for, everything I have worked for, everything I live for."

She raised an eyebrow and asked, "How so?" I realized I was frowning, because she started laughing. "I'm not judging, man. Don't worry. I just mean, I don't understand."

"Look, Sunni," I began. "I became a minister because I felt that I could make a difference in people's lives. My father was a traveling salesman, and his work only helped his company. My uncle was a steel worker, and he helped his company. I wanted to help people."

Sunni nodded. "Okay."

"Well, right here, right now, the world has its eyes on New York. People want to stop a war. They want to stop an unfair draft. They want peace. So do I."

"Well said, preacher boy."

We looked out the window as we sipped our coffee.

Across the street, a band of Hare Krishnas danced down the sidewalk, singing and shaking tambourines.

Sunni asked, "They want peace, too. Aren't you after the same thing?"

The question had a depth to it that belied its simplicity. "In some ways, yes." I said. "I'm just more comfortable with my beliefs, my understandings, my traditions."

Sunni giggled. "That's good, 'cause I'm having a hard time picturing you with a shaved head and wearing a robe." She reached out a hand and touched my hair. Her touch was electric. I felt like we could have talked for hours.

"What about you?" I asked. "What brings a journalism student to an SDS shop printing bad copy on a cheap printing press?"

"Bad copy? I wrote that stuff," she said.

"Sorry. I meant 'promising.'"

"Well, I believe in the cause, like you," Sunni said. "I know some former students who are in Vietnam right now and I'd like for them to come home. Alive," she added. "Plus, if I'm going to be able to write about something, I have to live it, right?"

"Makes sense to me."

We chatted for another thirty minutes, and then waded back through the street and gave flyers to anyone who would accept one. About an hour into it, she pulled me aside and said, "I've gotta get back to the dorm."

"Wait. Can I get your phone number?" I asked.

Without hesitation, she dictated it and I jotted it down on the back of one of the blue sheets of paper. I made sure to stuff that one in my back pocket.

I handed out every one of the remaining flyers and headed back to the little hotel where I was staying for the night. I considered calling Sunni, but didn't want to seem too eager.

The morning of April 15 came with all the promise of a new world. The city, with all of its refuse and sour smells, seemed to me like the brightest and cleanest place on earth. I felt as if the things that were going to happen that day would shape the direction of our world forever, and I was there to be a part of it.

I grabbed breakfast at the same little diner where Sunni and I had shared coffee the night before, hoping she might be there. I tried calling her from a phone booth outside the diner, but a sleepy female voice told me she had already left for "that parade thing."

Around 9:30 a.m., I headed toward Central Park, a few blocks west. *White Room* by Cream blasted from a third-story apartment window. The tension inside coiled like a spring as I neared the park. The same crowd I'd marveled at the day before was here, moving into the park. They were young, old, white, black, dressed up, dressed out—and all very excited.

Organizers herded us into one area of the park. Pete Seeger sang *Where Have All The Flowers Gone*, and Phil Ochs followed him with *Draft Dodger Rag* as dozens of young men, huddled at the foot of the stage, retrieved draft cards from their wallets and lit them on fire unceremoniously in protest of the unjust draft system. Several outstanding speakers, including Stokely Carmichael, took a turn firing up the crowd.

Then some people with bodyguards gathered at one end of the crowd and started walking south. The march was led by a group carrying a banner that read *Vietnam Veterans Against the War*. Hundreds of thousands of us began to follow.

It's really not that far from Central Park to the United Nations Building. But the two-mile march took forever. We walked slowly. We sang *We Shall Overcome*. We chanted. We all locked arms, and some beautiful girl with a gorgeous smile and huge breasts squeezed my right arm tightly.

The parade was everything I had hoped for: exciting and energizing and thoroughly intoxicating. The diverse crowd, the rousing speeches, the electricity in the air all came together in a way I had never experienced before.

We slowly made our way down Park Avenue to the United Nations Plaza. There, Dr. Martin Luther King, Jr.

implored members of the UN to convince the United
States to end the war in Vietnam.

The trip back to Florida was as raucous as it could
be. People were singing and shouting most of the way to
Atlanta. Wine and weed were passed freely from seat to
seat. Whenever one of the protestors got off the bus,
everyone would cheer as if he or she had just graduated
from college. Everyone said goodbye with a "See you in
Washington," referring to the upcoming march at the
Pentagon in November.

Neither Maverick nor Knight was on my homeward
bound bus, and I never saw them again. But I did make
friends with some really far-out people. There were
Butterfly and Track, both heading to Nashville,
Tennessee, where Track hoped to record an album. There
was Don Albee, going back home to North Carolina to
teach eighth grade biology. There were several kids
heading to various colleges across the eastern seaboard.
And there was me, heading back to my church in
Springlake, Florida.

The strange thing about returning from an
emotional event like the Spring Motivation for Peace is
that you feel changed, and you assume that everything
else has changed as well. But that wasn't the case. As our
bus headed south out of Atlanta, young airmen boarded at
every stop. At the bus station in Macon, Georgia, I
watched silently as all were transferred to another bus
bound for Robins Air Force Base. I wondered how many
might be headed for Vietnam, and how many might never
return home. We still had a long way to go.

After the bus arrived in Springlake, I hitched a ride
eight blocks to my house and put my stuff away. Then, on
a whim, I called Sunni.

"Hello?"

"Oh, you're in!" I said, sounding more like an overly
protective father than a friend.

"Hi, Stephen," she said. "Where are you?"

"Well, I wanted to call and let you know that I
arrived home safely." I was sure that sounded lame.

"Good. I'm glad to hear it. Did you enjoy the

march?"

"It was so cool," I said.

"I thought so, too," she said.

"Listen, Sunni. Stay in touch, okay?"

"Sure."

"If you come down to Florida, you can always hang out at my place."

"I don't know. What kind of scandal would those little old ladies in your church cook up if they knew we were sleeping under the same roof unchaperoned?"

"I'll get a chaperone."

She laughed. "Maybe I'll take you up on that sometime. I love Florida."

"Anytime."

We said our goodbyes and hung up the phone. I seriously doubted that I would ever see her again. The chemistry was there on my end, but I wasn't sure how she felt, and the distance between us was a big roadblock.

But, as my mother used to say, you never know until you know.

* * *

November 1967

I returned from my protest trip to Washington full of fight and anger and righteous indignation. I was proud of what we had done and believed that our protests would bring an end to the Vietnam War. But the country was still strongly divided. Tens of thousands of young men had died in Southeast Asia, and as many people who marched in New York were fighting in rice paddies in South Vietnam.

I became bolder than before. I posted newspaper clippings of the event on a bulletin board in my office and talked about it openly in Sunday School classes, youth discussion groups, and among my friends. Somehow, the Spring Motivation for Peace rally had become a part of me. I couldn't look at the American flag without recalling the songs, the chants, or the words spoken in New York on that powerful day in April.

It's amazing how insignificant such seemingly pivotal moments in our lives can be when life takes a left-hand turn. My rally focus was put on hold the day the church secretary transferred an emergency call to my office. Graham was out of town on a minister's retreat (probably on the golf course), so I was the minister in charge.

"Hello," I answered in the most polite, ministerial voice I could manage. "This is Reverend Phillips. How can I—"

The caller cut me off. "Stephen. This is Ray Franklin." His voice was shaky. "I just got a call from the hospital. Tim's been in a car accident. He's been taken to the hospital."

I felt like the air had been knocked out of me. Tim? Accident? All I could get out was, "Does Katie know?"

"She's on her way to the hospital now. I wanted to call you before heading there myself. "

I took a quick breath to steady myself and said, "Ray, I'll meet you there."

He hung up before I could say, "Bye."

I gave what little information I had to the secretary and told her that I was on my way to the hospital.

Grabbing my tweed jacket and, as a last minute thought, my Bible, I headed for the door. My Volkswagen was parked in the minister's reserved parking space. I climbed in, cranked up the engine and sped to the hospital.

My mind was racing. What had happened? What would I say? How serious was it? How could I comfort my friends in such a time of pain and grief? Were others involved in the accident, and what would I say to their families? Would Tim . . . I stopped myself from finishing that question.

The clergy parking space was empty, so I took it and dashed inside. The County Hospital was a fairly new facility. People were proud of the modern, clean building. I couldn't be bothered to notice at that moment. What good was a new hospital if Tim were beyond help? What comfort was there in having the newest and brightest place in which to die?

Katie Franklin was sitting on a bench in the waiting room, looking every bit as distraught as I expected. She was sobbing uncontrollably into her handkerchief. For a moment, I froze. In theory, my seminary training, preaching conferences, volumes of books and hours of Bible study had prepared me for this, but in practice, I was speechless. Tim Franklin. I couldn't accept it.

At that moment, Katie looked up from her handkerchief, and seeing the pain in her eyes as she stood to greet me kicked me into gear. I went to her with open arms and she buried her face in my shoulder and wept uncontrollably. I stood still and let her cry. It wasn't necessary to say anything. My presence in that antiseptic, cold place at this special time of incredible need said enough.

I blocked out the rest of the world. I ignored the strange sounds, the voices of the intercom, the doctors and nurses passing by. I was just one soul there to support another. And, more than any other time in my life, more than the march in New York, the sermons from the pulpit, the late night conversations with doubting friends, more than all of that, I felt purpose.

Ray arrived a few minutes later, and I stepped aside for him to wrap his arms around his wife. I guided the terrified couple to a sofa, where they sat glued together.

Katie forced herself to calm down enough to bring us up to speed on the situation. Between dabs of a handkerchief and a few intermittent sniffs, she told us what had happened.

"Tim was on his way home from school. He was out on County Line Road by that corner where Wagoner's Field is all overgrown. You know . . . you can't see around that corner. Well, Tim pulled out and someone ran the stop sign and . . . and they plowed into him at about fifty miles an hour."

I didn't want to shift the focus, but I needed to find

out if any other church members were in need of support. "Is the other driver okay?" I asked gently.

"He walked away without a scratch," she said. "He was a salesman passing through from Jacksonville."

I breathed a quiet sigh of relief.

"And Tim?" Ray asked, his voice strained. I'd avoided that question. I was terrified of the answer.

"He's in surgery," Katie said. "His left leg is shattered and his right leg's broken in two places, and . . ." She started crying again. "There may be other internal injuries. They don't know. They don't know if he will make it through the surgery."

Ray and Katie hugged each other again. I waited as they tried to steady themselves, and then asked, "Where is Rob?"

Katie slowly pulled away and said, "Rob. He's at basketball practice. He—he doesn't know."

I sensed that it may be a while before we had any more information, and I felt that I could be most helpful now by uniting the Franklins. "Would you like for me to go get him and bring him here?"

Ray turned to me and nodded.

As I headed toward the parking lot, I realized that I hadn't prayed with the couple yet. At the same moment, I realized that I had no idea what to say. My mind was totally blank. So I continued walking toward my car, determined to sort this all out later.

* * *

I parked by the gym and turned off the VW. Entering through the side door, I saw the team running some strange drill where students would pass off the ball and run to opposite sides of the court. I located Coach Bridges and walked briskly in his direction.

"Excuse me, Coach," I said. "I'm Reverend Stephen Phillips. I'm Rob's minister."

The coach stopped and looked at me like I had all the nerve in the world to interrupt one of his important basketball practices. "Yeah?"

"Rob's brother has been in a serious car accident. I need to take Rob to the hospital to be with his family immediately."

"Oh," he said. "Yes, of course. Okay."

Rob had seen me enter the gym and had been watching me talk with his coach. He clearly sensed that something was wrong. When I made eye contact with him, he immediately started walking toward me. His friend, Larry, followed him.

I met Rob halfway across the floor and shared the news that no one should ever have to hear about a loved one. "Rob. Tim's been in a car accident." As I spoke, the words sounded separate from me, as if I could hear them, but they couldn't possibly be coming from my lips.

"Oh my God," Rob said. "What happened? Is he okay? Where is he? Where are my parents?"

Larry put a hand on his shoulder to steady him. I nodded in thanks and answered a couple of Rob's questions. "He's in the hospital and I told your folks that I would bring you there. They are waiting for you."

"Is he all right?" he repeated.

"He's having a tough time, Rob, but let's not panic. Are you ready to go?"

"Yes."

"I'll go with you," Larry said, following us.

Larry folded himself up into the backseat and Rob climbed into the front. I couldn't see anything out of my rearview mirror because Larry's Afro was blocking the view, so I had to shift and squirm to see around him as I backed out of the parking space.

"How bad is it?" Rob asked.

I didn't know whether I should tell what I knew or wait until he heard it all from his parents. I decided it would be best not to make his parents repeat the painful details. "Both his legs are pretty banged up. They didn't know if he had any internal injuries when I left."

"What happened?"

"What I heard was that some out-of-towner ran a stop sign and broadsided him. I don't know anything other than that."

"How's the car?"

I shrugged my shoulders because I had no idea.

I've never driven so carefully and self-consciously in my life. I watched every pedestrian, every oncoming car, paralyzed with the irrational fear of getting into a wreck with Rob in the car on the way to see his injured brother. Such would be an unspeakably terrible tragedy.

We arrived at the hospital, and Rob and Larry ran ahead of me inside. By the time I arrived in the waiting room, the four people were standing in a large huddle, arms wrapped around each other. I stood slightly apart from them to give them space. Ray looked up from the huddle, saw me, and motioned me to them with a wave of his hand.

* * *

We stayed together in the waiting room for hours. Larry had called his parents from one of the hospital's two pay phones shortly after we had arrived, and within thirty minutes, Mr. and Mrs. Watson joined us in our vigil.

At one point, I asked the group to pray with me for Tim. It wasn't a very profound prayer. Nor was it memorable. But it was simple, a plea for help.

After the prayer, it dawned on me that we were setting a very real example of interracial unity in this bright hospital room. Two families of different races were joined at a time of crisis. If it could happen here, it could happen throughout our country as well.

We settled in on vinyl couches in the lobby and waited. Despite the gravity of this situation, one by one, we let our guard down.

Ray started it off. He leaned forward and spoke softly to Bill and Marilyn. "People have come into the hardware store with the weirdest projects over the last few months. This old guy who lives out on the east side of town, Johnson was his name, he wanted to install running water in an outhouse."

Bill said, "Come again?"

"No lie. He wanted to run water into his outhouse

so he could add a sink and a flushing toilet."

Bill shook his head.

Most of us had tuned into Ray's story, so he sat back and described other quirky projects in the most animated way I have ever seen from him. Ray's conversation was helping Katie relax. She leaned against his shoulder as he told more tales.

"Just last week," he said, "we had a farmer who bought hundreds of feet of insulation for his barn. He said he wanted to keep his cows warm this winter."

"That's crazy," Bill said.

Rob and Larry lightened up as well. They played a brief game of one-on-one, using crumpled up newspapers as basketballs and the hospital garbage can as a basket. When they became too rambunctious, Ray and Bill made them stop playing.

Katie stared off into space for a while and said, "I remember when he bought that Camaro. He had saved up his money from working at the auto supply store for two years. Last summer, he bought one of the first used Camaros that went on sale."

"It was a bad car," Rob said. Then, with a quick look to his dad, he added, "But Tim never drove it recklessly or anything."

The Watsons excused themselves at about 8:30 p.m., saying they had to get Larry home to do some homework.

Then, just after 9:00 p.m., the doctor came out and said that it looked like Tim was stabilizing. He invited Katie and Ray to come inside to see him, but warned them he may not be conscious yet.

I waited with Rob.

"So, how you doing, man?" I asked.

"I'm cool," he said.

"Your brother will make it," I said.

Rob was silent a moment. Then he said, "Thanks for coming to get me. I can't think of anyone else I'd rather tell me about something, you know, like this."

I smiled and squeezed his shoulder gently. We waited in silence, looking at old issues of National

Geographic and watching the clock on the wall. Moments like this were once in a lifetime. I was glad I was there.

* * *

I felt a soft but firm hand on my shoulder. Katie said, "Stephen, you should go home and rest."

I opened my eyes, realizing I had dozed off. "What time is it?"

"It's almost midnight," she said.

"Tim?"

"He's sleeping. The last thing we heard was that his legs will take a long time and some work to heal up."

"Did they find anything else?"

"No, thank God."

"Yes, thank God."

She smiled and said, "Why don't you go on home?"

I nodded and pulled myself up from the couch. "I'm going to take a look at the miracle kid," I said.

I slipped into Tim's room and stood by his bed. His legs were wrapped up in casts. He had an IV in one arm and some machine was making strange noises nearby. I reached down and placed a hand on his bare arm. "God," I prayed, "thank you for allowing me to be a part of this family tonight and to know the wonder of such love. Thank you for sparing Tim. Continue to work to heal him."

After a moment of silence, I added, "And thank you for letting me serve in Springlake. Amen."

We took turns staying with Tim for a week. Since I was young and single, naturally I took the midnight shift. Katie would stay there during the day and Ray would come and go to relieve her. Bill and Marilyn did what they could now and then.

Gradually, Tim came around. Within the week, he was bandaged up, put in a wheelchair and sent home. Needless to say, he was very sad about his Camaro. That car had been his pride and joy. We prayed for him regularly at church. Many of the members put some dinners together for the Franklin family during the days right after the accident. We all came together in a powerful way for the family. People gave up their time and energy and resources because a family in their circle was hurting. That kind of compassion was a valuable commodity in Springlake—in any town, really.

* * *

June 1968

In 1968, the world was shocked first in April and again in June by tragic and senseless deaths.

First Dr. Martin Luther King, Jr. was gunned down in Memphis. I was so glad that I had heard him speak in New York.

Then, a few months later, Bobby Kennedy was killed in a hotel kitchen in Los Angeles. I remember sitting in my living room the night that Bobby was killed and thinking, *Why do they kill the great ones?*

I wasn't alone. The world mourned the loss of both influential men.

I wondered what the world would be like in the future if either had survived.

* * *

December 1968

Every Christmas season, First Methodist sponsored a Living Nativity scene next to Main Street in front of the church. Years ago, someone had constructed a crude manger, which could be easily assembled before Christmas and disassembled after the holidays. Kids in the church would dress up in their parents' bathrobes to portray the major characters in the nativity scene: Mary, Joseph, the Wise Men, and the Shepherds.

One of the nearby farmers would donate a calf and a goat, which would be tied near the manger. People from all around Springlake would make a point of driving by and viewing our Living Nativity scene each year.

Even in Florida, December was a cold month. We

scheduled the kids to take turns, rotating in and out of the scene. We set up makeshift spotlights, donated by Springlake Hardware, but they were barely strong enough to light the manger. They did nothing to keep the children warm. In between their shifts out in the manger, the kids would chug down cups of hot chocolate, so they were happy. It was a great tradition.

As the associate minister, it was one of my duties to oversee the Living Nativity each year. Late one night, three days before Christmas, I was closing up the church building when I saw some movement near the manger. At first, I thought the Kirkpatricks had left their animals behind and figured I'd have to wait until they came back for them. But then I remembered seeing them leave with both animals at around 9:30 p.m.

I walked back over to the crude structure, now dark since we had unplugged the lights at the end of the evening's performance. I could see a figure rustling in the hay on the floor of the manger.

"Hey," I called.

The figure didn't move.

I walked closer. "Who's there?"

No answer. I moved closer, curious but cautious.

"Who's there?" I repeated.

"Just me, Baby Jesus," said a male voice.

A female giggled.

"What?" I said. "Come out of there."

Slowly, the figure unrolled, stood up and stumbled out of the manger. He was a young man with long hair down around his shoulders, a grungy beard and the accent of a pod of pigs. He wore a pullover cotton shirt and dirty, ragged blue jeans. He was skinny, and looked like he hadn't eaten for a week. Looking down, I saw he was wearing sandals. Even in the dim light, his toenails looked filthy.

He eyed me lazily. "You're not the fuzz, are you?"

"No. I'm a minister here," I said. His stench was all around. I stepped back for fresh air.

"Far out." He turned and gave a two-fingered whistle. "Missy. Come out. It's all right."

An equally thin, equally dirty and equally underdressed girl of no more than nineteen or twenty crawled out of the manger on her hands and knees. "Baaaaah," she said, and giggled some more. "I'm just one of the sheep." She stood up beside the man.

"Who *are* you?" I asked, shocked to see a young girl in this sort of situation.

"Man, we were passing through and we needed a place to crash," he said. "My name's Dave. This is my lady, Missy. We came down from Detroit. This is the warmest place around at this time of night. It's really better than the bushes, and when the lights are on, we can almost roast marshmallows."

"When was the last time you had a full meal?" I asked. The cold was beginning to bite through my thick jacket. I pulled it tighter around my chest.

"A full meal? God, I can't remember," Dave said. "We usually get some scraps here and there." He stamped his feet as if to shake the cold.

"We had lunch at a soup kitchen in Macon last Monday," Missy said.

"Don't you have some relatives or someone you can visit?" I asked.

Dave shook his head. "Man, we came to Florida to get out of the cold. I didn't know it got this cold down here."

Missy snapped at him, "Yeah. You said it was always warm here. I believed you."

"How could I know? I've never been here before. You've seen the postcards, Missy. Everything *looked* warm."

"Take it easy," I said.

Just then, a police car turned the corner in front of the manger. The spotlight on the cruiser came on and was turned to shine directly on us. Someone inside the car rolled down the window and yelled, "What's going on, here?"

I walked over to the driver's side of the car. "Good evening, Officer," I said. "My name is Stephen Phillips. I'm the associate minister at First Methodist Church."

He nodded. "I know who you are. My sister's a member here."

I looked inside the car and could barely make out the name on his uniform. "Thank you for your help, Officer Rawlings," I said. "I'm just closing things up for the night. Did you see our manger scene earlier this evening?"

"I seen it," he said. "Who are they?" he asked, motioning toward the young couple.

"Just a couple of vagrants, asking for some help," I said. "I'm going to take care of them."

"You ain't in any trouble, are you, Pastor?" he asked, his eyes locked onto mine for telltale signs of distress.

I smiled. "No, sir. Not at all."

"All right, boy. Give us a call if you need anything."

"Thank you, again, Officer."

I walked back to the manger, where Dave and Missy were waiting. "He's one of our city's finest, watching over the town. Nothing to worry about."

I weighed my options. I could take the couple to the police station and let them spend the night in jail, but Officer Rawlings had just left and it would seem odd to take them there after telling him everything was all right. The senior minister had a small contingency fund that he sometimes used to provide a hotel for vagrants, usually in return for some minor work around the church. I had no fund and no work for this young couple. They both looked half-starved, and I was beginning to feel a little hungry myself. So, I settled on taking them to Springlake Diner. I knew it would still be open, and thought I should at least get them something to eat before sending them on their way.

As we entered the diner, I was pretty sure we were a strange-looking trio. I was wearing a sweater over a dress shirt and tie, a sport coat and corduroy slacks. Plus nicely polished shoes. My new friends were dressed in cotton shirts and extremely worn bell-bottom blue jeans. And tattered, dirty sandals. I smelled a bit like Brut; they smelled as if they hadn't had a bath in a week. Dave's hair was long and stringy, down around his shoulders. Missy's was long and straight. It flowed down to the small of her back, and was actually surprisingly healthy-looking. Mine was longer than most men my age, but in a stylish, deliberate sort of way. And, it was shampoo-clean.

"Guys," I said, divvying up the menus. "Dinner's on me. Have whatever you want."

They sure did.

"Uh, I'll have the pot roast, with potatoes, green beans, creamed corn and biscuits, please ma'am," Dave said as the waitress jotted down his order.

"And I would like ham, mashed potatoes, green beans and fried okra," said Missy.

Both ordered large glasses of iced tea.

"Just bring me a slice of pecan pie, please," I said.

They ate like this was their last supper, sopping up every drop and scooping up every morsel. As they ate, we talked.

"So, what's your story?" I asked.

"We're hiking around America, man. We're exploring the vast, open spaces of our wonderful country." He zoned out for moment, then slipped back in. "We're like the pioneers, man. We don't follow maps or stuff like that. We just go where life takes us."

"Some of the pioneers had maps, you know."

"Really? Far out. Where'd they get them?"

"Other pioneers, I imagine."

"Oh, yeah, man. And the Indians. I'll bet they had maps."

"So, where do you sleep?"

"Usually out under the stars. In the woods. You know."

"What if it rains?"

"Well, sometimes we'll sleep in a bus depot. If it's raining, they usually let us stay."

"And if they don't?"

"Well, lots of places have these little overhangs and porches. In Virginia, we slept on a porch swing at somebody's house. They never knew we were there."

Missy chimed in, "Sometimes we find some other freaks like us who are camping out in the woods. It gets fun, then. We all build a fire, and someone may lift some pork or something and we make a pretty good stew."

"Yeah, man," Dave agreed. "That's fun. And the state parks are good places to stay. They often have these little covered areas with picnic tables. If we don't get caught, we can sleep under a picnic table for a week." His tone became more serious. "Man. Did you know that our country has some of the most beautiful parks in the world?"

I nodded. "Where all have you been?"

"Oh, wow. Like everywhere. We were in New York and Pennsylvania, and went down to Washington, DC. Then we went back to Kentucky and worked on a commune there for a while. It's been a weird trip."

"Do you have a car? How do you travel?"

"Oh, that's easy, man," Dave said. "We hitch."

"Hitch? As in hitch-hike?"

"Yeah, man. It's really easy, especially with Missy."

I raised an eyebrow.

"Yeah, man," he said. "A lot of people wouldn't stop for me, but since I have a chick with me, they figure I'm safe." He was still for a second, looking around absent-mindedly, then he was back. "Yeah. They think I'm safe 'cause she's with me."

"Are *you* safe?" I asked.

"Sure, man. I won't hurt you."

"No, Dave. I mean, is it safe for you and Missy? Aren't you afraid someone might hurt you or her?"

"Why, man? We don't have anything worth stealing, and we're good company."

I stared at him for second. "Do you do a lot of drugs?"

"Is it obvious?" Dave asked. "Yeah. I guess we do a lot of drugs."

"Which ones?

"Oh, wow, man. We've done Mary Jane . . . Hey, in fact, we still have four or five joints. You wanna toke?"

"Uh, no thanks," I said.

"It's good stuff, man."

"I'm sure it is," I said. "What else?"

"Well, we dropped acid in Frisco . . . Oh, yeah, man. We've been to San Francisco. I forgot about that. And to Montana and Oklahoma. Wow. How could I forget? I must be losing my freakin' mind." Then he just stared at me with the blankest stare for a good minute. "What?"

". . . you were listing the drugs?"

"Dave," Missy giggled. "You're such a space cadet."

"Wow. You're right." He shook his head several times. "That's about it. We stay away from the hard stuff. I don't like heroin or coke. Mostly grass."

Missy excused herself and went to the ladies' room.

I leaned across the table and spoke softly. "Dave. Do you have protection?"

He leaned toward me and whispered back, "Yes, Father. I keep a little pocketknife in my backpack."

I shook my head. "No, Dave. I'm a minister, not a priest. I mean protection to keep Missy from getting pregnant."

"Oh. That. Wow, man. Sorry. I really am spacey tonight," Dave said. "Yeah. Well, no. Sometimes." He had a proud look on his face and shook his head up and down.

"Dave," I said. "You've got to be careful."

"What do I need to worry about?" he asked. "We love each other, and if she did get pregnant, I think I'd be a pretty good dad. Yeah."

I held up a hand, "Please promise me you'll be careful."

He raised three fingers on his right hand in the Boy Scout sign. "Scout's honor," he said.

"You were a Boy Scout?"

"Yeah. I almost made First Class."

Missy came back from the restroom and slid in next to Dave. "So, what have you boys been talkin' about?"

"Just getting to know each other better," I said. "So where are you from?"

"I grew up on a farm near Indianapolis," she said.

"She really knows her farm stuff," Dave said. "We can be walking through a field, and she'll stop, pick up some plant, and tell me to taste it right there. We have a gourmet picnic right in the middle of nowhere," he said.

"What about money?" I asked.

"You should know, man. Money is the root of all evil," Dave said.

"Actually, it's *love* of money that is the root of all evil."

"Really?" He stared off into space again. "Wow . . . That makes sense, man. How'd I get that wrong?"

"A lot of people do," I said. "But what about you? Do you work?"

"Yeah. When we can and when we need to."

Missy spoke up. "We worked at a little daycare in Jacksonville last week. The little babies were so cute."

"Someone trusted you with babies?"

"Oh, yeah, man," she said. "Dave is really pretty good with children . . . When he stays focused."

"I'll bet he is."

They had both cleaned their plates, so I ordered some pecan pie for them and some coffee for me.

"No coffee for us," Dave said. "Missy doesn't drink coffee 'cause of the caffeine in it."

That made me chuckle. "So, my friends," I said. "What do we do from here? It's going to be a cold night. It may get below freezing. I don't feel safe taking you back to the nativity scene."

"We'll be fine, man," Dave said.

"I could take you to the police station, but I don't know if they'd put you up for the night or not."

They both gave me a blank stare. They didn't seem to like that idea.

I looked across the parking lot at the First National Bank sign. It displayed the time and the temperature. At 10:45 p.m., it was twenty-eight degrees. After a few minutes of silence, I said, "Look, you two. I can't let you sleep outside tonight. You'll freeze. I've got an extra bedroom and bathroom at my place. You can stay with me."

"Far out, man," Dave said. "Are you sure? We won't be in the way, or anything, will we, Missy?"

"No, honey," she added.

"I'm trusting you," I said, not at all sure why I was.

"You can count on me," Dave said, and he gave me the Boy Scout salute again.

I paid the bill and we headed out to my Volkswagen, parked out front. Dave squeezed into the back and sat sideways, placing his feet on the floor behind me so he could fit. Missy slid into the passenger's seat. As we drove to my house, they both thanked me profusely.

"This is so nice of you," Missy said, placing her hand softly on my arm.

Dave added, "Yeah. I don't know what to say."

That's a first, I thought.

* * *

That night, I slept very little. I worried about the seemingly normal couple stealing everything I had. I worried that Dave might be crazy, like that guy in *Psycho*, and he might come into my room at night wielding a giant carving knife, even though I knew I didn't have any giant carving knives in the house. I worried that someone in the church might see them leaving and assume that I was doing drugs.

The couple took a shower before bed. I think they shared it, because I only heard it turn on and off once.

* * *

The house had cooled down a bit the next morning. I walked through the chilly living room and into the kitchen to fix a pot of coffee.

Dave was still asleep. I could hear him snoring behind the bedroom door across the room.

The snoring grew louder as the door opened and Missy slipped out into the kitchen wearing nothing but Dave's cotton shirt, which barely covered her at all. They had washed clothes during the night, and the shirt actually looked kind of nice when it was clean.

"Is the coffee ready?" Missy asked.

"I thought you didn't drink coffee," I said.

"I don't around Dave," she said. "He doesn't like it,

so he doesn't drink it. Can you imagine him, wound up on caffeine?"

I rolled my eyes.

"Where are the cups?" she asked.

I pointed to the cabinet above the counter and she padded over to get herself one. As she reached up into the cabinet, the shirt slid up her thighs, revealing how very little she was wearing that morning. It surprised me. She was truly very sexy, and very appealing.

Grabbing a cup, she turned to see if I was watching. I looked away quickly, but I was too late.

"Do you like what you see?" she asked. "I can show you more if you want."

"Huh?" I said stupidly. "But you're with Dave and I'm a min— "

"So what?" She filled the cup with black coffee. "We're free spirits with free love, Preacher," she said, slinking back to the kitchen table where I was sitting. She put the coffee cup down and wrapped her fingers around it for warmth. Then she added, "He don't care."

"But I would," I said. "It wouldn't be right. Not for me."

She gave me a sheepish, little-girl pout that made me wonder if she was even eighteen yet. Then she dropped the pout and changed into the wanton flirtatious temptress. "You sure?"

"Yeah," I said, a little disconcerted. "Afraid so. But flattered."

"If you change your mind, let me know." She skipped back to the second bedroom. I heard her jump on the bed, rousing the sleeping, snoring giant. Giggles and laughter soon turned into sounds of rustling covers and soft moans. Then, more loud snoring.

I pulled some eggs from the refrigerator and beat them together in a bowl with some salt and pepper. I scrambled the mixture and tossed some toast in the toaster. While the eggs were cooking in one frying pan, I added some bacon to another. I pounded a big pot with a wooden spoon and announced loud enough to wake a snoring behemoth, "Come to breakfast."

The sleepy guests stumbled into the kitchen where I served up their hot breakfast, complete with milk and orange juice. They ate breakfast like they had eaten dinner the night before.

I sat down opposite Dave. "So, guys. What's next?"

Dave ran his hands through his long hair and groaned. "Man, I don't know. I thought we might head to Tampa. I heard there's a shelter there that might put us up for a couple of nights."

"Shelter?" I asked. "Who runs it?"

"I think it's the Sallies," he said. "Yeah. The Salvation Army. A guy in Gainesville told me they have beds and breakfast, and they'll let you stay up to three nights."

"Then what?"

"Hell if I know," he said. "Oh, sorry Father. I just keep moving on, like a rolling stone." He paused for a painfully long moment and said, "Do you like The Rolling Stones?"

"Yeah. I like the Stones. I'll tell you what. I'll take you to the bus station, buy you a couple of tickets, and get you to Tampa, okay?"

"Groovy, man," Dave said. "I'm like, really blown away."

"Just . . ." I said. "Promise me you'll be careful. It's a dangerous world out there, and you need to make sure you and Missy are safe."

"Yes, sir," he said, giving me a Boy Scout salute once again, this time with his left hand.

* * *

That morning, I took Dave and Missy to the Greyhound Bus Station and put them on a bus bound for Tampa. Dave wrapped his giant arms around me and gave me a big bear hug. Missy gave a much more sensuous hug, or at least, that was how it felt to me when she pressed her tiny body against mine.

I waved to both of them as they boarded the bus, thinking about how many people I'd met in this transient world, and wondering if I'd ever see these particular two again.

We live in a crazy world, I thought, *where sex is free, food is a luxury and traveling around the country without any responsibilities is "groovy."*

* * *

January 1969

I couldn't get Dave and Missy out of my mind. I worried that they had no place to go on our frigid Florida nights. I contacted associate ministers in the Baptist and Presbyterian churches, and we met to talk about what could be done to help homeless kids during the winter season. We drew up some quick plans, called special board meetings, got permission and started recruiting volunteers.

In Florida, a freeze could be deadly, particularly to the citrus industry. Farmers would spend all night in the groves, burning old tires to keep the orange and grapefruit trees as warm as possible. You could drive up Highway 27 and see pillars of black smoke rising from the groves for miles.

The next major freeze hit Florida around mid-January. We posted some handmade signs around town announcing that a temporary shelter would be open that night. I had no idea if anyone would respond, but recruited five volunteers to help just in case. We opened the doors of His Place, stocked the kitchen with hot chocolate and coffee, and waited. No one came that night, and I let the volunteers go home at about midnight.

The next night, another freeze was scheduled, and we had some volunteers from the Presbyterian Church scheduled to join us for our homeless vigil. I had put up some flyers in the bus station to advertise our Cold Night Shelter.

About 10:30 p.m., a lady opened the door softly and peered inside. I went to greet her. "Hi. Welcome. I'm Steve."

"I heard that we could stay here tonight," she said timidly.

"Absolutely," I said. "Come in."

"There's no charge, right?" the small, frail woman asked. "Cause I ain't got no money."

"You're welcome here, ma'am," I said.

"And my kids?"

"You've got kids?" I asked, surprised.

She turned back to the door, and opened it. Two children, both under seven years old, stood outside in the cold. The volunteers rushed over to welcome the young family inside. Since they were the only family who came on that first night, they pretty much had the place to themselves. Mom slept on the sofa and the two children slept on beanbag chairs.

We sent three volunteers home around midnight, and I stayed up with the two who remained. The next morning, we served doughnuts, coffee and a nice egg casserole that one of the volunteers who had gone home at midnight brought back early in the morning. "I couldn't let those two little children go hungry without a warm meal in their stomachs," she explained.

The next week was fairly mild for January, and then another cold snap came through at the end of the month. That night, volunteers from the Baptist Church joined us.

At 9:30 p.m., there was a soft knock at the door. I opened it, and saw that it was the frail little lady from the week before. Jesse, as she had introduced herself. Her children rushed inside and were welcomed by the volunteers. They were given hot chocolate and coffee and some snacks.

Still standing at the door, Jesse asked, "Can the others come inside too?"

"Others?" I echoed. I opened the door wider and looked past her. There were close to fifty people standing outside.

The volunteers snapped into action. We rushed everyone inside and handed out blankets and hot drinks. We found places for them all to sleep. There were so many of them that we had to use the floor, guys on one side of the house and girls on the other. It wasn't much, but they were happy. By midnight, everyone had quieted down and we all settled in for the night.

We had to call in reinforcements to have enough volunteers on hand to serve breakfast, but we managed to provide everyone with a warm meal and a warm place to stay.

We had four more nights that winter when the temperature dropped below freezing. We opened the doors, and the homeless came in healthy numbers. The most we had on a single night was fifty-eight women, thirty-one men and seventeen children.

Most of the people who came to us were just down on their luck. Some had lost their jobs. Others were migrant workers, looking for work in the Florida fields. Some were hippies, traveling from town to town like gypsies. Some were white. Some were black. All needed help.

One morning after a particularly cold night, one elderly lady grabbed my hand and said, "You saved our lives."

I honestly felt as if they'd somehow saved mine, too.

SANCTUARY SIX

The Gym

"Gladiators fought for their lives in the
coliseums of Ancient Rome. Today, we battle for
dignity, purpose and character on the court."

— Note on Coach Bridges' desk

COACH BILL BRIDGES

September 1969

The new school building was a facility built with pride. The concrete block walls were spotless. Sparkling glass on the windows welcomed in the brilliant Florida sunlight. Even the metal door handles gleamed.

The science department had the latest in technological gadgetry, from chrome Bunsen burners to shiny glass aquariums to rows of microscopes lining the windowsills with mirrors pointed sunward.

Other departments benefited, as well. The history department had huge twenty-seven-inch televisions suspended from the ceiling of each room. The math department had incorporated blackboards on more than one wall of each room. New foreign language departments now taught Spanish and French in addition to the traditional Latin.

But the new facility came with a cost. Taxpayers had to vote in a sales tax increase to fund the elaborate facility. They were told it was a new day. Humans were in outer space. The U.S. was winning the Cold War. Science was leading mankind to new horizons brighter and greater than ever before. Such changes demanded better skills, and such skills could only be learned with a new educational system.

In addition, the Elementary and Secondary Education Legislation Act now required that black students in Florida be integrated into public schools with white students and none of the existing high school facilities were large enough to accommodate all of the black and white students in the area. So the citizens of Springlake voted to build a new high school.

* * *

Coach Bill Bridges felt like he was finally home. He walked into the brand new gymnasium of Springlake High knowing that this was *his* territory. He had lobbied, politicked and begged to be made head basketball coach of the Springlake Spartans. The head coach of the old Springlake High had built a solid legacy. During his fifteen years at the old high school, the team had won seven state championships. They had been runners-up on four other occasions. But his time for fame and glory was over.

It was time for new blood, and Coach Bridges welcomed the chance to prove himself. He felt a tinge of guilt about some things he had told some people about the former coach. About how he didn't seem to relate to the new generation and how he wouldn't make the best use of the new facilities. But that was behind him now. Bridges had paid his dues. He had coached junior high basketball in an old school with a gym that should have been condemned long ago. This was his moment.

He had watched the new gymnasium being built along with the new school for almost a year. He had seen the brick masons laying concrete blocks. He was even able to advise the board on the new parquet floor, which incorporated a mosaic pattern of wood pieces glued together for both an appealing look and a strong hold.

Now, with school just two weeks away, he stepped into this wonderful new gymnasium. Fluorescent lights overhead illuminated every shadowy area. The Springlake Spartans logo stood prominently on the wall behind the home team bleachers. New scoreboards stood at each end of the gym, and the paint on the floor looked like it had been baked on.

Coach Bridges was especially fond of the smell: the scent of high-quality wood tickled his nostrils. A salesman over at Springlake Hardware had said that the smell was actually the highly toxic glue holding the floor together, but Bill didn't care. This gymnasium was a special place where he would help mold young minds and bodies to play the wonderful game of basketball.

* * *

School started and Coach Bridges couldn't wait for basketball tryouts. He knew all of the junior and senior ball players who had played at Springlake Junior High. He didn't know any of the players from George Washington Carver, since they had just been integrated into one school this year.

State regulations prevented the team from meeting before a certain date, but Coach Bridges let it be known that the new gym would be open for individuals to practice on their own, starting the second day of school. Naturally, he and his assistant coach would be there to observe and chaperone, but no formal practice would take place.

They sat in the top row of the bleachers, watching the boys shoot on the floor below them. There were about twenty-five boys in the gym. He recognized several of the boys from previous teams: Franklin, Watson, Young and Bowden were shooting jump shots from way too far out, trying to impress and intimidate any new players. But the ball has to go in to be impressive, so the shots just made the boys look bad.

There were seven black boys, including Watson. The Carver boys all looked like they had played ball before, if not organized.

There were six basketball nets in the gym: one on each end, and four that were used for practice along the sides of the court. Within ten minutes, most of the boys had gravitated to one end of the floor or the other: six black players on one side and the rest of the players at the opposite side.

Coach Bridges could see that after only two days of

forced integration, the two races were not yet mingling freely. He also saw, with some relief, that one of the boys who had tried out in the seventh grade, the one his teammates had nicknamed Crew Cut Kinney, was not on the court. That kid had struggled with his anger. It was good that he wasn't trying out this year. They didn't need that additional headache. Besides, the kid wasn't that good a ball player. Coach Bridges believed in a disciplined approach to basketball. His plays were based on staying in constant control of the ball. A hothead like Kinney would not make a good Springlake Spartan.

* * *

November 1969

Coach Bridges posted an announcement on the bulletin board outside the gym that said that tryouts would start on November 3, a month before the season began. Players came to the gym every afternoon, and Bridges took them through various drills and practices, evaluating each hopeful.

In addition, he and the other coaches checked background and academic information on each player. Two of the black players had to be removed from tryouts because their grades were below the minimum requirement. One quit because of a past record with the law. Four white players dropped out during tryout week; they either realized that they didn't have a chance of making the team or they didn't want to work that hard.

Bridges was on the floor when yet another white player dropped out. They were running block-out rebounding drills. The players were paired up, half on defense and the other half on offense. The assistant coach would toss the ball against the backboard and those on defense would pivot, face the basket and square off so that their bodies, backs now to their offensive counterpart, would be "in position" to get the rebound.

If the ball came their way, they were to leap into the air, grab it and pull it down while swinging their elbows one way or the other. This served to prevent the offensive player from getting to the ball. It was an effective maneuver if done correctly. It also tended to bruise some players' ribs.

Just before tryouts, one of the black students had come to his office and asked if he could play basketball. He was big, with a round chest, thick thighs, and arms that promised tremendous physical strength.

"Why haven't I seen you on the floor 'til now?"

"I've been at football practice, Coach," he said. "I play defensive guard.

"What's your name, son?"

"Gerald Green, but my friends call me King."

"We'll see how well you play."

Practice had gone well until the rebounding drill.

King blocked out his offensive opponent and jumped as high as he could raise his two-hundred-plus pounds. He grabbed the ball and brought it down to his stomach with a wide swing of his elbows. His left elbow caught Jeff Williams upside the head and the lanky boy went down with a thud. He bounced back up looking for blood.

The two squared off, and even though King was easily fifty pounds heavier than him, Jeff was ready to dance. "You did that on purpose, you black son of a bitch."

"Of course I did, boy," King said. "That's what the Coach told me to do."

It seemed to dawn on Williams then that he didn't have a chance in a fight with King. He also probably realized that being a forward on this team would lead to flare-ups like this one all season long. He turned and headed toward the showers. "I've got better things to do than this," he huffed.

By the end of the week, sixteen boys remained. It wasn't difficult for Coach Bridges to trim off the four poorest players. He posted the names of the twelve team members on the bulletin board on Friday.

* * *

December 1969

He hated pep rallies. He had managed to schedule only one each year when he taught junior high school. He wished he could do the same at Springlake High.

Pep rallies were all about emotion. Basketball, on the other hand, was all about control. Emotion had no place on the basketball court. Players who got emotional made bad shots and bad passes. They fouled needlessly. They missed free throws. So Bridges hated pep rallies on principle.

But the athletic director had insisted, so a pep rally was scheduled. The 1969-70 basketball team stood proudly at center court with their reluctant coach at their side. They joined their fellow students in the Pledge of Allegiance, the player introductions and the efforts to lead cheers by the cheerleaders.

A pep rally resembles an old time tent revival, Bridges thought while watching the event from center court. Crowds file into place, expecting a moving and motivational message. Upbeat music by the pep band helps the crowd stay entranced. Banners and pompoms stir up feelings. Individuals challenge the audience to support the cause and follow the leader. Then, at the moment when everything comes to a fever pitch, the leader—him, in this case—steps to the podium to deliver the divinely inspired message.

The problem was that Bridges was not good at delivering messages, and when he did deliver them, they were anything but divinely inspired. He tried. He wrote out speeches and practiced them in front of the mirror. He just didn't have that gene.

It came to his turn, so he stepped to the podium, leaned in to the microphone, and said, "Uh . . ." He felt great drops of sweat drip down his forehead. He looked down at the speech he had written three days ago. Sweat drops fell from his wet brow and splattered on the page, blurring the words. In desperation, he decided to wing it. "We're glad you came out to the pep rally today. The boys are looking forward to a great season. We've worked real hard to get ready. This is your 1969-1970 varsity team."

Someone in the crowd began clapping, and lackluster applause followed.

Coach Bridges continued, "Come to the game tonight to watch us beat Tampa."

The coach returned to the team, grateful when the pep band started playing because it took attention away from him. Cheerleaders ran out on the floor and began kicking their legs high into the air, flashing skin and cotton panties while they skipped to the music.

And then, thank God, the pep rally was over.

* * *

Coach Bridges faced his first challenge in the first game of the season.

The opener against the Tampa Titans was tough. Tampa won the tip-off and relayed the ball quickly down the court for an easy layup. They pressed from the get-go, and stole the ball for another two.

Eventually, Franklin and Watson were able to get the ball down the court and set up the offense. King grabbed a bounce pass, turned and promptly had his shot blocked by the six-foot-six center from Tampa. By the end of the first quarter, the Spartans were down twenty-one to twelve.

The second quarter was a painful repeat of the first. The Spartans caved in to the full-court press. Whenever they did manage to get the ball over the half-court line, they never seemed to be able to set up the offense. Open players were ignored. Shots were blocked. Passes were deflected. It was going to be a long night for the fans, the team and Coach Bridges.

He watched helplessly from the sidelines as Tampa destroyed them. They would steal the ball and run with it, again and again. They didn't waste time setting up an offense; just took the ball to the hole, over and over. By halftime, Tampa was leading by twenty-four points.

"What are you thinking out there?" Bridges yelled in the locker room during halftime. "Control the ball.

Bring the ball down the floor. Set up for the good shot."

None of the boys looked up from the floor. They were not proud of the first half.

"Get out there and run the offense. Run the offense," he yelled. His throat hurt. At this rate, he wasn't going to have a voice by Christmas.

When the Spartans were warming up for the second half, he pulled the two guards aside. "Boys," he said. "If we don't set up the offense, we aren't going to score any points. Set it up. Run the plays!"

The second half started with some promise. King somehow managed to tap the toss to Franklin, who nailed a long pass to Watson on the way to the goal. Thirty seconds later, they got lucky again and King was open beneath the boards. Watson connected with him and the Spartans had another two-pointer.

"Run the plays," Bridges shouted from the sidelines. "No show-boating. Implement. Control the ball."

Watson shot Bridges a confused look, apparently questioning his instructions. Bridges replaced him at the next time-out.

When the final buzzer sounded, Springlake walked through the exit doors humiliated in a seventy-six to forty-one rout. The fans were disappointed. The coach was disappointed. The faculty was disappointed. But the players were by far the most disappointed.

Coach Bridges called a special Saturday morning practice and sent the boys to the showers. It was going to be a long, long season.

* * *

It was a few days before Christmas, and the Springlake Spartans had managed a mere two wins out of nine games. The fans were taking it hard. Attendance had dropped proportionately to the number of times the players dropped the ball. *The Springlake Tribune* printed very critical columns about the team and their hopes for a break-even season. Bill Bridges told his wife that all he wanted from Santa Claus was a few more wins. It was a dismal time to be on the Springlake Spartans basketball team.

A week before the holiday break, the Spartans traveled to Lakeland to face one of their main rivals. The Lakeland High team was merciless, stealing pass after pass and running up the score as fast as the scoreboard could record it.

Bridges had scouted Lakeland and knew that they had a short guard who was destined for greatness. Calvin Shaw stood a little over five and a half feet tall, but made up for his height by being unbelievably quick. He could snatch the ball away from a guard and run downcourt for the layup before the guard even realized he had lost the ball. College scouts had already come to several of his games, and the rumor mill hinted that he would play for one of the southeast basketball college giants.

Calvin didn't disappoint his home team crowd when they played against Springlake. By the end of the night, he had scored thirty-eight of the team's seventy-four points, an incredible accomplishment. As players shook hands with their opponents at the end of the game, Bridges overheard him thank the guards, Franklin and Young, for helping him secure his upcoming college scholarship.

The bus ride home, like all bus rides so far that season, was dark and quiet. Other teams shouted cheers, told jokes and sang songs to make the long bus rides more enjoyable. But the Springlake bus was as quiet as a hearse. Coach Bridges, sitting at the front of the dark bus, did nothing to hide his disappointment. When the players started whispering to the cheerleaders in the back of the bus, he demanded, "Quiet down. Why don't you give some thought to the game we just lost?"

Then, unexpectedly, something happened to change the mood. They drove passed a manger scene someone had constructed in front of their house. Way in the back, King's deep bass voice began to sing *Away in a Manger*. The fact that it was so close to Christmas, combined with the raw beauty of King's deep voice, lifted everyone's spirits. The rest of the kids on the bus began to sing along with King, and the sound, on that cold, empty and dark night, was very welcome.

The group followed up with other Christmas carols, like *We Three Kings* and even *Deck the Halls*. Then they sang the *Star-Spangled Banner*. Bridges allowed it all without interruption. Hell, he figured he couldn't stop it anyway.

Just before pulling into the school parking lot, King broke into a solo of *Amazing Grace*, and the bus became very still as everyone listened. He hadn't finished yet when the doors of the bus opened, and no one moved. They waited quietly for the gifted young man to finish his song before peacefully filing off the bus and going home.

* * *

Coach Smith, the athletic director at Springlake High, glared across his desk at Coach Bridges. Smith was also the head football coach. Naturally, that meant that the football program had virtually everything it could possibly want. It also meant that the other athletic departments had to scramble for whatever resources they needed.

"I'm hearing a lot of concerns from the community about the basketball team, Bill. What are you now, two and nine?"

"Eight, Coach. We're two and eight."

"That doesn't sound good."

Bill couldn't take his eyes off the shiny trophies sitting in glass boxes along one side of the room.

"What's going on?" Smith demanded.

"We're adjusting," Bridges said. "It takes time." He hated being called on the carpet like this, especially when he felt like he was doing his best.

"Seems to me like the competition adjusted fairly quickly," Coach Smith said. "*Everyone* seems to have adjusted quite well . . . except us."

Now, Coach Bridges felt like he was being backed into a corner. "I don't know. I get the feeling that the coach from George Washington Carver didn't prepare his boys as well as I thought." He raised his hands and held an imaginary basketball. "Most of them have pretty good individual skills, but they don't think strategically. They're not disciplined. They don't play like a team. I don't think they've had to do that before."

Coach Smith cocked his head to one side. "They went twenty-five and five last year," he said.

Now Coach Bridges was getting frustrated. "It's just going to take a little longer than I had hoped," he said.

"Look, Bill. Parents are calling. The principal is asking questions. I even got a call from the pastor of First Baptist Church yesterday. They all want to know what happened to their championship team."

"We'll get there. I've seen some progress."

"Just do whatever it takes to stop the bleeding," Coach Smith said. "Whatever it takes."

* * *

The last game before Christmas break was against the Bryan High Bengals, possibly the worst team in the division, at least on paper. Coach Bridges was desperate to end the calendar year with a win.

The first quarter looked fairly good, with both teams giving and taking field goals. Watson outran and outshot his opponent on the Bryan team. However, Bryan's rebounding was a notch or two above Springlake's and that made up for the difference enough to keep the game close.

Bryan also had a center who was taller and faster than King. The Springlake center could muscle his way to the boards, but his opponent could outjump him. Both centers fought for turf throughout the night. In the end, King outlasted the Bryan center with fewer fouls. Bryan's center made his fifth foul in the final quarter when he blocked a short jumper but lost his balance and fell across King's shoulders. Before the whistle blew, the player was heading toward the bench.

"C'mon now, King," Bridges shouted from the

bench. "We need these."

King made both free throws. The score was tied up with a minute to go in the last quarter.

At that point, the Bryan guards slowly brought the ball down the court. When the ball crossed center court, they began tossing it back and forth. It was obvious that they were "freezing" the ball to let the time run out. Without their star center, Bryan's only hope was to keep the Spartans from getting the ball and outscoring them.

"Foul him," Bridges yelled from the bench. It was a chance they had to take. If the Bryan guard missed one of the two free throws, the Spartans could bring the ball down and score the winning basket. Franklin rushed his opponent, who turned his back to protect the ball. With twenty-five seconds left, he grabbed the offensive guard in a bear hug and the referee called the foul. Unfortunately, the guard made both free throws.

With Coach Bridges yelling "Set up the good shot," the Spartan guards quickly brought the ball down the floor. They began to run their play, bounce passing the ball to King in the center and crossing in front of him, using his huge frame as a screen. Watson came around the top of the key and King passed him the ball. Watson faked a pass to Franklin, dribbled to his right and took the jumper.

Coach Bridges yelled, "Nooo!" He was too late. Luckily, the ball swished through the net, tying the score, but one of Bryan's guards grabbed the ball and put his hands together to signal a time out.

Bridges was furious. "What are you doing taking a jump shot at the top of the key with twelve seconds to go in the game?" he yelled in Watson's face. "I told you to work for the good shot. To control the ball."

"It felt like I had the shot, Coach," the black guard said. "I made the bucket."

"And they have the ball with a full twelve seconds to score the winning goal. You don't throw the ball away like that with twelve seconds on the clock."

Larry Watson lowered his face and stared at the floor.

"Listen," Bridges said to the starting team in the huddle. "We can't let them score. We can't foul them, but we've got to get that ball." He pointed to the big guy. "King, you take the man bringing the ball in on the sideline. Do everything you can to keep him from in-bounding the ball. Be in his face. Yell, scream, shout and wave your arms. Act like an ape. I don't care. Just don't let him bring the ball in."

He pointed at Franklin. "You play off your man just a hair. When they throw the ball in, you go after it."

The team put their hands in the center of the huddle, shouted "Go!" and took to the floor.

King didn't just *look* like a madman. The coach's comments seemed to make him furious for real. He waved his arms and shouted at the top of his lungs. The Bengals player had a hard time concentrating enough to find an open man. The referee was bouncing his hand up and down, counting the seconds the player had left to pass the ball inbounds.

At the last possible second—in fact, according to many Springlake fans, after the time limit was up—he fired a bounce pass to one of the guards.

Franklin lunged for the ball, missing it by an inch. The guard grabbed it while the clock ticked down, and he charged the goal, heading in for a layup. Springlake's two forwards both jumped as high as they could to block his shot. At the last second, with both feet off the ground, he slipped a pass to the Bryan forward on the opposite side of the foul lane, who laid the ball up against the backboard and into the basket.

The buzzer sounded before the ball hit the floor.

Bryan fans streamed out onto the floor to congratulate their team on the victory. Coach Bridges and the Springlake team walked dejectedly to the locker room and the showers. The bus was quiet on the way home, and no one had to ask the players to keep silent. King didn't sing. No one said a thing. In the back of his mind, a nagging, pesky thought was eating away at Coach Bridges. *It's all about control.* Tonight, his team lost control. Tonight, he lost control. *It's all about control.*

* * *

January 1970

Over Christmas, Coach Bridges felt like he experienced a deathbed conversion and was now a new man. After New Year's, his practices were different. Most of the time was spent on ball handling. Passing, dribbling, and free throws were the priority.

The coach was in the locker room after practice when he overheard some of the boys talking.

"I don't understand how passing and dribbling is going to get us points," Young said.

"Can't hurt. It's not like you scored any points when we practiced shooting," Wells quipped.

The next game was at the end of the week. On the last day of practice, the team ran a full-practice scrimmage. Coach Bridges had the first team do nothing but freeze the ball. The other players did everything they could to get the ball from their opponents. At the end of practice, Coach Bridges called the boys together.

"Gentlemen," he started. "We have a new game plan. We are going to keep control of the game by implementing a full-game freeze. This will give us an advantage over teams that don't have our ball-handling skills. This will give us our wins." The players were stunned by this unconventional tactic. "Now, hit the showers and be on the bus tomorrow at 4:00 p.m."

The gym cleared out and Coach Bridges walked out onto the floor to pick up a basketball that had been left behind. He stood at center court of the gleaming facility that he had been entrusted with, feeling all the weight of his decision pressing down on him. *God, I hope this works.*

* * *

The Spartans had not yet played Chambly this season. Coach Bridges walked into the gym at Chambly High more nervous than ever before. This was the epitome of slow-motion risk-taking.

Chambly got the tip and scored within the first thirty seconds. Then, Springlake brought the ball down and sat on it. They used a three-guard formation to take advantage of their better ball-handlers, and the three guards tossed the ball around in the backcourt for most of the quarter.

Every now and then a guard would dribble the ball into the front court to obey league rules that required the ball to cross a certain line every so many seconds. Then they'd toss the ball out to a guard in the backcourt and the process would start again.

After a couple of minutes, the Chambly coach figured out what was happening, and began yelling at his guards to foul. Someone finally did, and the Springlake player sank the free throw.

Chambly rushed the ball down the court, visibly shaken by the change in game strategy. They were playing right into Coach Bridges' hands. As soon as they crossed mid-court, they were met by the pressure of a one-three-one defense. The guard with the ball got boxed into a corner and tried to pass to his teammate, but Watson was there to pick off the pass and sprint in for the layup.

The Chambly coach, now down three to two, called time out. They managed to bring the ball in, but Wells stole it from their guard and fed Franklin for a layup, sending Springlake ahead five to two.

Chambly brought the ball down the court again and scored as quickly as they could. When it was Springlake's turn, they froze the ball for the remainder of the quarter. At halftime, the score was Springlake nine and Chambly eight.

"It's working, boys," Coach Bridges told them in the locker room. "Stay with the game plan and control the ball. These guys don't know what hit them."

The second half was a repeat of the first, and at the end of the game, Springlake went home with a twenty-two to twenty victory.

* * *

Coach Bridges was called into the athletic director's office early on Monday morning.

"What the hell is going on, Coach?" Smith demanded.

"You said to do whatever it takes," Bridges replied. "This is what it takes."

"They're laughing at us," Smith yelled.

"We won," Bridges said calmly. He wasn't about to back down.

"Yeah, but it was a hollow victory."

"But still a plus in the win column."

"Do you plan on freezing the rest of the season?"

"If that's what it takes."

"Why can't you play traditional Springlake basketball, Bridges?"

"Look, Coach," Bridges explained. "These boys aren't ready to play the control type of game that Springlake has used for a decade. The colored boys—I mean, the Carver boys—certainly aren't there. They only want to run and shoot."

"So why don't you run and shoot?"

"That's not how the game is played. It should be disciplined, controlled and strategic," Coach Bridges said. "The full-game freeze evens the playing field. It worked at Chambly."

"Understand this," Smith warned. "You're taking a huge risk here. This is a gamble. If it backfires, you'll be coaching elementary school."

Working in elementary school doesn't sound half bad, Coach Bridges fumed on his way out the door.

* * *

Coach Bridges felt that his boys were ready for the next game against Lakeland High, the rival team that had humiliated them when the two teams first met in December. Their star guard, Calvin Shaw, was now averaging twenty-eight points a game.

Bridges stumbled across a quotation from Eleanor Roosevelt the morning before the big game: "People grow through experience if they meet life honestly and courageously. This is how character is built."

Today, he thought, *we're going to help that little monkey from Lakeland develop a little character through an honest experience.*

Calvin took the first shot of the game and sunk the fifteen-foot jumper. It looked like a normal game until the Springlake guards brought the ball down the court and froze it. Frustration rose among the Lakeland players, particularly for Shaw. Bridges noted that they were visibly more aggressive than Chambly High had been. It didn't take them long to foul Franklin, and Franklin repaid the favor by sinking the free throw. By the end of the first half, Lakeland led thirteen to ten.

Lakeland came out strong after halftime, pressuring the guards mercilessly. But that just allowed the skilled ball handlers to show off their moves and bring the ball up court where King was waiting for the easy hook shoot.

Bridges shouted, "Two minutes," to let the guards know that the game was almost over. Lakeland held a razor thin lead of two points. Springlake had the ball and was demonstrating its one-hit wonder: how to pass the ball.

Calvin Shaw was visibly frustrated. The twenty-eight-point guard had scored only twelve points tonight. This would definitely hurt his game point average and his chance for a prime basketball scholarship. He worked harder than anyone to steal the ball, but even he was unsuccessful.

With thirty seconds to go, Young passed the ball to King on the baseline. The big man looked for Watson coming across the lane, but saw that he was covered. He passed the ball back out to Young, who relayed it to Franklin. By the time it reached Franklin, King had come across the lane and was setting the pick of all picks for the guard. Franklin faked left and drove right with less than ten seconds on the clock. He went up for the layup, stretching as high as his five-foot-nine frame would let him.

From out of nowhere, a desperate Calvin Shaw leapt to block the shot after climbing over the mountain of a center who had set the pick moments before. His fingers narrowly missed the ball, but his entire frame came crashing down on the Franklin's shoulders. The referee's whistle blew just before the ball rolled around the rim twice and fell in.

Three seconds on the clock. No time outs. Tie score, twenty-four to twenty-four. Ten players and about three hundred screaming fans. Talk about pressure.

Franklin stood at the foul line and breathed deeply. Coach Bridges shouted at the other guard, "After he makes the free throw, get everyone back down the floor fast. Don't press. No press."

Two Springlake players were already waiting by the other goal. Watson and Young were at the half-court line. No one was lined up under the board to rebound a possibly missed foul shot.

Franklin balanced the ball in his hands and stared at the goal. He bent his knees slightly, brought the ball up past his face and let it go, holding his right hand in the air after the shot. The ball fell through without touching the net.

The Lakeland forward grabbed the ball, took one step out of bounds and hurled it down court to one of the guards. He relayed the ball across the court to Calvin, who dribbled once and leapt into the air for the jumper. Three Springlake players followed him, arms flailing to block the shot. The ball bounced off the front of the rim and the game was over. The hometown Spartan crowd went wild. Calvin, held to twelve points, sulked off the floor. The fans flocked their four-and-eight heroes as if they'd just won the state championship.

Coach Bridges watched as Franklin slipped through the mob to get close enough to the sullen Shaw to say, "Good luck with that scholarship."

Victory, even cheap victory, was sweet.

* * *

Coach Bridges congratulated the Springlake team in the locker room and then waited behind in his office. The crowd quickly dispersed to go celebrate at the drive-in or at the new McDonalds that had opened in November.

The custodians started sweeping up after the game. Bridges walked back to center court. The building seemed somehow friendlier now. A few days ago it was cold and intimidating. Now, empty but still resonating with the sounds of hundreds of screaming fans, squeaking shoes on polished floors, and the bounce of the ball, it seemed familiar. It felt like home. He relished the moment.

* * *

The next five games went by in a flash. Springlake won two of them, but still faced a losing season.

The fans grew tired of watching their home team play catch, and attendance continued to dwindle. Bridges sensed that the players were frustrated with not being able to take anything but the surest of shots.

The visiting teams were coming up with ways to combat the full-game freeze. Most used a tough, full-court man-to-man defense to try to shake the ball loose before the Springlake players could cross the half-court line.

The Pinedale High coach sent in his worst player at the start of the game with instructions to do nothing but foul. Since the first five non-shooting fouls of the half resulted in one-shot free throws, it would cost no more than five points. He fouled out in the first three minutes of the game, but his team led by five points after that.

One team gave them a healthy dose of their own medicine. After winning the tip-off, the visiting team froze the ball most of the game. The most boring, waste-of-time game on the books ended with Springlake winning seven to six.

The crowd was becoming as annoyed as the players. They began to boo when the Springlake guards set up for the stall. One night, half of the crowd brought pillows and faked a "sleep-in" during the game. Some kids even wore pajamas.

The life of a coach can be tremendously rewarding or terribly frustrating based on a few points in a few games. Coach Bridges' life went from one extreme to another almost overnight. He felt the glares and dirty looks in the hallways and in the classrooms. He felt waves of hostility in the local stores. He thought he heard nasty comments when he walked down the street.

He didn't know if he could make the full-game freeze last the entire season. At some point, he would have to go back to playing traditional ball. But he knew the boys weren't ready for Springlake-style command and control basketball. He feared that some of the boys would *never* be ready. He was beginning to believe that the traditional way of doing things might not be effective any longer.

"Whatever it takes" had quickly become bad advice. He was miserable. *What do you do,* he wondered, *when the place you once called home stops feeling safe and inviting?*

SANCTUARY SEVEN

Springlake, the World, and the Rest of It

"Sanctuary is not going to be a place of doom. It will be a place of life and living."

— Linda Gholston

September 1969

The world turns day after day, and with each revolution, new changes occur. What was commonplace yesterday is out of date today. What is new and exciting today is boring tomorrow.

The world experiences growth pains as old standards are replaced by new ideas. Music becomes a battle cry for a generation seeking meaning. Wars are waged, wars are protested. Fashions change for the sake of change. Politicians come and go. Authority is challenged.

In Springlake, Florida, the kids now wore their hair long like the hippies in San Francisco. They were beginning to adopt new attitudes about authority and life in general. *The Springlake Tribune* announced a drug abuse "epidemic" when marijuana was seized at a Saturday night teen party.

Florida schools had experimented with voluntary integration and talk was that the federal government was going to resort to forced integration by busing kids across town to desegregated schools in the coming year. Many people, white and black, were frightened.

Traditionalists didn't take this lying down. The Ku Klux Klan stepped up its efforts. Crime increased and white people moved farther out of town. Springlake struggled with all-encompassing change along with the rest of the nation. Nothing would ever be the same again.

* * *

During the last weeks of summer, people could talk about nothing but desegregation. *The Springlake Tribune* was filled with editorials and letters decrying the new policy. But the policy could not be deterred.

The halls of Springlake High rumbled with the sound of new student chatter, fueled by the new desegregation ruling. Even though the school was now integrated, the students themselves remained segregated. Pockets of black students and white students gathered here and there across the campus. People of one race glared at people of another. On the first day of school, it looked like it would take a long, long time for the new policies to work.

Fights broke out here and there during the first weeks. A black senior claimed a white junior had made a racist comment, and fists flew. A white junior claimed a black junior was staring at his girlfriend, and he wrestled him down the front steps of the school. Two girls started a fight in the girls' restroom. Students refused to tolerate each other.

Teachers tended to hide out in classrooms or teachers' lounges until the day was over. Then, they quickly packed up their belongings and went home. Finally, school administrators hired off-duty policemen to patrol the halls, and on the surface, the conflicts seemed to die down. But within each student, the tension was ratcheting up.

Football may well have been the savior of Springlake High. When black and white students were touted as role models, students became more accepting. Name-calling turned into name cheering, and the frigid feelings of the past began to thaw.

With the exception of a skirmish here or there, student life became routine once again. Generally, black and white students remained in separate groups, but they did learn to coexist.

Still, coexistence is not the same as peace, and tolerance is not the same as acceptance.

* * *

January 1970

"Another loss," Rob said, dragging himself into the locker room after their eleventh loss. "We suck."

"Yeah, and the crowd's getting tired of the freeze," Larry added.

They both slumped down on the bench and began to unlace their shoes.

"How much worse can it get?"

"Listen up," Coach Bridges yelled. "This was a tough one to lose, but we're coming around. Practice on Monday, as usual. We'll be ready for Tampa next week."

The players quickly showered and filed out of the steamy locker room. Rob and Larry were among the first to leave. The unusually chilly temperature outside made them feel even more isolated than the loss they had just suffered.

Karen, Rob's girlfriend, was waiting by Larry's car in the parking lot when the two defeated Spartans walked slowly to the car. Bundled up in a navy peacoat, she still had to hug herself to keep the cold out.

"Hi, honey," she said as she gently kissed Rob on the cheek. Then she gave Larry a quick hug. "C'mon, boys. Are you going to be depressed all night?"

Larry unlocked the door and climbed into the driver's seat of his Chevy II, and Karen slid in beside him from the passenger's side where Rob had opened the door. Rob slid in next and wrapped his arm around her shoulders.

As Larry backed out of the parking lot, Rob took a deep breath and said, "I'm starving. Let's get something to eat."

"Man, I ain't hungry," Larry said.

"Me neither," Karen said. "But if you're hungry we can go to that new restaurant."

"Naw. Everybody would be there. I really don't want to see anyone from school."

Larry said, "We could drive to Lakeland. Won't be any Springlake kids there."

"Too far," Karen said. "I have to be home by 11:30

or my dad will kill me."

"Let's just go to Pete's," Rob suggested. Pete's was a little diner that had opened quietly on the edge of town a couple of months ago. It wasn't cool enough for most of the kids to go to, but they made the best cheeseburgers in town, and Rob was in the mood for a greasy cheeseburger.

"Cool," said Larry. "Pete's it is."

It took less than ten minutes to slip through the streets of Springlake to the outskirts of town.

"Marsha was at the game tonight," Karen said to Larry.

"So?"

"You know she's interested in you."

"Karen, I'm no mind reader. I don't know that."

"Well, why don't you ask her out?"

"I don't know . . ."

"Let's double date next weekend."

"We've got games on Friday and Saturday," Rob said.

"Jeez," Karen said, feigning irritation. "How am I supposed to play Cupid if you guys are always playing basketball?"

"I'm not so sure we're 'playing' basketball," Rob said with a shrug. Larry chuckled and nodded.

Only three cars were in the parking lot. Pete wasn't doing a lot of business tonight.

"I don't know how he stays open," Larry said.

"I'll be right back," Rob said. He climbed out of the little Chevy and ran inside.

* * *

"He sure does get bummed out about the games," Karen said after Rob had left. She had slid across the bench seat and leaned against the closed door so she could face Larry.

"Cut him some slack. He's serious about b-ball." Larry turned up the heater in the little car.

"I wish he was as serious about me," she said.

"Are you kidding? You're all he talks about off the

floor, and sometimes while he's on the floor. The man is obsessed."

"Yeah?" she asked. She smiled when Larry nodded. "So what about you, Larry? Who do you obsess about?"

"You don't know her, girl."

"Oh, so there is someone."

"Yeah. I met her over Christmas. She goes to my cousin's school in Tampa."

"Does this mystery girl have a name?"

"Grace," Larry said. "She's really cool. She plans to go to NYU in a couple of years. She has this big 'fro and wears long, dangly earrings."

"Well, listen now," Karen said. "I've gotta meet Miss Amazing Grace. I don't know if I approve of my friend dating someone I've never met."

Larry chuckled. "You'd like her, Karen."

* * *

"What can I get you, hon?" the waitress asked, holding an order pad in hand.

"Take out please," Rob said.

"Do you want to see a menu?"

"No, ma'am. I'll take a double bacon cheeseburger, large fries and three Cokes."

The waitress jotted down his order, attached it to a metal clip on a rotating carousel, and spun it around to face the kitchen. "Order up," she yelled.

Rob looked around the restaurant. There wasn't much to look at. Pete needed a decorator. A clock hung on one wall and a framed dollar bill hung by the cash register. The rest of the wall space was blank.

A couple of old men were sipping coffee at one table and one man was eating a late dinner alone at another. His eyes went back to the two men at the table. They were both looking at him. He nodded his head toward them.

"Hello, young feller," one of the men said. "Did you go to the game tonight?"

"Yes, sir. I was there."

"So, who won?" asked the other man.

"Pinedale. Twenty-five to nineteen."

"Shaw," the old man spat. "This is the worst team we've had in years."

I didn't see you on the floor, old man, Rob thought. "It's a rebuilding year, sir," he said, careful to show no disrespect.

"Rebuilding, my ass," the old man said. "Springlake has always had a good basketball team. Now that they've got a new school and a new coach, they've all gone flabby."

Rob noticed that the old coot was missing most of his teeth. *How can he eat a hamburger?* he wondered.

"It's that no good coach," the other old man said. "He wouldn't know how to coach a basketball team if his life depended on it."

"You know what it is," the first man said. "It's them niggers. We used to win State. That is, before that stinkin' integration was forced on us."

The third old man in the room, sitting at a separate table, chimed in. "That's right. They don't know how to play team basketball. They just all want to run and shoot the ball."

"I think the coach oughta kick them all off the team. Go out with a squad of white boys and show the state what kinda ball white boys play."

"Out of curiosity, *sir*," Rob asked. "How many games have you been to this year?"

"Don't need to go to no games," the old man said. "I read about it in *The Springlake Tribune.*"

"Well, the team's working real hard," Rob said. "The competition is really tough this year."

"Shaw," the man repeated. "The competition's always been tough. It's them niggers."

As soon as the waitress said, "Your order's ready," Rob turned away from the trio of pseudo-commentators. He paid and took the brown bag and three Styrofoam cups out to the car.

Good thing they didn't look out the window, he thought, seeing his black friend and his white girlfriend talking in the front seat.

* * *

But someone else had seen the pair in the front seat.

The pick-up truck slowly drove by Pete's, heading toward the Fast-Trac gas station. Cale had told his parents that he was going to the game, but instead, as he always did for home games, he and his friends met out at Wagoner's Field where they built a bonfire and drank beer. He hated basketball.

"Hey, look who's parking at Pete's," Cale said as they drove by the restaurant. "Ain't that Larry Watson, that nigger on the basketball team?"

"So?" the other kid in the car said. He was fairly bombed and wasn't paying attention to the scenery.

"He's with a white girl," Cale exclaimed suddenly. "That ain't right."

"No, he ain't . . . well I'll be damned."

They slowed a bit. "I can't make out who it is, but she's as white as snow," Cale said. "I knew it was gonna come to this." He took another sip of his beer. "Goddamn niggers moved into our schools. Now they're moving in on our women."

"What are we going to do about it?"

Cale thought long and hard as they drove away.

* * *

Rob jogged out to the car, bag in hand. He appeared so suddenly that Karen almost fell out of the passenger seat when he opened the door.

"Easy, man," Larry said.

Rob helped Karen back up and she slid across the seat so he could climb into the car. He opened the bag, passed the little bag of fries to Karen to share, and took a big bite of his cheeseburger.

"So you're going to take me home with the smell of onion and bacon and hamburger on your breath? No goodnight kiss for you."

In response, Rob exhaled long and deep into the

car.

"Whew, boy," Larry said, waving one hand in front of his nose. "I can smell that from way over here."

They laughed and joked their way past Wagoner's Field to Karen's house. She lived quite a ways out of town, so it took some time to get there. Larry plugged a cassette into the deck hanging below the dashboard and they listened to Sgt. Pepper all the way there. They pulled into her driveway, and Rob got out to walk her to the door.

"Make it fast, you two," Larry said. "I've gotta be home before dawn."

"Thanks for the ride, Larry," Karen said. "See you next week."

Rob and Karen walked to her front door holding hands. "You gonna be okay?" she asked.

"Yeah. Basketball's just got me down."

"You're good at it," she said. "People who are good are tough on themselves."

Rob turned her around to face him and wrapped his arms around her waist.

"I know you can figure this out," she said.

They kissed tenderly.

The porch lights suddenly burst on, surprising them.

"There's my cue," Karen said. "G'night."

"Night Kar."

Karen went inside and Rob walked back to the car.

"You, my friend, are one lucky man," Larry said as they drove away.

"Lucky at love but unlucky at basketball."

* * *

Cale made a phone call while his friend filled up the truck in the self-serve lane. Within a few minutes, two more trucks pulled into the gas station. Cale walked over to the driver's side of the first truck.

"Man," Cale said. "Did you bring the whole freakin' Army?"

"We were playing poker when you called. You're

sure about what you saw?" the driver asked. Cale could smell stale beer on his breath.

"I'm telling you, Donnie. The niggers are dating white girls. It ain't right."

"Listen. We've gotta make an example," Donnie said. "Like my big brother did back in fifty-eight. Do you know where they are?"

"Naw. Not now. But I know where the black boy lives," Cale said. "An apartment over in Nigger Town. We can drive by and see if he's home."

Cale got into his truck and the three vehicles drove off toward the railroad tracks. They pulled to a stop at County Line Road when, all of a sudden, a dark blue Chevy II sped past.

"Oh my God," Cale shouted. He stuck his head out of the driver's window and shouted to the driver behind him. "That's him. That's the son of a bitch!"

"Get him," Donnie yelled, and Cale's tires squealed off as he chased down Larry's car. Three pickup trucks roared down the road, pursuing the little Chevy II. Cale switched his lights to high beam and came up fast on the unsuspecting driver in the other car. The trees bordering the road made the darkness seem twice as dark.

The convoy came up on a sharp turn in the road and the Chevy II braked fast and turned to the right. Cale had to slam on his brakes to avoid crashing into the ditch. The other two trucks narrowly missed smashing into the rear end of Cale's truck.

The Chevy II sped off into the night.

Cale quickly regained his composure and pressed down on the gas pedal to catch up again. They made up the distance fast, and reached the Chevy as they were nearing Wagoner's Field. This time, Cale didn't hesitate. He plowed the big front bumper of his Dodge into the rear end of the small car. The impact temporarily bounced the little car ahead, but Cale was back on him like a flea on a dog. He rammed him again.

The Chevy II swerved left and right and then went into a spin before sliding off the slick road and into the ditch beside Wagoner's. Cale pulled his truck to a stop in front of the wrecked Chevy II, and the other two trucks boxed it in from behind. Angry white boys climbed out of the cabs of the trucks and surrounded the car. Some had baseball bats and sticks. One had a long, heavy chain and was swinging it by his leg.

"Get out of the car, nigger," Donnie said.

Nobody inside the car moved. In a rage, Donnie swung the bat and cracked the rear window of the car. "Get out, now."

Cale joined in. "Come on, nigger. You've stepped over the line, boy. You're gonna regret you ever came into our world."

Larry opened the car door and stumbled outside into the freezing cold night. He was dazed. The door on the other side opened and Rob fell out. He climbed to his feet and leaned against the car for support. He had struck his head and blood was dripping down his forehead.

"Where's the girl?" Donnie demanded.

After a pause, Rob said, "We took her home."

"You sick son of a bitch." Donnie swung the bat at Larry. It caught him in the small of the back and dropped him to his knees.

Rob ran around the front of the car and yelled, "Stop it."

"You nigger loving faggot," one of the drivers said, and he punched Rob in the belly. He went down like a bag of rocks.

"We're tired of you niggers and queers screwing up our town," one of the boys said. He struck the stunned and injured Larry with a glancing blow on the side of his face, hard enough to dislocate his jaw. Larry cried out in pain.

"We don't like your kind here."

"Why don't you go back to Africa where you belong?"

"I'm an American," Larry managed to say.

"Don't you say that," Cale shouted. "You ain't got no right to call yourself an American."

Rob and Larry managed to crawl together in front of the headlights of the battered Chevy.

"You think you're hot stuff on the basketball team,

don't you?" Cale said as he took another swing at Larry. The blow was short, glancing off his shoulder, but he kept going. "You think you're cool at school, don't you?" He swung again, and this time Larry just managed to block it.

"Well, we're going to teach you a real school lesson," Cale said. Three of the boys came around the side of the car.

One of the attackers pulled Larry to his feet and gripped him around the neck. Donnie reached into his pocket and extracted a slender switchblade knife. He held the knife into the light as the blade flashed out from the casing. He came closer to Larry and pressed the blade against his sweaty neck. "So you think you can hang out with white chicks, right boy?"

Larry groaned in pain.

He pressed the blade harder against Larry's neck, pushing him back against the wrecked Chevy II. "I've always wondered if niggers bleed red," he said. He pulled the knife from Larry's throat and cut a deep, long slice in his forearm.

Larry yelled.

"Damn," Donnie said. "It *is* red."

Larry managed to grasp his left forearm with his right hand to staunch the bleeding.

But Donnie wasn't finished. "Let's castrate this little black piggy right here, right now," he said lowering the blade to Larry's crotch.

"Fuckin' A," someone said.

"Do it!"

He pulled both hands to the waist of Larry's jeans and began to tug on his belt.

The movement forced him to turn the knife away from Larry's skin. It also caused the guy holding Larry to loosen his grip.

Rob saw his chance and lunged at Donnie, knocking him off his feet and into Cale. Donnie, in his semi-inebriated state, accidentally dug his switchblade into Cale's soft belly about an inch. Cale let out a squeal that caused all his friends to jump back. Larry squirmed free and shoved his captor into the ditch. He turned toward the fence. "Run!" he screamed. Rob was right behind him and the two clambered up the ditch to the edge of the field. There was confusion behind them as the attackers sorted themselves out.

Rob and Larry grabbed the barbwire and scaled the fence. Spikes of steel ripped through their clothes and tore through their flesh. Blood spattered the cold ground. But it was better than the alternative.

"Shit. Get them," one of the boys yelled, heading for the fence.

"No, wait," Donnie shouted. "Get the trucks. It'll be faster."

Everyone got back into the trucks. Two boys grabbed bats and climbed into the truck bed. They screamed like demons as the trucks fired up and screeched off toward the entrance to Wagoner's Field.

The driveway had a cattle gate made of metal train track rails running perpendicular to the drive, embedded into the road. There was a space of a few inches between each rail, which was enough to prevent cows and horses from trying to cross. Cars, tractors, trucks, and anything else on wheels could pass over the rails with just a few mild bumps—if the vehicle was driven slowly.

Cale's truck hit the gate at about fifty miles per hour. It bounced up and down like a bronco at the rodeo and sped into the field. Halfway in, he stopped the truck and jumped out, yelling, "Come on, nigger. There's no place to run."

The other two trucks drove over the cattle gate more carefully and stopped as soon as they were past it.

Cale stopped his screaming and drove back to meet up with them. They all climbed out.

"We've got 'em now, man," Cale said. "There's no way out of this field but through this gate."

"All right, then," Donnie said. "Cale, you guys wait here. Blake and I will drive back into the field and find them."

"What about the other side of the field?" one of the drivers asked.

"It's fenced in. Besides, there's a big canal that

borders the property over there." Cale knew this field well. This was where, at a rally back in '67, he'd vowed to do right by his country. He was getting more excited by the moment. "I wouldn't wade through that shit if my life depended on it. There are gators and snakes and God knows what in that water."

The two trucks drove back into the darkness where the boys had run. Halfway in the headlights split off into two directions. Their screams and shouts, followed by the gunning of truck engines, echoed through the night.

* * *

Battered, beaten and confused, Rob and Larry were running for their lives.

They ran as fast as their beaten bodies could take them toward the opposite side of the field. Rob felt his temple throbbing like a pounding drum.

Larry was breathing heavily and clutching his side. "Man. We are in so much trouble. We can't get over the canal back here."

"Yes, we can. We can get out by the old rope swing," Rob said. "We can swing over and run back to town and call the cops. The police will be here before they know we're gone."

"You trust the pigs more than I do, brother," Larry said between gasps of air.

They staggered to the edge of the canal and turned left, back toward town. The odor from the dank water was enough to choke a horse.

About a hundred yards away they came across the old oak tree with the huge branch that extended over the canal. The old rope swing that they had suspended from the branch years ago was still there, tied to the trunk of the tree.

"Is it going to hold?" Larry asked. He was really more concerned about whether *he* could hold on to the rope.

"Guess we'll know in a minute," Rob answered.

He gave it several firm tugs and it seemed to be in good

shape.

"You know, we're about twice as heavy as we were back then," Larry cautioned.

"Maybe you are, fat boy," Rob said. "I'm going across." With that he grabbed the rope, leapt up into the air and swung across the canal. He cleared the other shore by a good three feet and dropped safely to the other side. "Piece of cake, man. C'mon," he said, trying to muffle his pain from the effort of the swing.

Larry didn't hesitate. He retrieved the rope, jumped up and grabbed it as high as he could. The piercing sting of stretching his aching body made him cry out. Hanging on for dear life, he soared across the divide. He dropped beside Rob and let out a sharp cry when he hit the ground. Rob helped Larry up and both boys started running as fast as their injured bodies would take them down the paved road back to town.

Back at the gate, Cale and the others continued to yell into the darkness, threatening to do all manner of harm to Larry. Eventually, they quieted down. Cale sat on the hood of his truck, leaning back against the windshield, and lit up a cigarette. The other boy stood watch, peering into the darkness.

The stars shone brightly and the sky glowed like a Baptist church ceiling during candlelight service on Christmas Eve. Under different circumstances, even these boys would have been awestruck.

Eventually, the darting headlights of the two search trucks came together at the opposite side of the field. The trucks sat still, side by side for a few moments, then started heading back toward the gate.

"I can't believe it. They got away," Donnie said before climbing out of his truck. "It looks like they jumped the creek on some kid's rope swing."

Donnie turned and faced Cale directly. "You're sure about this thing, right? This nigger was with a white girl."

"Saw it with my own fuckin' eyes."

"How far is it back to town?" Donnie turned and gazed into the darkness where the swing crossed the canal.

"From that part of the field? I'd say about half a mile."

"We might can catch them if we hurry."

* * *

Rob and Larry ran until they came upon the streetlights of town. Then they slowed to a jog, gasping at each painful breath.

The Springlake police department was in the center of town, near the churches, the post office and the downtown banks. They decided to go straight there.

From behind them, they could hear the roar of truck engines. They threw their broken bodies into some bushes in front of the courthouse, a few blocks from the police department.

The trucks sped by. They cruised down the side streets, drivers and passengers obviously looking for them.

"Shit. This is bad," Larry said.

They pressed themselves into the soft sand bed and tried not to move. The trucks slowly passed.

* * *

Cale pulled over to the curb and told his partner to get out of the car and search on foot.

"Where are you going?" he asked.

"I've gotta run an errand." Cale drove away from the search team down Plant Street. Lighting a cigarette to calm his nerves, he pulled into the back parking lot of Springlake Hardware and quickly shut off his lights. He had come to this store enough to know every product they sold and exactly where it was shelved.

He ran to the back door, carrying a tire iron. He looked up and down the streets of the dark neighborhood and could see no one. Reaching back, he swung the tire iron against the door, shattering glass and setting off a loud alarm bell.

Cale knew exactly where to go in the store. He had wanted this particular handgun for several months. He had asked the salesman several times to take it out of the case so he could see how it felt in his hands. He also knew where they kept the bullets.

He grabbed a handful of shells and loaded the gun. On his way out he stumbled over some kerosene cans someone had stacked by the back door. As he ran through the door, the cigarette fell from his lips into a pool of kerosene. Within seconds, the flames had consumed the tiny back office. Panicked, Cale stuffed the Smith & Wesson '38 in the waistband of his pants, jumped into his truck and tore off into the night, ignoring the burning hardware store behind him.

* * *

Katie turned off *The Tonight Show with Johnny Carson*. She nudged Ray to wake him up. "Honey," she said. "I'm worried. The game must have ended over an hour ago, and Rob still isn't home."

"He's probably out celebrating," Ray said, his eyes still closed.

"What would they have to celebrate? Scoring more than two dozen points?"

"I don't know. What am I supposed to do?"

Katie thought for a moment. "Send Tim. Ask Tim to go look for him."

Ray climbed out of his recliner, walked down the hall and knocked on Tim's door. "Tim? Timmy? You still up?"

"Yeah, Dad," came Tim's voice from inside the room.

Ray opened the door. Tim was lying on the bed watching the *Tonight Show* on a portable black and white TV. "Rob's not home yet. It would make your mom feel better if you drove into town to look for him."

"Okay, Dad," Tim said. He sat up in bed and put his feet on the floor. Reaching down, he picked up a pair of jeans and pulled them on. Ray could see the scars on his legs before he covered them with the slacks.

He pulled himself up to his feet and hobbled toward

the kitchen. He grabbed the cane by the bedroom doorway, which he still used for support since the accident two years ago. Grabbing the car keys off the kitchen table, he headed out in search of his little brother.

* * *

Rob whispered to Larry, "I've got an idea."

"Okay," Larry said. "I'm ready for one. I feel like I'm sitting in a rice paddy somewhere in North Vietnam. If we don't do something soon, we're gonna be found."

"Look. Let's go north two blocks. We can break into my church and call the police from there."

"You sure? Break into your church?" Larry asked.

"It's the closest phone that's not out in the open," Rob said. "I know a Sunday School classroom where the window is usually open."

They crawled out of the bushes and ran down the road, dodging streetlights. It hurt them both to run, but when they drew near the big brick church building, they both broke into a sprint. They darted through the bushes and along the wall until Rob raised a hand. "Stop. Here it is."

He pushed on the top part of the window and it raised two inches. Prying his fingers at the bottom, he pulled and the widow slid easily up. He climbed inside, stepping on a table beneath the window. Larry followed.

"How'd you know about this?" Larry asked, looking around the kindergarten classroom.

Rob chuckled. "My kindergarten teacher used to like to have the window open during Sunday School. She never locked it."

"But that must have been years ago."

"Some things never change," Rob said.

Just as Larry was reaching back up to pull the window closed, the headlight of a car passed by and the boys scrambled out of sight.

* * *

Larry followed Rob through the door and down the hall toward the stairs to the main area of the church. Rob held his finger to his lips and said, "Shhh. No lights. Someone might see us."

They crept up the stairs to the second floor. Halfway down the hall, they found the phone on the wall, put there to allow children to call home after choir practice. Rob picked up the phone and spun the rotary dial to zero. Larry went over to the window to stand watch.

"Connect me to the police office," Rob said after the operator answered the phone. In a few moments, he said, "I need help. I know this is going to sound crazy, but some guys just beat up my friend and me and we need the police right now."

There was a pause.

"No, I'm not high. I'm not drunk, either. I'm at First United Methodist Church, and there are some very bad people trying to kill us."

Another pause.

"Oh. Okay. But get here as soon as you can, all right?" He hung up the phone and looked at Larry. "They're on the other side of the city at a hardware store fire. It may be an hour before they can get over here," Rob answered. He briefly wondered if it might be the store where his dad worked that was on fire, but he had bigger things to worry about at the moment.

He and Larry slipped down the hall and sat in the first row of pews. There are places that are supposed to be quiet, where silence is right and peaceful and safe. A church sanctuary is one of those places. For the first time in an hour, the two boys relaxed.

The streetlights outside danced against the stained-glass windows, giving the interior of the sanctuary a fantasy-like feeling. Rob took a deep breath and breathed in the odor of unlit wax candles, freshly vacuumed carpets and the cherrywood of the pews and fixtures. It felt good to be home.

* * *

Cale caught up with the rest of his friends in front of the county courthouse. Their number had grown as others heard about the nigger who was with the white chick. Cale felt a bit exposed with the stolen gun in his pants, but he listened intently as the small crowd talked about the incident.

One of the new guys said, "I thought I saw something over at the Methodist Church when I drove by. Let's go over there and look around."

The crowd was quickly becoming a mob, as more young men were called to join the attack on the church. They marched through the streets until they came to the front of the church building.

Two boys slipped away from the crowd and went around to the back. They scrambled through the bushes, trying the windows as they went to see if any were unlocked.

Finding the window to the kindergarten classroom unlatched, they opened it and crawled inside.

* * *

Rob thought he heard a noise in the hall. He sat up straight and cocked his head so he could hear better.

There it was again. A creaking sound, like when people are tiptoeing and they put their weight on the wrong floorboard.

Rob reached over and shook Larry. "Someone's here," he whispered.

"Maybe it's the cops."

Rob shook his head. "They wouldn't be sneaking around. Listen."

The two boys slowly stood up and walked over to the doorway leading out into the hall. Rob grabbed one of the brass candleholders and held it over his head, ready to strike. They crept through the door and ran straight into Reverend Stephen Phillips.

"God," Rob yelled in shock.

"No, just me, Stephen, although He's probably around here somewhere too."

"What are you doing here this late?" Rob asked.

"It's our night to host the homeless shelter," the minister answered. "So, I'm playing host. I thought I might get a book from my office to pass the t—" He stopped and pulled both boys into the light of a nearby window. "Are you guys all right? What happened?"

"We got jumped," Rob answered. "Some guys in some pickup trucks are trying to kill us."

"Why on earth would someone be trying to kill you?" Stephen asked.

Rob said, "I have no idea. But just look at us." In this case, seeing was believing. "So we came here to call the police."

"Well, you came to the right place," Stephen said. "Did you reach them?"

"Yeah." Rob said. "They're fighting a fire on the other side of town, but should be here soon."

"Good. Then it's only a matter of time."

Suddenly, there was a loud banging sound on the front doors of the sanctuary.

They stopped and stared, first at the doors, then at each other.

"Do you think that's the police?" Larry asked.

"That would be *really* fast," Rob said.

"Wait here," Stephen whispered.

They didn't listen. They all walked up the aisle to the front door. Opening it, Stephen quickly stepped outside into the freezing winter air and closed the door behind him. He was met by an angry mob in the portico. "The homeless shelter is closed for the evening, gentlemen. We have to close the doors at 10:00 p.m." he said, playing for time.

"We ain't here for no homeless shelter," Donnie said. "We're here for the nig—for the black boy. We know he's in there. Bring him out."

"I'm sorry, friend. There are several black people in the shelter, but it's in the house across the street over there," Stephen answered. "We don't discriminate."

"That ain't what I'm talking about and I think you know it," Donnie said. "We want that black kid from

Springlake High."

"I'm sorry, but I can't help you," Stephen said.

Donnie pushed up through the crowd and got into Stephen's face. "Let me make this clear, preacher boy," he threatened. "We'll go right through you if we have to, but we're gonna get what we came for."

Stephen stepped back from the young man. "You've been drinking tonight, haven't you? Man, you need some gum."

That only made Donnie angrier. He swung a fast, hard right and caught Stephen in the chin. The minister fell back onto the steps. He kicked him in the stomach with pointed-toe boots.

"Stay down you stupid fag," he snarled.

Someone grabbed the silver door handles and yanked hard on them. "They're locked," he yelled to Donnie.

"The Rev's probably got a set of keys on him," Donnie said. "Search his pockets."

Stephen was dazed and stunned, having no experience with street fighting. Hands reached down to grab him, and he rolled out of reach. He pushed himself against the wall and took a deep breath to help him think.

"Give us the keys, preacher," Donnie said, walking toward him. "You can give us the keys, or we can take them from you. Your choice."

At that moment, Stephen didn't like either option.

* * *

Tim had driven by the empty gym parking lot, the new drive-in restaurant, the new shopping mall and even Pete's Restaurant, but had not seen Larry's blue Chevy II. He drove out by Karen's house, but the lights were off and Larry's car wasn't there.

On the way back to town, by Wagoner's Field, he passed the wrecked car in the ditch. He backed up and got out to inspect the vehicle, his heart in his throat.

"No, God. Not another car accident," he prayed quietly.

No one was in the car. Relieved, Tim figured they must have walked back to town. He quickly returned to his car and began a slow drive back to town, scanning the shoulders of the highway for any sign of movement.

His drive took him all the way to the downtown area without any luck. The streets were empty and no one was out. Even the theater was closed for the night. Assuming that Rob had made it home while he was out searching for him, Tim turned up Main Street and headed for the house.

While driving by First United Methodist Church, he noticed a crowd of men gathered at the front doors. He made a quick turn into one of the parking spaces and got out of the car. Leaning on his cane, he climbed the stairs as fast as he could. Two or three older guys were having an argument in the middle of the mob. Someone was on his hands and knees in front of the crowd. As he got closer, Tim could hear their words.

"Look, preach. Give us the keys or we'll take them from you."

Alarmed, Tim saw Stephen huddled up against the door. "What is going on, here?" he yelled.

One of the younger guys in the crowd turned in his direction. "Hey. That's the nigger-lover's brother." Instantly, the crowd turned on Tim.

"Where is he?" one of the young men demanded.

Tim was speechless. He has no idea what was going on. "Hold on a minute," he said. "What are you talking about?"

"We're looking for your faggot brother and his nigger friend," someone said.

"Why? What did they do?"

"That ain't your problem. Tell us where he is."

"Rob's at home," Tim said, thinking quickly. "I just left the house a few minutes ago, and he was going to bed."

Confusion rippled through the crowd like smoke in a burning house.

"That ain't right," one boy said. "I saw him climb into the church through a window 'bout a half hour ago."

"Must have been somebody else," Tim said.

"What are you doing out driving around this late?" one of the crowd demanded.

Again, Tim thought fast. "It's my shift at the homeless shelter," he answered matter-of-factly. "Our church lets homeless people stay in that house on cold nights. I volunteered for the late shift."

By then, Stephen had managed to rise to his feet. "Y'all go on home, now, and we won't call the police."

The men looked at each other and shuffled their feet, waiting for someone to make the next move. Finally, Donnie said, "Maybe he's right. Let's take care of this tomorrow." He turned to Tim. "Tell your nigger-loving brother that we're gonna git them both."

The crowd started to break up, and Tim made his way to where Reverend Phillips was leaning against the church door. "Are you okay, man?"

Stephen nodded. "Thanks for your help. I don't know if I could have kept them out if you hadn't shown up. That was fast thinking, too."

They both breathed a sigh of relief.

* * *

Rob and Larry were leaning hard against the large wooden doors of the church, listening closely to the squabble outside. Rob could see Larry's hands shaking in the dark.

"It's gonna be all right," he said.

"I know, I know."

Suddenly they were slammed hard from behind against the doors.

* * *

Four boys smashed through the wooden doors, knocking Stephen and Tim to the front porch of the church. They all fell in a heap of flesh and wood at the top of the steps.

"There he is," yelled Cale when he saw Larry. The mob, now numbering about twenty, turned around and

rushed the doors. They pushed the fugitives, along with
Tim and Stephen, up against the wall beside the shattered
doorway.

One of the boys said, "Donnie. We snuck into the
church and caught these punks listening at the front
door."

"Liar," someone yelled at the minister. "You said
they weren't here."

"Let's hang 'em all," someone shouted.

Donnie muscled his face up close to Larry's. "You've
been messin' around with white women, boy," he said.

"What?"

He delivered a sharp blow to Larry's gut. He
doubled over in pain.

"We don't like niggers taking our white girls," he
continued.

Larry struggled to resist Donnie's verbal and
physical confrontation.

Suddenly, from across the street, someone yelled,
"What the hell are you doing?"

The boys on the porch turned and looked down the
steps into the faces of more than seventy homeless people.
Black, white, male, female, they stood together as one,
demanding an explanation. The homeless crowd moved
quickly up the steps of the church to confront the much
smaller mob of white boys.

"It ain't none of your business," Donnie yelled, with
a little less bravado than before.

"Yeah, it *is* our business, boy," one of the black men
yelled back. "This church is looking out for us, so we're
looking out for it." The crowd of homeless moved closer to
the steps of the church.

At that moment, Cale raised the Smith & Wesson
'38 and pulled the trigger twice. It was all he knew to do in
the frenzy and hysteria around him. He thought he was
doing the right thing. He thought it was what his friends
wanted. But in reality, he didn't think at all. He just
acted.

Both bullets missed Larry and bore deep into
Stephen's chest. He was slammed against the wall,

leaving blood and scraps of flesh and clothing against the rough brick facade. He crumpled to a heap in the doorway of his church.

The sound of gunshots stopped everyone, but just for a moment. In that brief second, a hundred minds worked to decipher what had happened. The mob of white boys at the top of the steps scattered, jumping walls and leaping banisters to get as far away as possible.

The homeless crowd moved forward quickly to find out what had happened and what could be done. Rob and Tim knelt beside their fallen pastor. "Get a doctor," Tim yelled at the top of his lungs. "Somebody get a doctor. Get a doctor."

Larry pressed back against the wall of the church, wanting it to swallow him up and protect him from the madness around him. He had just looked death in its redneck face, and he was terrified.

Just then, the Springlake police cruiser rounded the corner. When Officer Rawlings saw the mob at the top of the church steps, he switched on his lights and siren and called for backup. The crowd of homeless people scattered, but not before a couple of them wrestled Cale Kinney to the ground.

By the time Rawlings reached Kinney, the boy's nose was broken and a concussion was beginning to set in. Someone handed the '38 to the officer and told him the boy had fired it, and the minister had been hit. The officer quickly handcuffed the boy to the rails of the stairs, and raced back to the squad car to call for an ambulance.

OBITUARY

The friends and members of First United Methodist Church of Springlake mourn the death of their Associate Minister, The Reverend Stephen Michael Phillips.

Reverend Phillips was a member of the Florida Conference of the United Methodist Church. He served on the staff of First United Methodist Church of Springlake from 1966 to 1970, assisting in the preaching, visitation and counseling duties of the church. While on the staff, Phillips organized a ministry to help and house homeless people on cold evenings, serving as many as seventy-five persons a night.

Phillips received his Bachelor's Degree from Florida Southern College in Lakeland, Florida, and his Master's of Divinity from Candler School of Theology at Emory University in Atlanta, Georgia.

Phillips is survived by his mother and father, Susanna and John Phillips, of Miami, Florida.

A memorial service will be held in the sanctuary of First United Methodist Church on Saturday, January 24, 1970, at 2:00 p.m. The public is invited.

EULOGY

Tim Franklin stood behind the pulpit facing the crowded, well-lit sanctuary, grasping his notes in his shaking hands. Ladies from the Methodist Women's group, dressed elegantly in their Sunday best, and men his father knew from the now-destroyed hardware store waited patiently here and there among the crowd. Hundreds of students, black and white, sat together, filling most of the ornate pews. In the back, shadowed beneath the balcony, dozens of homeless people sat reverently and respectfully. A couple of boys who were in the mob that chased Larry and Rob on that tragic night squirmed nervously in the back row.

The open casket stood in front of the altar rail.

Organ music played, scripture was read, and comforting words were spoken, reminding everyone in this beautiful, lavish sanctuary of the wonderful life Reverend Stephen Phillips had lived.

Now it was Tim's turn. He raised his head and spoke from his heart. "In times of madness, individuals stop reasoning for themselves and allow others to determine for them what is right and what is wrong, what is just and what is unjust, what is good and what is bad. These are times of desperation, and in such times desperate things happen.

"Different circumstances could have brought different consequences. But the world is kinda crazy these days. Stories about riots in far-away cities, newspaper articles inciting hatred and anger, protest speeches that confuse us more than inform us, comments stated in back rooms and hallways, actions taken by those who want to control others, and fears of the uniformed and ignorant came to a conclusion in one dramatic moment last Saturday night. Like an object balanced on a cliff, our world tilted and fell, changing everything forever. It changed my town, my school, my church . . . me.

"I will miss Stephen Phillips and the long, deep talks we had, the compassion he showed everyone, and his strong and sincere desire to make a difference.

"You have made a difference, Stephen, in my life and in the lives of all of us here. Thank you."

ACKNOWLEDGEMENTS

Special thanks and appreciation to Bonnie Hearn Hill and Sadie Scapillato for their editing prowess, and to the wonderful folks at Novel Voices Press Inc. for their faithful support.

And, of course, gratitude to my wife, Kay, for the time and support to write.

ABOUT THE AUTHOR

Sharpton is a child of the sixties—a Baby Boomer's Boomer. He grew up in a small town in Florida with white and black water fountains, white and black bathrooms, and white and black theaters. Junior high and high school brought both voluntary and enforced desegregation.

He watched The Beatles on *The Ed Sullivan Show*, Vietnam on the Nightly News, and the first moon landing with its grainy black and white images. Rock and roll music blasted through his eight-track player. Bell-bottom jeans hugged his hips. He was one of the last to sign up for the draft, one of the first to pump his own gas, and one of millions who wore his hair longer than his dad liked.

He holds a bachelor's degree from Asbury University and two master's degrees with honors, the first from Wheaton College and the second from Rollins College. He has served as a church youth director, a corporate trainer for major Fortune 500 companies, and a college professor of business.

Ben lives in Roswell, Georgia, with his wife, Kay, and their two (barely) teenage children, along with a boxer named Grace and a chubby beagle named Peanut.

For more information on this author, please visit *www.bensharpton.com.*